WHY SHE FLED

A MAK AND WILTON THRILLER
BOOK 4

ADDISON MICHAEL

2025 Pages & Pie Publishing

ISBN: 979-8-9862920-9-0

Library of Congress Catalogue-in-Publication Data

Michael, Addison

Why she fled: a mak and wilton thriller/Addison Michael

Cover Design by Art by Karri

Editing by Tiffany Avery and Jayne Shaw

www.addisonmichael.com

Thank you to family, the supportive thriller writer community, and dedicated readers. I would not have written book number ten without you

PROLOGUE
GREG WILTON

Nineteen Years Ago…

Shania Woodstone was the girl Greg had spent late nights and long summer days dreaming about. With her straight brown hair that touched her waist and big brown eyes framed by thick, black eyelashes, a light smattering of freckles covering the bridge of her nose, and a smile that lit up the room, Greg was *gone* over her. Shania had heart-shaped lips that were always shiny with pink lip gloss that smelled like bubble gum. Greg only knew that because one time in the sixth grade, he and his friends had played that stupid spin-the-bottle game. Greg had gotten lucky when his bottle had landed on Shania. She had developed earlier than the other girls, and every guy wanted her.

It was more than that for Greg. He had loved Shania since she'd moved there in the second grade. It had only taken him eight years to get up the courage to ask her out. If he'd known how quickly she'd say *yes*, he would have asked her out sooner. But now, as he watched her socialize, Greg wished he'd taken her somewhere else for their first date.

They were in the old, abandoned cabin just off the stone quarry outside of town—The Cliffs, they called it—a popular party place where they'd all hung out for years. Tonight, the cabin had gotten crowded, the temperature rising exponentially with each body that shoved into the cabin. There was too much competing for Shania's attention here.

It wasn't her fault really. She'd also known these other kids at the party since the second grade. Take Beth Donovan, for instance. Beth was Shania's best friend. It was rare for one of them to be seen anywhere without the other. Beth was here with a guy named Jacob Greenly. Jacob was a year older than they were. He was harmless, but Greg knew he would get tired of Beth. Beth was pretty, but she was too high-maintenance and talked way too much.

As Greg turned from the keg holding two cups of cheap beer from the tap, he noticed Trevan Collins edging his way closer to Shania, who stood on the other side of the room next to a ratty leather couch. Trevan was a tall, good-looking kid who most girls drooled over. He'd been chosen to play varsity football tight end, the spot Greg felt sure he was going to get, leaving Greg stuck on JV. It made Trevan pretty cocky. Having beaten Greg to Shania's side, Trevan was now flirting with Greg's girl.

"Back off, Collins," Greg snapped, slightly out of breath from rushing across the room. He pushed Trevan back with his elbow and presented Shania with a drink.

"You got a problem, Wilton?" Trevan's face lost its charm as he put his shoulders back and puffed out his chest, making himself appear bigger.

Greg stepped into Trevan's personal space, imitating Trevan's stance. Trevan had already taken Greg's spot on the football team. There was no way Greg was letting him have Shania too. "Back off my girl!"

"Really? She's *your* girl?" Trevan sneered. "Maybe you should ask her what she thinks of that."

"That's enough, boys," Shania blushed as she sipped the beer.

"Tell him you're here with me," Greg challenged, his eyes still on Trevan.

"Yeah, Greg and I came together," Shania confirmed.

"Well, tell him you're leaving with me," Trevan growled back.

Greg's eyes flew to Shania's face.

Shania's mouth dropped open. "I didn't—"

Alcohol and testosterone flowing through their veins, Greg turned his anger on Trevan. He could tell by Shania's reaction that Trevan was lying. He shoved Trevan so hard that Trevan's back slammed into an old wooden cabinet.

Trevan pushed off the cabinet like a springboard and flew into Greg. Bodies crashed together and then into the alcohol stacked on a rickety card table. Two legs of the table collapsed, and bottles slid to the floor. The sound of broken glass twinkled over the loud voices of the crowd.

"Let's take this outside!" Trevan, ever the hot head, yelled. "Winner takes Shania home."

"You're on!" Greg agreed as the two tramped toward the door.

"Uh, I didn't agree to that," Shania called out. "I think I'll just go home with Beth."

Not listening, Greg followed Trevan outside where the cool air slapped him in the face. He threw the first punch. Everyone knew most fights got broken up within the first five minutes, so the winner was usually the one who threw first.

Greg's fist connected with Trevan's face, knocking him backward. Trevan rebounded quickly, light on his feet, as he threw a hook that landed against Greg's ribs. A small crowd had followed them out.

Fight, fight, fight, they chanted.

For the next ten minutes, the crowd gasped and cheered as Trevan and Greg bloodied each other's faces and punched stomachs, ribs, and any other body part that got in the way.

Then they heard a yell somewhere in the distance. "Police!"

In mass chaos, the crowd scattered. Underage drinking at parties was still a huge offense in this little town. Trevan and Greg, still locked together but now on the ground, tumbled, kneeing and pinning each other like it had become a UFC fight.

"Knock it off, guys!" Davey Stinnert was coming in quick. "Didn't you hear? Police!"

Jacob Greenly and Beth Donovan still stood in place rather closely, eyes locked on the two fighters. Beth looked a little green and Jacob stared in sick fascination.

Out of nowhere, Shania stumbled toward the boys. She giggled obnoxiously as she tried to focus. "Oh, boys!"

"Is she trashed?" Jacob asked.

"I dunno," Beth said. "I didn't even think she drank that much."

"Fine," Shania slurred. "You can both take me home."

"Uh, Shania?" Beth stepped forward. "You okay?"

"Hey!" Davey's voice was loud beside them. "Watch out for—"

It all happened too quick. One minute, Shania was bobbling after the boys, who were still rolling around on the ground dangerously close to the cliff. The next minute, Shania was flapping her arms like she was fighting for her balance.

Beth rushed forward in an effort to save her friend.

"Shania!" Beth's voice pitched upward in a scream. She arrived just as Shania lost her fight with gravity. Beth reached out, but it was too late. Shania had pitched over the edge of the cliff.

A shrill, eerie scream was the only sound in the night, until it cut off abruptly.

For a moment, no one moved. On the ground, Trevan and Greg were frozen in an awkward embrace. Beth stared in horror with an arm still outstretched over empty air. Jacob stood beside Davey, both of them gaping like fish, eyes huge and unblinking.

Then all hell broke loose.

"Police! Everybody, freeze! Put your hands in the air!" Three police officers, guns drawn, descended on the teenagers. The flashlights they held swung from kid to kid, temporarily blinding them.

A loud wail sounded from somewhere deep inside Beth.

"I'm Officer Pottstaff." A tall, intimidating man flashed a badge. "Someone better explain what the hell is going on here!"

The two other officers stood silent, waiting for an explanation.

"She's gone!" Beth wailed.

"What?" Pottstaff snapped. "Who?"

"My friend—she just went over the edge." Beth's words were now coming out in a hysterical torrent. She pointed down over the side of the cliff. For a moment, no one spoke. Hearing Beth's words made it more real. It hadn't been a figment of their imagination. Shania had gone over the cliff. She was now at the bottom.

Officer Pottstaff stalked over to Beth, planted his feet, and shined his flashlight over the edge. He gasped and then cursed. "Who is that?"

"Shania Woodstone," Beth stammered, having a hard time getting out her best friend's name.

One of the other officers pulled out a phone and called for an ambulance.

"You!" Pottstaff shined his flashlight at Beth, Trevan, and Greg, who were now sitting on the ground, valiantly trying to hold back tears. Jacob and Davey were standing stoic, frozen in their places. "You been drinking?"

No one said a word.

Pottstaff nodded. He made some signal to the other officers. The officers swooped in and handcuffed Davey and Jacob. Pottstaff handcuffed Beth. "You have the right to remain silent. Anything you say can and will be held against you—"

"What are the charges?" Greg asked, looking like he might make a run for it.

"I wouldn't do that if I were you, son," Pottstaff said as one officer took Davey and Jacob up to the squad car. He nudged Beth to start walking. The other officer cuffed Greg and Trevan and began leading them up the hill to a second squad car.

"I said, what are the charges?" Greg asked again more loudly.

"Murder."

1

———————

WILTON

Ashes to ashes, dust to dust... Stephen Wilton listened to the monotone drone of the clergy man. Standing apart from the small crowd of mourners, a few feet up the hill, Stephen watched as they lowered David Stinnert's coffin into the ground.

It was hard to believe that five short days ago, David had taken a bullet for Stephen. David had been best friends with Greg Wilton, Stephen's brother. David had confessed and spent time in prison for the murder of Greg Wilton. Which Stephen thought was true until he had discovered photographic evidence that showed David Stinnert was innocent of that murder.

There had been no money for a funeral for David—until—the local funeral home had received an anonymous donation covering the cost of a burial. It was the least Stephen could do. Stephen was alive right now because of David's sacrifice.

Stephen had never had a civilian intentionally protect *him*. That single action had rocked his whole perspective. It made him feel like he was part of something that was much bigger than himself. With that realization came another feeling—

guilt. Since that night, Stephen had been questioning if the life he lived was worth another man's life.

Stephen gulped down the knot in his throat and surveyed the small crowd. He half expected Beth Donovan to make an appearance. Not that she would be seen in public right now. Beth was the last of the teenagers alive who had been coerced into working for a drug trafficking ring at sixteen years old. It was the beginning of the very ring the marshals now sought to take down for good. But, as Stephen scanned the crowd, the trees, and parked cars, he knew Beth wasn't here. She was long gone. He thought he might never see her again, and he didn't know how he felt about that. It was like the strong feelings he'd had for her when they had been together had faded to nothing more than concern when she drove away. Out of his life. Like all the others.

That left five people in attendance. Distant relatives from the look of it. Davey's mom and sister had died in a car accident before he'd been released from prison. If that was really how they died. Nothing was what it seemed anymore. Stephen would never take the first explanation—the logical one—as fact again. He would forever question everything.

As he watched mourners step forward and throw dirt on David's coffin that had been lowered into the Earth, Stephen's eyes flicked to where he knew his brother, Greg, was buried. Eighteen years ago, in this exact cemetery, Stephen had attended a service just like this one. Though the turnout had been better, he could see the sixteen-year-old version of himself throwing dirt on Greg's coffin and watching it lower in the ground.

Until that moment in Stephen's life, nothing bad had ever happened to him. His parents were still together, and he had a great childhood. He'd gotten the grades he wanted without much effort, he'd played key positions in sports, and he had several good friends. Greg's death had overwhelmed him with so many emotions he had never felt before. He hadn't known what to do with the pain.

He remembered how his throat had hurt from holding back the tears, but he'd been trying to be a man. He wouldn't allow himself to cry. Not when his mother was so broken over this. She hadn't stopped sobbing since the police officer had told his parents the news on their doorstep that fateful day. Instead, Stephen had decided to follow his dad's lead, watching how strong he was, showing no emotions while he comforted his mom, meeting her needs.

When Greg's funeral was over, the pain in his chest remained. He wanted to hug his mom, to comfort her, but his dad seemed to have that covered. He watched his dad put his arm around his mom and turn to leave. Stephen had fallen in line behind them, following them to the parking lot and quietly getting into the back of the car. He wasn't needed then or for the rest of that day. So, he decided to visit his girlfriend. She'd been so sweet and sympathetic. He needed an escape from this new reality—the one where his brother wasn't in it. He'd lost his virginity that night. It had been the distraction he needed to take his mind off the pain.

Stephen blinked at the memory. *Odd,* he thought, *I forgot about that.* He stared hard in the direction of where he knew Greg's tombstone was located. He knew he should go pay his respects. He was here, after all. But those old emotions—the ones that threatened to overwhelm him—crept up. *Some other day,* he told himself. After all, he had a birthday party to get to.

Taking one more look around at the small crowd, Stephen turned away, got into his car, and left. He'd come to pay his respects to David Stinnert, the man who had saved him, and now it was time to go. He knew he would forever be grateful to him. *In fact,* he vowed to himself, *when I kill Senator Lang-*

sten, I'll do it in David's name. He'd avenge them all—Greg, David, and Trevan.

A short while later, Stephen pulled up to the airport and parked the car he'd been driving in a rental parking spot and dropped the keys off. He glanced at his phone when it indicated a text message.

Mak: *ETA? Plans in place.*

Stephen: *Just got to the airport. I'll text when I touch down.*

Mak: *Talk soon!*

Stephen shook his head as he mindlessly navigated airline procedures until he found himself on the plane heading back home. He had a feeling this next step in tracking the crime ring would have him working closely with fellow marshals, police officers, and likely, the FBI. He would need to follow protocol until he had a chance at Langsten. Despite his inability to separate his personal life from his business life, Stephen knew he had no choice but to keep things strictly professional, biding his time until he could take out the senator. With any luck, he could make it look like an accident.

In the meantime, Stephen had one stop to make before he arrived at the birthday party.

2

MAK

Cake, check. Ice cream, check. Decorations in place, check. Noise makers and party hats, check. Now they just had to wait until Harper arrived with her new best friend, Anna Wilton.

Mak moved the curtain for the tenth time to check outside for any impending arrivals. Then she looked at her husband, John, and smiled, her green eyes lighting up in excitement. John had always been in charge of parties since Mak was away so often on business. But Mak, feeling full of energy having just come off a medical leave, had taken charge.

"I got this one," Mak had insisted while John had quirked a brow comically at her. Taking it as a challenge, Mak had jumped right in, organizing a surprise birthday party in record time. Which was why relatives, friends from Harper's dance class, and even a few neighbors all stood in a place where they could duck, squat, or stand behind a door when Harper arrived.

She would never admit it to John, but planning this party had been way harder than she'd anticipated. In fact, she didn't know if she could have pulled it off had it not been for

Paige Friesen, Stephen's baby mama, coming to the rescue with a promise to bring Anna and take them to the park so the guests had time to arrive.

The sound of a car door slamming had everyone scurrying for cover. When the front door opened, Wilton stepped through and quickly said, "It's just me. But I did pass their car driving slowly in this direction. They'll be here soon, so stay down."

Mak nodded, annoyance slipping easily from her face as Wilton handed her birthday candles she had forgotten to pick up. She watched him find a hiding spot next to her dad and shake his hand. Who knew that her partner would fuse so easily into her life?

This time when a car door slammed, Mak moved the curtains to see Paige and her husband, James, get out of the car and open the back doors of a minivan to let the girls out. In minutes, Paige and James each emerged with a baby on a hip, and two energetic best friends—Harper and Anna.

"They're here!" Mak hissed and went to find a spot to hide herself.

Minutes later, their newly four-year-old, Harper, walked through the door looking shocked when her family and friends all jumped out at her.

"Ohmigosh!" Harper squealed and jumped on her toes. She spotted the person nearest to her and yelled, "Uncle Jay!"

A tall man with strong biceps who looked similar to Mak reached down and picked Harper up and spun her around. "Hey, little tike!"

"I'm not little anymore!" Harper declared.

"You're right," Jay said as he placed her back on her feet.

"Hi, daddy!" Anna smiled as Stephen gave her a warm bear hug. Mak knew it was hard on Stephen not to see his daughter more regularly, but knew Stephen did the best he could to prioritize her.

"Go say *hi* to your friends," Mak instructed and watched as Harper scurried off with Anna on her heels to greet all the party guests. Mak noticed Stephen and his family all standing near her brother, Jay, and turned to introduce them.

"My brother, Jay. Jay, this is Stephen, Paige, and James. Paige is married to James and these are their adorable twins." Mak tickled a foot on each child who squealed in turn and kicked at her. "Stephen is my work partner and Paige shares Anna with him."

Jay looked where Mak was pointing to a blond, curly headed girl following Harper around. "Ah, the new best friend. It's nice to meet you all. I'm the better-looking sibling—"

"No one cares, Jay." Mak rolled her eyes. She reached up to smooth a few stray hairs that always seemed to escape her auburn-colored ponytail.

"Ouch. Sore spot." Jay grinned.

"Please, it's your only claim to fame. Clearly, dad loves me more." Mak stuck her tongue out at her brother.

"Are you guys still fighting over who I love more?" Larry entered the conversation from nowhere. Everyone laughed.

"Well?" Mak put her hands on her hips.

"Depends on who I'm in the car with," Larry quipped.

"Yeah, yeah," Mak said as she turned to go survey the present table. She turned back when she was out of range of her dad but still had a line of sight to her annoying older brother.

It's me, she mouthed.

Jay shook his head and turned back to his new friends.

The next few hours were a whirlwind of games, presents, cake, singing "Happy Birthday," and sending gift bags home with Harper's friends. Thank God, John helped with that one. Mak hadn't even known that was a tradition when hosting a birthday party.

It had been tiring, but Mak knew she was going back on a case Monday. It was nice to make the best of the time she had off. With her job, it really was quality over quantity.

After every party guest had left, and she and John worked to clean up, Harper ran up to her and wrapped her arms around Mak's waist.

"Thank you, mommy! Best party ever. Love you!" Then she ran out of the room.

Mak turned at the sound of John's rumble of laughter.

"Best party ever. Looks like you just became the new party committee." John gave her a hug and kissed the top of Mak's head.

Mak pulled away abruptly. "Are you kidding? I'm exhausted! We'll do the next one together."

"Agreed."

As John pulled her back in, Mak knew despite her complaints, she wouldn't have changed today for anything in the world. Who knew how long this next case would take her away?

As she thought about the senator, the trafficking ring, and Wilton's brother, she knew this case was going to be tougher than any other she'd worked up until now.

3

———————

BETH

Unbeknownst to her parents, Beth Donovan had been living in the basement of her parents' home for the past five days. No one was more shocked than she was when her former US Marshal boyfriend, Stephen Wilton, had let her go without so much as a trip to the police station. While she'd been grateful, it had left her without an immediate plan. Not to mention the cast on her hand that made everything difficult. Even driving took twice the amount of time it normally would. Who knew driving one-handed would be so hard?

Taking responsibility for her own life when she was wanted by extremely dangerous men meant she had to keep herself hidden. Airports had cameras and required ID. Her own home was off limits because it was the first place anyone would think to search for her. Not that she had many friends, but the few she had would be in immediate danger just by housing her. Not to mention the questions they would have.

That's when she realized she still had the key to the back door of her parents' walk-out basement. Beth knew they lived in a rural area and didn't so much as lock their car doors, let alone have an alarm system. Her parents were trusting like that.

At first, Beth thought she'd just stay in the shed at the back of their ten-acre property. She could access it from a dirt road not visible from the house, and because of all the trees, the shed was nearly hidden on the property. But when she got there and jimmied the door open, she realized the nights were going to get cold and there would be too many critters she wouldn't be able to see in the dark.

Shivering to herself, Beth pulled her recognizable red, compact car into the abandoned shed and made the short trek to her parents' home. This would give her time to think through what to do next. She needed to disappear—permanently. Travel as far away as possible and change her identity and her appearance. It was the only way she could survive.

In the meantime, the basement was comfortable. Beth knew her parents would never find her here, since her mom sometimes complained that they couldn't go downstairs anymore due to her bad back and her dad's iffy knee. Because this was the place where Beth had lived when she was still at home, all her childhood things were still here. Her mom had kept her room like a tomb, capturing her essence during her worst years—high school. And though her old bed was less comfortable than she remembered, it had welcomed her home.

The shower in the bathroom connected to her old bedroom was a perk, though Beth had to wrap a plastic bag around her newly formed cast to clean herself. That had been a process. Her left hand was broken, and luckily, her right hand was dominant, but Beth still found it a struggle and awkward to navigate.

She ate and slept when her parents left for their volunteer jobs. It was hard to come up with a solid plan for where to go next because once she stepped back out in the "real world," anything could happen. Even the best plans couldn't account for every possible conflict that might arise. Perhaps that's why she'd never tried to run from *them* before.

Beth might have stayed at her parents' house longer had it not been for a loud knocking on the fifth day and her mom's perky voice as she answered the door.

"I'm Officer Johnson. Sorry to bother you, ma'am, but we're looking for your daughter, Beth. You seen her lately?"

The man's voice wasn't familiar, and Beth had a sneaking suspicion he was no officer. Beth bolted off her bed where she'd been lounging and grabbed the backpack purse she'd found in her closet, left behind during her high school years. She'd been lucky to find a few items of clothing that still fit, which she'd pre-packed in the small pack for this very moment. She quickly slipped on her tennis shoes.

"No," Beth's mom answered. *"What's going on? Is Beth in some kind of trouble?"*

"We just got a report that she's gone missing," the man said. *"Mind if I look around?"*

That was Beth's cue to leave. She grabbed the backpack and slung it over her shoulder, let herself out the back door, careful to latch it behind her, and ran. The sun was down and there was no moon in sight. She didn't wait to give anyone time to look out the window and spot her. She just ran the dirt road to the shed, got in her car, backed out, and drove. It wasn't too far-fetched to think they would look for her at her parents' house. She was going to have to be smarter to stay ahead.

4

WILTON

Driving back to the office, Stephen thought about the disastrous meeting he'd had with Mak, Deputy Director Sikes, and Alyah Smith before he'd left for the funeral.

David had left Stephen with one clue, which had contained the name of the man who killed his brother. But David's dried, brown-red blood had marred the name. It was Alyah Smith who showed up with the final piece. Alyah, the District Attorney who'd formerly worked in their US Marshal office in Kansas City, had transferred to a career in Washington, DC.

Alyah showed up in the US Marshal office when he least expected to see her, just in time to decipher David's note. It said *Senator Langsten.* But naming the man who'd killed Stephen's brother wasn't all Alyah had to tell them. She had stolen a copy of a plan containing important details on an illegal operation headed up by Langsten. The plan—a manifest—had names, addresses, and bank account information, all stored on a zip drive.

In the pocket of her jeans, she'd held that key piece of evidence they needed to take down the senator and everyone else who had been working with him over the years. Evidence they had turned over to the FBI. Stephen knew their office, along with marshals all over the US, would likely be commissioned to find and capture each criminal mentioned. It would be a huge undertaking.

But Stephen had been more worried about protecting Alyah. What had she been thinking? He'd asked her to look around, not try to get herself killed. In the middle of a heated debate on whether Alyah would accept the witness protection they offered her, Stephen quietly excused himself, got in his car, and drove to the airport for David's funeral. He'd be lying if he said he hadn't used the trip as an excuse to get out of town to think about what he needed to do next.

Alyah Smith was the one woman who Stephen could not stop thinking about. They had connected deeply, bonding over the loss of her sister, Carley, solidifying the start of a strong relationship, only for Alyah to call it all off before it had even begun. She'd taken the job in Washington, DC, to further her career. Later, she'd admitted she also took the job to put distance between her and Stephen and the feelings she had for him. His job struck fear in her heart. She didn't want to always wonder if Stephen was coming home at night.

Stephen hopped out of his Tahoe, turning his focus to the meeting he was heading into. He was exactly on time to the morning brief, wearing a pair of black jeans and a dark grey polo shirt with his coffee in a to-go cup the way he liked it, hot and black.

He entered the room to find everyone was already there. Stephen's eyes widened and he paused, double-checking the time on his watch. He didn't usually miss a detail like when a meeting started. He self-consciously ran a hand through his unruly blond curls. His phone reminder told him he was on time, which meant they were early. He sighed in relief and strode into the room. He sat down, nodding to Mak and his boss, Sikes.

Warring emotions flooded him as his eyes fell on Alyah. Apparently, she had not gone into witness protection after all because here she sat at the wooden conference room table with the US Marshal emblem etched on top. Did she suddenly not care about her safety? She sure cared a lot when she was using it as the reason to break things off with Stephen.

"What's Alyah doing here?" Stephen whispered quietly to Mak as he slid into the seat right next to her. "I thought she was going into WITSEC."

"Good morning to you, too," Mak quipped sarcastically and answered in her typical, direct fashion. "Don't worry, we've assigned Alyah a protective detail. They decided as long as she was here—in this building with us—she would be safe."

"We need to get her out of town," Stephen breathed, worry etched on his brow.

Alyah sat forward, her long brown hair falling around her petite shoulders as her green eyes held Stephen's blue ones as she answered. "*We* will. As soon as I get all the information in the hands of the right people, I'll be on a plane out of here in mindless solitary confinement—I mean, protection."

Heat crawled up Stephen's neck as he watched Alyah smile with false sweetness and sit back in her seat. He hadn't meant for her to hear him.

Sikes fiddled with his remote control, looking up. There were two screens now. Some things had changed since Stephen's leave. One screen showed a Zoom waiting room. The other screen showed a picture that should have been jarring, but Stephen found himself slightly desensitized after memorizing every detail of it for the past six months. Only, now the picture had more than just one focal point—his brother minutes before he was killed.

Thanks to a contact from his former police station, the picture had been cleaned up to reveal not only a picture of a criminal with a gun to Greg Wilton's head, but the background where a group of teenagers stood, all of them Greg's friends, watching helplessly, faces in fear and agony. Stephen didn't even want to think about the therapy it would take to function after witnessing such a heinous act. The majority of those teenagers, turned adults, were now dead. Only one had survived, Beth Donovan, and she had fled.

"Good morning, Stephen," Sikes greeted, then he turned his attention to the screen. "Ah! There you are. Good morning, Trey. Trey Masterson is the FBI Director, located in Washington, DC."

All eyes lifted to the screen as a man with a short crew cut and stern look on his face appeared on Zoom. He wore black-rimmed glasses, which only added to his severity.

"Good morning, Deputy Director," Masterson greeted formally.

"Sikes is fine," he corrected.

Masterson nodded curtly. "I have my team on speaker listening in. We have agents from the Midwest states all the way to Washington, DC, on the call today. For the sake of time, we'll skip all their introductions and keep this to a core team for now. Until we have a plan and assignments to take this ring down, I will be your point of contact and will dispatch my team as I see fit."

"Yes," Sikes matched his tone. "As you know, during the course of the last six months, we've been working on apprehending criminals we've found to be connected to a drug and sex-trafficking ring. When we put one man away, we discovered that there are more people involved. We now have evidence that this ring is farther reaching than just the state of Missouri, which is why we called the FBI in to help take this thing down once and for all."

"Right," Masterson agreed. "Let's get started."

"Senator Joseph Langsten," Sikes announced. He turned his attention to Alyah Smith. She looked beautiful today. She always looked put together and professional. Stephen's problem was he'd given his heart to her, and she'd given it back. She'd left him, admitting the need to put physical distance between them. Stephen discovered with dismay that neither the distance nor the time had lessened his feelings for her as he watched her rise from her seat.

The anger and frustration left Stephen abruptly and in the void of that pent-up resentment, he realized he was letting his personal feelings interfere with his professional life, and he needed to pull it together.

Alyah stood confidently and pointed her clicker at the computer, quickly sharing her screen with Masterson. A picture of Senator Langsten now filled the screen. In the photo, Langsten's hand clasped the hand of Mickey Upton in a handshake, his head tilted close. He had aged well and his hair was shorter, but it was unmistakably him.

"This picture was taken at a rally in Oklahoma approximately two weeks ago. It shows that Senator Langsten is well-acquainted with the criminal, Mickey Upton, who was allegedly heading up a drug and sex-trafficking ring—"

"Allegedly nothing!" Mak interrupted.

Sikes gave Mak a warning look and Mak wisely shut her mouth.

"Further digging through files confirmed that Mickey Upton, who you know is a disgraced former senator, and Senator Langsten, are more than acquaintances. They are friends," Alyah confirmed.

"Being friends with a criminal doesn't make you guilty," Stephen commented.

"No, but murdering Wilton's brother in cold blood sure does," Mak commented.

"Just playing devil's advocate for the sake of what a lawyer in a court of law might say. We need to make sure we get this guy," Stephen answered.

"True," Alyah pointed and clicked at the screen again revealing another picture. This one was a long bank ledger of transactions. "I believe this will prove that Senator Langsten is paying Mickey Upton for services that are unknown to us at this time."

"I know what they are!" Mak raised her hand sarcastically but lowered it when Sikes leveled her again.

"We all do," Alyah acknowledged Mak's comment. "But to Stephen's point, it has to be proven in a court of law."

"No missing pieces," Sikes stated. "We need to take down the whole ring. The entire operation at one time. Now that we know who the players are, no need to give them a heads up."

"Saving the women they are holding hostage in the process!" Mak passionately added.

Sikes nodded.

Alyah took the zip drive she'd been protecting and inserted it into the computer. Its contents displayed up on the screen where the picture had been. "Here you will find maps of highways that I believe are routes used to traffic women." She clicked open another file. "Here, you will find a spreadsheet full of names to investigate—a complete planning manifest."

"How did you obtain this information, Alyah?" Stephen spoke, aware of the hard edge in his tone.

Alyah regarded him quietly for a second. "I was working with Senator Langsten on a case—"

"Is this going to be admissible in court?" Stephen cut in. "Attorney-client privilege and whatnot?"

"Yes, we do have attorney-client privilege. And I'm well aware of the law. Which is why I'm not telling you *why* the senator needed my services. However, it did give me access to other information in his office such as this bank statement and these spreadsheets. This is not a part of my case with him, nor is it covered under our agreement."

Stephen took a deep breath in and held it, then slowly released the tingle of fear that crept up his spine. "You could have gotten yourself killed."

"You were the one who told me to look around!" Alyah swiveled and stared Stephen down. "So, I did."

"I told you to be careful," Stephen answered. "Not put yourself into the line of fire!"

"At least you know who killed your brother now," Mak jumped in to defend Alyah.

"Alyah is not a trained marshal. It's not a position we should be putting her in." Stephen sat up straighter.

Alyah glared at him.

No one blinked for a few seconds.

"You're welcome, Stephen," Alyah stated quietly, her beautiful red lips lifted in a smirk, her green eyes cold as steel and filled with anger.

"At ease, you two," Sikes commanded, a low growl to his tone.

Alyah sat back down, but Stephen noticed a pink flush had crept into her cheeks.

"Okay," Masterson said as he cleared his throat. "So, what we have is photographic evidence of Senator Langsten minutes before he killed Greg Wilton. Do I understand that we have a witness who was also at the scene who can testify to the murder as well?"

"We did, but her whereabouts are currently unknown," Stephen answered quickly.

Mak snapped her mouth shut, but Stephen knew she

wanted to point the finger at him for that. She would be right. He did let Beth leave.

"Okay," Masterson continued, getting them back on track. "We have bank statements that prove Langsten was paying Upton for something, but we don't have evidence of what that something is."

"Right," Alyah confirmed.

Sikes put his hands on the table. "And we have a manifest with maps, routes, and names so we can officially investigate how far this ring goes and who these people are."

"That's where we come in," Masterson jumped in. "It's going to be a big job to round up as many people involved all at once, so we don't tip them off and have our criminals go into hiding."

"That's why we need a solid plan," Stephen said.

"We're going to need a warrant to cover a more thorough search of Langsten's office. Can we assume Ms. Smith can go back in to show us where she found this information once we have the warrant?" Masterson asked.

They all knew what Masterson was doing. They needed the warrant to cover their tracks and make sure no one ever suspected them of taking evidence illegally. This was tricky, considering this evidence is what would give them the right to go do a thorough search.

"Yes," Alyah said.

"No," Stephen answered simultaneously. "It's not her job to play detective. She put herself in enough danger. For once, can't we just play this straight and do our job by the book? Go in, apprehend the criminal, get a search warrant, and uncover the rest of the information safely while Langsten sits in a cell?"

Sikes shrugged. "It's about timing, Wilton. If we rush this, we might be ensuring that information gets dumped—erased, shredded, deleted—to cover tracks. Alyah is in a position where Langsten trusts her. How do you feel about showing the FBI where to look when we get the warrant, Alyah?"

Stephen saw it. Just a flash of fear, but it was real enough that he opened his mouth to protest.

Alyah cut in before Stephen could speak. "Langsten trusted me. I had full access to his office, his files, his bank statement, and his phone. Then something changed. I think he might suspect me now."

"What changed?" Sikes asked.

"He started canceling meetings and dismissing me from normally scheduled duties," Alyah admitted.

Stephen's jaw dropped. "Which means you're in danger and need to stay as far away from DC as possible!"

"He's right." Sikes glanced up at Masterson, whose expression looked pensive. "It's our job to protect Alyah, but we can use her as a consultant from far away. Not to mention, we are still hoping that one of the guys we have apprehended—Upton, Allister, or Pottstaff—gets sick of sitting in those cells and starts talking."

"Yes, in the meantime, you two—" Sikes pointed to Mak and Wilton, "are going to DC to watch Langsten."

"Okay." Stephen nodded to Sikes. Finally, a plan that made sense.

Mak crossed her arms over her chest. "With all due respect, don't you think sending in two marshals will spook Langsten? That's a sure way to get him to start dumping and covering."

"True," Sikes agreed. "Which is why you will be there in an undercover capacity. You lay low and if your cover gets blown, make it look like you're visiting friends in DC. Heck, we can make it look like you're thinking about a transfer."

"Won't work," Stephen said flatly.

"I beg your pardon?" Sikes' face instantly turned red.

Stephen straightened up in his chair. "No more games. No more undercover. This man killed my brother. The minute he sees me, he'll know why I'm there. We have enough to make a quiet arrest."

"Word will leak. We can't risk it," Masterson jumped in.

"Then, you need to send someone else," Stephen asserted.

No one said a word.

"I need a minute," Stephen got up and stalked out of the room, unwilling to consider what really had him spooked. While working in this close of proximity to Alyah again was the last thing he needed, his reasoning went even deeper. The minute Stephen found himself in a room with Senator Langsten, he didn't trust himself not to seek revenge. Langsten didn't deserve a trial. He deserved the same fate he'd dealt to countless others.

Give him time... Stephen could hear the words float behind him as he walked out the door of the conference room. He kept on walking out of the building. No amount of time would fix the anger in his hardening heart. Or the bigger problem that lurked there. An emotion that was more prominent than any others—fear.

5

ALYAH

Alyah watched as Stephen Wilton walked out of the conference room, taking his storm of emotions with him. She understood his feelings because she was struggling with them too. Though she couldn't guess what had triggered him, she knew very well what she was feeling. She was in love with Stephen. She had been for a while. Her attraction to him had been instantaneous, with his striking blue eyes, wayward curly blond hair, and the confidence he wore in his slim but muscular frame. She had been drawn to him.

She had hated him before she knew him, at least, that's what she told herself. He had let her sister, Carley, die. Oh, she had known about his relationship with Carley. Alyah had made it her business to know what her sister was doing, even if Carley had wanted nothing to do with her. The company Carley kept tended to be wild and borderline criminal. Which is why Alyah had judged that Stephen was the same way.

When Alyah first approached Stephen Wilton, it hadn't been professional courtesy—though she told herself it was her job to weed out any corruption. Rather, it had been personal curiosity. A desire to see the man who'd loved her sister then let her die. She hadn't expected to see the gut-wrenching sorrow on his face that mirrored her own. Stephen was many things, but she saw who he was from the beginning. She'd recognized his self-torture and desire to fix himself and his mistake. She'd fallen hard and fast. Then, she'd run away. His reputation around the office, that dreadful nickname—Love 'Em and Leave 'Em Wilton—had only been one strike against him. She could see that he was more than that.

What had scared her away was the fear that something would happen to him on the job, and she would get a phone call that it was him this time who would not be coming home. Losing her estranged sister had been hard. Losing him, well, she wasn't sure she could survive that. So, she left him first. It hadn't taken her much distance to realize her mistake. She had nothing but time in the quiet moments to process that close connection she'd felt to him.

Then Stephen had started calling her. She'd let the calls go to voicemail, hoping to discourage his efforts, trying to preserve her heart. But the messages he left destroyed the walls and boundaries she'd attempted to erect. They were true attempts to show her who he was. They only pulled her in further. Distance had not helped. It had made her ache for him.

Alyah had tried to stay away, but then Stephen left the message that Mak had been hurt. Alyah just reacted. She had to be there to comfort Stephen. She'd reconnected with her old team. She was reminded that the Kansas City office was full of good, solid people. They were so different than the politicians she had met in Washington, DC.

Sure, she'd had a salary increase, but she'd used every bit of that to update her wardrobe just to fit in. In Washington, DC, she found she could not take people at face value—at least, not the people she met and worked with. Everyone had an agenda, and not all of them were noble. She felt like a country mouse trying to cross a busy street in rush hour traffic. No matter how much time she gave it, she simply didn't belong there.

It had been a mistake to take the job. Until she realized the case Stephen was working on was connected to her case and people she now knew firsthand. She'd put the pieces together from the snatches of conversation she'd overheard when she went to see Mak.

But she hadn't known how much danger it would put her in. She hadn't been honest about that. After she'd found the picture of Micky Upton, she started paying more attention and watching Senator Langsten more closely. From her years of practicing as a lawyer, it wasn't hard for her brain to pick up patterns and anomalies. What was hard was pretending like she didn't know the truth.

She'd gotten lucky the day she discovered Langsten knew what Alyah had been up to. She didn't know how he knew she'd been snooping, but he did. Alyah had gotten to the senator's office early that morning and overheard his words through the door before she opened it.

"Alyah Smith knows the truth. Everything," Senator Langsten had said.

"What do you propose we do about that?" an unknown voice asked.

"We need to eliminate her," Langsten responded.

"How should we do that?"

"Make it look like an accident."

Alyah had to put her hand over her mouth to stifle her horror. Then she'd run. Fifteen minutes later, she'd gotten a text from Senator Langsten asking to meet outside the office. *Like a kill room,* Alyah thought as her mind filled in the blanks. Alyah had texted back, agreeing to the change, though in reality, she was moving farther away from the capitol. She requested to move the time and bought herself an extra hour. She had been right about all of it. She was in danger.

She'd driven to the airport without stopping to pack a bag and had gotten on the first plane straight to Kansas City, not surprised to find an active US Marshal team finishing up a case. She thought if she stayed close to her former team, she'd be protected. The part of her she was unwilling to acknowledge out loud knew the truth. She would never be safe until Senator Langsten was locked away. She should have said *yes* to witness protection, but she wanted to feel useful. She needed to help. To stay ahead of her fear.

Instead, two US Marshals had been assigned to accompany her around for the foreseeable future. Though it had been the cause of much angst before, Alyah was now glad her Kansas City home hadn't sold while she had been in Washington, DC. Living in it now gave her a sense of normalcy. Not to mention, her master bedroom had a connecting bathroom, so she didn't have to leave the suite unless she needed food or something in the main house. It was a good thing Alyah relished the feeling of sitting in her favorite oversized, felt chair in her large bedroom. It gave her a place to relax while the marshals took over the spare bedroom and couch in the main house.

"Alyah?" Mak's voice cut through Alyah's musings. "Meeting is adjourned. You okay?"

Alyah looked up at Mak and nodded. Alyah wanted to confess the depth of the trouble she was in, but she knew such a confession would result in her own confinement with nothing to do but wait. The other part of her desperately wanted to be like Mak—fearless, empowered, and laughing at shadows. For now, she'd settle with helping with the hunt for Langsten. Maybe Mak's fierceness would rub off on her.

"Good," Mak gave Alyah a mischievous smile. "Let's go get Wilton and bring him back here."

"Where did he go?" Alyah wondered.

"He's day drinking." Mak grinned.

"But it's not even eight-thirty in the morning! Where on earth did he find booze at this hour?"

"You'll see." Mak waved for Alyah to follow her.

Sheer curiosity made Alyah get up and follow Mak out the door. "Does he drink like this often?"

"No, this is a first." Mak pulled out her car keys.

"Why now?" Alyah asked.

"You're in town," Mak answered simply, walking out the door into the beautiful summer sun.

"Oh no, you don't," Alyah stopped walking abruptly. "I don't have a thing to do with his bad habits, that's one hundred percent on him."

Alyah would be damned if they tried to blame that on her. She'd been blamed for her mother's drinking growing up, then Carley's terrible behavior, and worse—for her own father leaving them.

"Spunky and true," Mak said as she opened the car door. "I like it. Life is more interesting when you're around."

Interesting was one way to put it. *Lively* would be more accurate. *Alive* was her goal. Who would she be when all this finished?

Only time would tell.

6

———————

BETH

With a burst of inspiration, Beth drove away from her parents' home and headed in the direction of her nearest relative. Uncle Donnie owned Don's Automart, which was located a few short hours away. She wasn't naïve enough to think she could drive a red car around for long without being easily spotted, so her goal was to ditch it.

When she arrived, she found an open spot at the back of Don's Automart and pulled her red car in to *hide* in plain sight. Just before eleven that night, she turned off the car and waited, watching to see if she was followed. Every decision she made had to be about survival. But then, she laughed bitterly to herself. When had that not been true?

Which is why Beth had pulled on a denim blue ballcap before she left. She wore a light black jacket (one she'd borrowed from her dad's closet since her cast didn't fit into anything that was her size), a baggy t-shirt, and a pair of leggings. There were running shoes on her feet because if she was honest with herself, and she had to be, she knew she might have to put them to good use at some point.

When Beth was confident that she hadn't been followed,

she reclined her seat as far as it could go and laid back. This wasn't the first time she'd spent a night in her car, and she was sure it wouldn't be the last.

At the first light of dawn, Beth woke. She knew the car lot wasn't open yet, but she got out of her car anyway, squared her shoulders, and walked into the office. She was betting that since Uncle Donnie was an early bird, she would catch him. Sure enough, less than five minutes later, she found herself in front of Uncle Donnie himself.

"Well, Beth Donovan!" Donnie exclaimed. "It's been years since I saw you last! How the heck have you been?"

Despite herself, Beth smiled. She forced herself to answer cheerfully. "Good."

Uncle Donnie and Aunt Carol had helped her out at a time in her life when things had been tough. They had taken Beth in when she found herself pregnant and her parents were at their wits end on account of Beth's *very unplanned pregnancy her freshman year*, as her parents liked to say. Her parents had also told Beth that she had gotten *lucky* that she had Lacy at the beginning of the summer. It had given Beth time to recover and be back for a fresh start to her old school where no one would be the wiser.

Her parents had been opposed to Beth moving back to the same school district until Beth had promised to allow her parents to raise Lacy and call her Beth's younger sister. It had never sat well with Beth, but she'd missed her friends terribly—mainly Shania. But Uncle Donnie and Aunt Carol had been so kind during that time, Beth had a special place for them in her heart.

In fact, this car lot was where Beth had bought her first car. Uncle Donnie loved to reminisce about the *good old days* every chance he got. He had some great stories about her dad. Ones that her dad would never tell. Beth had practically memorized the wild stories on account of how many times she'd heard them. It was nice to know her dad had been a flawed teenager once as well.

"How's Lacy?" Donnie asked.

Beth stiffened, then she formed a fake smile. "Great!"

"Good to hear that!" Donnie said as he paused and let his eyes wander to gaze out the window. "I still remember your dad's fortieth birthday party. There we were, having the time of our life, talking and laughing—a bit too loudly, I might add—drinking some, and I look over and there you are. Lacy might have been what—one? And you were on the floor with her on a blanket with a load of toys, playing with Lacy, as if no one else in that room existed."

Beth gulped. She remembered that night. They *had* been loud, and they had woken Lacy up. Her mom often told Beth to let Lacy cry because her mom believed it was good to let a baby self soothe. Beth whole-heartedly disagreed. She had snatched Lacy out of her crib and cuddled her close, then she'd set up toys in the corner of the room.

Before she could stop them, the introspective words that Beth had believed her whole life popped out. "I wasn't really a mom to her."

Donnie looked surprised. "I wouldn't say that. You did the best you could, given your arrangement." Beth knew Donnie was referencing her mom raising Lacy. "You were just so young."

Beth had to blink back sudden tears. She wouldn't cry. She didn't have time to cry. She took a deep breath. "Well, that's not why I came in," Beth tried to joke.

"Right," Donnie said, his voice adapting a business tone. "What brought you here?"

"Oh, I was hoping you'd buy the Mini Cooper from me," Beth tried to appear confident.

Donnie blinked. "Trade in?"

"No," Beth cleared her throat. "I'm just looking for a cash deal."

"What year is that? Heck, I'm the one who sold it to you. Let me check." Donnie toggled on his computer and pushed a few keys on his keyboard. "2012. You kept it in good condition?"

Beth nodded.

"Gosh, Beth." Donnie took his ball cap off and ruffled his hair underneath before putting it back on. "You know I'm gonna give you the best deal I can. I can give you forty-five hundred for it, but I don't know if I can get you that much cash right here, right now. I think we just made our deposit yesterday, and I don't know if we have that lying around the office. So, I'd be happy to give you what we have and write you a check for the rest—"

"No check, just cash," Beth interjected.

"I'd love to help you out, but..."

"What *do* you have?" Beth asked, not even trying to mask the desperation that leaked out in her words.

Donnie paused and studied Beth. He sat back in his seat. His eyes flicked to her cast. "I have to ask. Are you in some kind of trouble?" Concern etched his brow.

"Trouble?" Beth asked with an unconvincing laugh. "No, I just need to free up some cash."

"Beth, we probably have around three thousand sitting in our vault right now," Donnie admitted.

Beth gulped, realizing the difference, knowing that she would have to take a loss of fifteen hundred dollars.

"Not looking to take advantage of you..." Donnie told her. "I could keep a tab here and owe you the rest when you come back to town."

"I'll take it!" Beth reached across the desk to shake Donnie's hand.

"All right," he said doubtfully, grasping her hand. "Let me

just get the papers drawn up, and you can sign. Be right back."

"Thank you." Knowing paperwork took a bit of time, Beth leaned down to grab her phone out of her backpack purse. She was bent over and ruffled through the bare minimums she had jammed in there—a change of clothes, her wallet, a toothbrush—when she caught movement out of the corner of her eye. Outside the window to her right, Beth had a clear view of where she had parked her compact car. Two men stood by it. One was looking into the car, and the other was scanning the lot. When his face turned toward the window of Donnie's office, Beth lowered herself to the floor.

All breath whooshed out of Beth, and she was having a hard catching it. She tried to calm herself and think what to do. They were here—already. They had found her. From her position, she peaked toward the window to get a good look at them.

They were both fit and on the muscular side. One was a few inches taller than the other, but they looked similar. Maybe they were brothers or related in some way. Both had dark hair. One wore his hair shorter and had dark brown eyes that had no hint of emotion as he continued to scan. The other wore sunglasses. Any minute, they would come into the building and find her. She would be trapped in here. A panic sweat formed over her brow.

"Great news! We were able to come up with four thousand—"

Beth jumped and hit her head on the desk she had been half under as the door opened.

There was a pause as the door shut.

"Beth? What are you...?"

"Do you see those guys standing by my car?" Beth hissed as she pointed in the direction.

"Yes," Donnie's eyes flicked to the window, and his voice took on a concerned edge.

"I am in trouble. I can't get into it. But I need a way to get out of here undetected or a ride to Union Station. I was planning to get an Uber, but now…" Beth shook her head.

"Let's get the police on the phone—"

"No!" Beth shouted, then immediately lowered her voice. "No, please."

"I'm not harboring a fugitive, am I?" Donnie's laugh sounded strained and cautious.

"No," Beth looked up at Donnie, showing him the fear in her eyes.

Donnie walked over and shut the window blinds. He held her look for a minute, then went to his desk and palmed his keys. "Okay. Give me a minute."

Beth stayed where she was as Donnie left. She was entirely at his mercy. What had she been thinking? He could still choose to call the cops. For all she knew, that's exactly what he was doing right now. Just when her mind had started to spin out, Donnie was back.

"Okay, follow me." Donnie left the door open, and Beth followed him down a long hallway that led to a garage. Donnie opened the door and motioned toward the lifted white truck sitting in the bay. "Hop in back. Windows are tinted."

"Thank you!" Beth felt the tears again. *No, you don't have time for that,* her mind chastised her.

"Don't thank me yet. Let's get you on a train." Donnie got in the driver's seat and handed back a large envelope of money and papers for Beth to sign while they drove.

Beth tucked herself between the seat and the floorboard knowing she was going to have some questions to answer. She would tell him what she could and hope that Uncle Donnie would keep her secrets.

7

WILTON

Stephen stared into his drink, watching the liquid slosh over the rim. He had apparently sat it down too hard. He never drank at this time of day. It wasn't a good idea and he didn't plan to make it a habit. But Stephen had found this bar where cops and firefighters, whose days were flipped around due to night shifts, could come and relax. Here, it was okay to drink in the morning.

What was he thinking leaving such an important briefing meeting before it was over? In truth, he didn't know what had come over him. Despite his reputation for always keeping himself under control, his emotions felt anything but these days. He felt like his focus was slipping, too.

Where Stephen had always been very confident on the job, he now felt self-conscious. All it had taken to set him off was the fear that he was late to the meeting and Alyah's judgmental eyes. Alyah coming back was unsettling, but Stephen couldn't figure out if it was the only source of his angst. He knew he would have to leave again soon, and he couldn't protect Alyah while he was on the road.

Stephen sighed into his drink. So much was happening in

his life right now. He would be lying if he said the job wasn't wearing on him. They'd just finished a case, and they were already heading into the next one. Well, they were continuing the one they had been on. Either way, it looked like there would be no end to it any time soon.

Then there was the truth about his brother. Stephen had opted not to tell his parents that Davey hadn't killed Greg after all. That Greg's real murderer was still out there, and Stephen was hunting him. He kept telling himself that he would sit his parents down when this was all over, after they caught Joseph Langsten.

And Davey Stinnert's name had not officially been cleared yet. Stephen took a gulp of his seven and seven. Maybe there would have been more mourners at Davey's funeral had the public not thought he was still a murderer. Stephen could not erase that thought from his mind. In law enforcement, a chief of police would typically address the press and break the new evidence in a case. David Stinnert was not a murderer. He was a fall-guy.

To Stephen, he was a hero, and Stephen had said as much to David. David had sworn he was more of a villain. Still, David had saved Stephen's life. When he whittled away at the emotions, he discovered anger, fear, sadness, and an over-whelming sense of guilt.

What had David seen in Stephen that made him want to sacrifice his life for Stephen's? How could Stephen live a life that was worthy of that? Stephen didn't know the answer. Nor did he have a handle on what emotion showed up when. Stephen knew it wasn't a good look for him.

Sooner rather than later, Stephen was going to have to get control over all of this. Right now, he was just navigating a whole lot of change coming at him faster than he could process. Change was hard for anyone. For Stephen, it was like kryptonite.

8

MAK

Mak spotted Wilton sitting at Hole-in-the-Wall bar, a place known as a law enforcement hang-out. He was hunched over what looked like a seven and seven. She knew it was his go-to drink. But finding him drinking alone at the bar so early in the morning wasn't like him. But then, neither was leaving a meeting before it was over.

"Hey," Mak said as she sat on the bar stool next to him.

Stephen turned. His eyes immediately narrowed. "Come to talk some sense into me? Don't make me regret telling you I was here."

Mak turned unusually serious eyes on Wilton. "I would never."

They sat in silence for a few minutes. For once, Stephen broke it. "I think it's time for me to step back, Mak. This case has become way too personal for me. I can't see when I'm this close. I'm too invested and pushing to solve this for personal reasons. There's a line I think I'm crossing. I also have to consider if Langsten and his people might be pulling me into a trap. Am I involved in this because they want me to be, and I'm playing right into their plan? If so, how far does it go? Did they hire Alyah knowing that she was a link to me? Or worse, have I put her in danger when she was trying to stay far from it?"

Mak quirked her mouth to the side. "Stephen, I'm going to say this as a friend… you sound really paranoid. You and Alyah weren't together long enough for anyone to know. I'm pretty sure they offered her the job before you came into her life. And I have a new theory about you getting too personally invested in your cases."

"Oh?" Stephen asked. He finished his drink. "Do tell."

Mak ignored his sarcasm. "I think you being personally invested is what makes you great at this job. No one will ever care more about solving this case than you. Except me, of course." She turned to the bartender. "Sprite, please."

Stephen eyed her wearily. "Of course."

"I don't think you should consider that a weakness. It's more like a superpower."

"Well, personal or not, my priority is keeping Alyah safe in all this. What is Sikes thinking?" Stephen's fist pounded on the bar.

"I think it's Alyah's choice," Mak answered after a moment of contemplation.

"Why? Why would she choose to put herself in danger when she re-routed her whole life—took another job and ran away—just so she could protect herself?" Stephen's tortured expression met Mak's eyes.

"Maybe she's facing her fears now?" Mak suggested. "People change, Stephen."

"What if I can't keep her safe?" Stephen looked tortured.

"This is a choice Alyah is making. Maybe we should give her the respect of letting her help if she wants to. Our job is to keep her as safe as possible. But we all know, at the end of the day, that this job, this task, is dangerous. There's no guarantee here. We just have to live every day as if—"

"There's no tomorrow," Stephen finished Mak's mantra for her.

"Exactly." Mak put her finger on her nose.

"You don't think this seems strange?" Stephen pushed. "It goes against Alyah's character. She plays it straight and safe. This is risky and dangerous. What is she trying to prove?"

"Actually, I don't have to prove anything to anybody," a sharp voice answered from behind them.

Mak watched Stephen whirl around. Alyah stood there, still wearing her black high-waisted pants and silky forest green blouse that she'd worn to the meeting. Her hands were on her hips, and she tapped the toe of her shiny black stiletto. Her eyes held Stephen's attention. They shot daggers of anger and reminded Mak of how Alyah had acted when she first met Wilton. She certainly had been suspicious of him. Glancing at Wilton now, she could see it in his eyes. He loved it when Alyah was mad. He might even be provoking her anger.

"You told her I was here?" Stephen asked Mak the question, but his eyes never strayed from Alyah.

Mak's eyes volleyed back and forth between the two of them. Wilton was in dangerous territory. Alyah angry was a sight to behold.

"We came here together." Mak winced. Maybe she should have warned Wilton. "She stopped off at the restroom."

"Are you aware of what I do for a living as a District Attorney?" Alyah asked, her voice low but snappy. She didn't wait for an answer. "Prosecuting law breakers, attending trials, overseeing justice department operations, conducting investigations, and presenting evidence in a court of law. Does knowing that help you understand that what we are *proposing* is just me doing my job? Does it further help to know that all the evidence I've gathered to this point has been obtained legally? Whether you like it or not, I will continue to gather evidence until I see Senator Joseph Langsten behind bars."

Stephen waited a beat, glancing at Mak and then back at Alyah. Stephen crossed his arms over his pecs. "Oh, is it my turn to speak, counselor?"

Mak's eyes widened and she gave an almost imperceptible shake of her head as she turned quickly back to the Sprite the bartender had placed in front of her.

Alyah closed the gap between the two of them and pointed a finger at Stephen's chest. "You know, I can't tell if you lack confidence in my abilities to do my job or if you think I need protection from a big, strong man, but let me assure you, your opinion is not needed here."

Mak snorted loudly.

Stephen's face flushed in anger and Mak could see the red creeping up his neck. He opened his mouth to speak when words from several TV screens hanging around the bar interrupted their conversation.

Senator Joseph Langsten disappeared from his home late last night. His wife estimates his last known whereabouts were around midnight when he got up and didn't come back to bed.

A pretty woman who looked to be in her late fifties came on the screen, crying and clutching a note to her chest. Her hands were shaking, making it hard to see the message sprawled on it. "I found a note on my dining room table this morning. He's been abducted."

Diane Langsten said her husband was abducted from his own home in the middle of the night. If anyone has knowledge of the whereabouts of Senator Langsten, please call the tipline number at the bottom of the screen.

Eyes wide, Stephen threw money on the bar. Then he, Mak, and Alyah turned and hurried outside. While it had been entertaining listening to Alyah remind Stephen of his place and the equality women have fought for, the news report had Mak feeling serious. Mak and Alyah got in the Range Rover. Wilton wordlessly got into the back of the car. *How much did he drink?* Mak worried.

Mak had just buckled her seatbelt when her phone rang. Seeing it was her husband, John, Mak pushed the button to answer it as she reversed out of a parking space.

"Hey, babe!" Mak said, her voice clipped, her mind on getting back to the station. *Where had the senator disappeared to?*

"You alone?" he asked.

"No, Wilton and Alyah are in the car," Mak said. "I can take you off speaker."

"Hi, John!" Wilton called to the car console.

Mak rolled her eyes. She pushed another button and picked up her phone, putting it to her ear so only she could hear him. "What's up?"

"Sounds like you're busy," John commented.

"Well, yes," Mak breathed as she navigated traffic with one hand. "We just had a break in the case—and not a good one. We're heading back to get our orders. I have a feeling we'll need to get on a plane this afternoon."

"Okay," John drew out the word.

Mak went on alert. John knew this was part of the job. He never bristled over her sudden changes in schedule. "Is everything okay?"

"Yeah. I just have some news. A possible job opportunity—"

A car honked loudly as Mak jerked the wheel to narrowly avoid some jerk who flew into her lane. Mak swore softly.

Alyah gripped the bar over her head.

"Whoa!" Wilton yelped.

"Maybe you can call me back later?" John suggested.

"I will," Mak promised. "Love you."

"Love—"

Mak had hung up the phone before John finished the words.

"That dude almost hit us!" Wilton snickered.

"Ugh!" Mak exclaimed. "How much did you have to drink?"

"Just a few." Wilton promised.

"A few too many," Alyah muttered under her breath.

Mak whipped into a parking spot in front of the federal building and turned off the car. She turned to Wilton with all the aggravation she was feeling. "Just pull yourself together before we get in here, would you?"

Wilton nodded. "I'll be fine!"

"Good, because I don't have time to babysit you." Mak grumbled as they got out the car and pushed through the majestic US Marshal double doors.

9

BETH

Beth stared out at the scenery as it quickly flashed by on account of the speed of the train. She shifted, lightly holding her casted arm against her body. Sometimes her arm ached, and no matter how much she moved around, she could not get comfortable. Don's final words after she thanked him for going out of his way for her played in her brain on repeat.

"Your dad loves you, Beth," Don had said.

"He has a funny way of showing it," Beth stated.

"Yeah, he does. He's always struggled with that," Don agreed. *"Having said that, you're an adult and he doesn't need to know what or who you're running from. Neither do I. But you need to know you're not alone. People love you and can help you if you need it."*

"Thank you." Beth nodded and felt the tears well again. Emotions she had shoved down a long time—maybe years—threatened to spill over. No one could help her. She hadn't been able to keep her emotions in check since she'd gotten on the train.

A small commotion sounded, drawing Beth's attention. Beth tensed, instincts on edge. She couldn't see what was happening at first. Then, a child around three-years-old was running up the aisle and a worn-out looking mother followed closely, trying to get ahold of her daughter. The train made a turn, and the little girl fell into the wall. Surprised when she lost her balance, the child began to wail.

Patiently, the mother, having caught up to her, gently scooped the toddler and put her back on her feet. Then the mom squatted down to eye level.

"What did I tell you about running on the train?" the mother asked.

The girl tugged on her low pigtails and sniffled before she answered. "Not to."

"And you did it anyway, didn't you? You always have a choice. When you choose to disobey, you can get hurt. Are you hurt?" the mother looked her daughter over.

The little girl shook her head and wiped her tears. "No."

"Okay, you got lucky this time. You need to listen to mommy. Here, hold my hand." The mother straightened and offered her daughter her hand. The little girl obediently took it and together they walked away.

Beth's chest tightened. She remembered when Lacy was that age, her own blond hair tied in pigtails. Beth hadn't parented Lacy. She'd left that to her mom. But she couldn't help but wonder how different her life would have been if she'd just accepted her responsibility. Maybe they would have been like the mom and daughter on *Gilmore Girls*. Beth would have been imperfect as a mom, but she knew one thing. She'd have a better relationship with Lacy right now.

Instead, Beth was on the run, trying to put as much distance between her and Lacy as possible. *For Lacy's protection,* Beth kept telling herself. But maybe Beth needed to admit that she didn't know how to be close—to Lacy or to anyone, really—and staying away had always been the safest thing for everyone.

As Beth stared out the window, watching the scenery

speed by, she pulled her ballcap down over her eyes and let the tears fall. Once they started, she couldn't get them to stop. A great torrent of emotion flowed down her cheeks, washing away her past regrets, putting in motion the healing of her broken soul. She cried until she had nothing left. Until her eyes felt heavy, and she fell into fitful sleep. A sleep that she could not fully give herself to because she couldn't let her guard down.

The train glided to a stop and the automated voice told passengers they'd arrived at Chicago Union Station. Beth put her head up, feeling the dried, crusted tears on her cheeks and noticing the crick in her neck from hiding under her hat for so long. She lifted her head and looked out the window, her eyes searching. She had to assume she had been followed. Assuming she was safe would get her killed, which was almost like allowing an attack to happen.

Eyes scanning defensively, she noticed busy people exiting the train and heading toward the stairs that she assumed led to some main street in Chicago. The small crowd of fast-moving people were purpose driven. Maybe that's why she spotted the men. Her stomach lurched as two fit men fought against the flow of travelers, walking toward the train instead of away. They stood out with their stocky body types and muscular builds. Both wore black, and they caused quite the commotion with people moving in the opposite direction and giving them dirty looks. They were the same men who had been stalking her car back in Arkansas, and they were now rushing on the platform, pushing against the crowd of people who were trying to exit the train.

Beth's stomach lurched, temporarily frozen. She slumped low in her seat and watched the taller man go to the front of the train and the short one search the windows near the middle of the train. She knew who they were looking for. She needed to move before they found her. But before she could, the short man's eyes lifted to the window where she was staring and locked right onto hers.

Beth ducked down, but she knew it was too late. She'd stared straight into the menacing brown eyes of a handsome devil—likely a bouncer at a bar who could snap her in half if he got his hands on her.

If she wasn't sure if he recognized her, she became convinced when his movements became quick and jerky. He turned, shouted something, and pointed, which made the taller man look up to him and then toward her. Only, Beth wasn't sitting still anymore. She was moving. Reacting. In a matter of minutes, they were going to board this train and there would be no exit for her. How did they keep finding her?

10

MAK

When they entered the US Marshal office, they found a frenzy of activity. "The BOLO and APB have already been issued for Senator Langsten," a voice called out.

"Good," Sikes answered. He greeted the three of them at the door. "I assume you've heard the news?"

Mak nodded and fell in step with Sikes, following him back to his office, Alyah and Wilton on her heels. "We did. Think he knows we're onto him and is fleeing?"

"One hundred percent," Sikes agreed. "This is where you two get to shine. We have a criminal on the run. I don't envy your jobs. This guy could have access to just about any location anywhere in the world, but you need to find him and bring him in. We can't let him disappear."

"Speaking of…" Mak said. "Do we have him on a no-fly list?"

Sikes poked his head out of his office and shouted. "Yates, where are we on the no-fly list?"

"Got it! Good to go," a man shouted back.

"We've made contact with the Police Department of

Washington, DC, and requested a warrant to search Langsten's office and home," another voice called out.

Sikes nodded. "Good. Keep up the good work. I need to know every property the man owns—homes, rentals, properties under construction. We need intel on every business he signed his name to. Check business loans, cars, trucks, RVs, private jets, mistresses, his favorite hotels... Give me anything that tells us what direction the senator might be headed next."

"I can help with some of that," Alyah asserted. "Having worked with him closely, I know the man pretty well."

"Great, let me get you set up on a desk." Sikes walked away with Alyah.

Mak whirled to Stephen and gave him a warning look.

"Relax, I'm just a little tipsy. I'll be fine," Stephen assured Mak.

"Well, you're going to pull it together and drink coffee or eat something because we need your full attention to detail right now. Can we count on you? Are you in this?" Mak put her hands on Stephen's shoulders and shook him lightly.

Stephen stared at Mak, then nodded and went off toward the kitchen.

Sikes returned to Mak's side. "Is he okay?"

Mak shrugged and tried to joke. "Is Wilton ever *really* okay?"

Sikes didn't laugh. Instead, he gave Mak a serious look.

Mak sighed. "Don't worry, he'll pull it together."

"Good. We need him."

Wilton returned just as Sikes' phone rang. "Masterson," Sikes greeted as he closed his office door and put his phone on speaker.

"Sikes, what the hell is happening?" the FBI director wasted no time.

"That's what we're trying to figure out," Sikes answered.

"Let me give you the full details on my end. I assume you saw the news brief?" Masterson asked.

"Yes," Mak answered for Sikes. "Mak Cunningham here."

Wilton stood holding a steaming cup of coffee.

"And Wilton's here as well," Sikes stated.

"And Alyah Smith? Is she in the room?" Masterson asked.

"No," Sikes said quickly. "I can get her in here."

"Not yet," Masterson's answer was terse. "I have a theory that Alyah might have tipped him off, and he ran."

Stephen gasped. "You think Alyah tipped off Langsten?"

Mak gave him a warning look.

"Not directly… Well, again, this is just a theory. She was working with him, was she not?" It was a rhetorical question. "Maybe it spooked him when she came here. Not sure, but something made him take off."

"What about the letter the news referenced?" Mak asked. "They used the word *abducted.*"

"Yes, that was our doing. We were very selective with what information we put out and what we allowed Mrs. Langsten to say. Often, we silence the media. In this case, we needed to alert the general public that Langsten is missing so we can get reports if anyone sees him without creating a panic. We figure the more Langsten thinks he's in control, the less desperate he will be. We were sure to mention it was an abduction as opposed to what we all know this really is."

"Okay, so you *leaked* the news… Maybe next time, you could give us a heads up before you inform reporters?" Sikes gritted out.

"There was no time," Masterson said curtly. "The key to controlling the narrative is to strike fast before anyone else has a chance to spin it."

Mak rolled her eyes. Investigations and apprehending

criminals worked so much better when all agencies worked together. She had hoped this FBI director would prove to be more cooperative.

"Well, take us back to the beginning. What does the letter actually say?" Sikes asked.

"That's the thing." Masterson cleared his throat. "Mrs. Langsten wouldn't let us see it. She said it was written to her and her alone. Told us to come back with a search warrant."

"Hmm, does she really believe it's an abduction?" Mak asked.

"Sounds to me like she knows how to play the game of politics," Sikes said. "She won't say a word that will come back to bite her later."

"How did he know we were onto him?" Wilton asked.

"That's the awkward part of all of this," Masterson said quickly. "I hate to circle back to this, but we need to rule out that DA Alyah Smith tipped him off before she came here."

"She's one of us!" Wilton bristled. "She comes straight from this office. She's as honest as they come. Why would you think that?"

"Something made the senator run before we even made any moves. We need to consider that there's a leak some-where," Masterson retorted.

"She's not the leak." Wilton clenched his jaw. "Don't forget she reports to the Attorney General. How trustworthy is *he*?"

Sikes shot Wilton a warning glance.

"Fair point," Masterson conceded. "We have my office looking for the source of how Langsten might have gotten tipped off. We need to know where the senator got his intel, and we're considering all possibilities at this point."

"Well, you can cross Alyah off that list." Stephen's eyes watched Alyah through the clear glass of Sikes' office wall as she spoke to a group of US Marshals. Both Mak and Sikes followed his gaze.

"Keep her close. Either for observation or protection, you decide. I need to know how he knew we're onto him." Masterson cleared his throat.

"What about Pottstaff?" Mak asked suddenly.

"Who?" Masterson asked abruptly.

"Sherriff Obediah Pottstaff was just arrested for working in conjunction with the trafficking ring. Could Pottstaff have gotten information out to Langsten via his lawyer to warn him?" Mak pondered.

"Is this Pottstaff loyal to Langsten?" Masterson wondered.

"Not sure. I think it might be a toxic loyalty. I can only tell you when we showed Pottstaff a picture of Langsten and asked him to ID the senator, Pottstaff looked scared," Mak said, rapping her knuckles on Sikes' desk for emphasis. "Pottstaff was likely protecting the senator. I'd put money on it."

"Okay, someone get back in front of Pottstaff and get some information out of him," Masterson ordered.

Sikes nodded. "We need to interview Mrs. Langsten—in person. Let's get you two on a flight out. We'll get you a warrant. I would like to see that letter."

Mak and Wilton nodded.

"Okay, sounds like a plan," Masterson agreed. "We'll keep working on the leak on our end. We're looking into everyone on that manifest so we're in place to take them all down at once when we find the senator."

Masterson hung up the phone.

Wilton gave them a look that told them he was sobered enough to mean what he said. "I don't care how you do it, but issue permanent protective detail to Alyah. She doesn't leave our sight. I don't trust Langsten. If he thinks she figured something out, he'll come for her. And we all know what he'll do if he gets her."

Three sets of eyes swung to the capable, in-charge woman who stood issuing orders and conversing with other marshals. Wilton wasn't wrong. Mak's gut told her that Alyah was in danger.

11

BETH

Beth grabbed her backpack purse and ran to the aisle. Only, instead of running toward the front, she ran toward the back of the train. There had to be an emergency exit. Her only thought was of getting off this train undetected while the two hitmen got on and started searching for her.

Beth looked back, causing her to run smack into an older man wearing a Union Station logo on a polo and a name badge that said *Bill*. Her arm under her protective cast throbbed on impact. He put out a hand to steady her and slow her down.

"Woah, easy there, little lady. The exit is up front," Bill informed her while pointing his finger.

Beth had two options. She could push past him, potentially knocking him down in the process, or... Beth turned to see the men had boarded the train. In a panic, Beth scooted around Bill, causing him to turn around and block her from their view with his broad body.

"Doesn't this train have an emergency exit?" Beth asked breathlessly.

"Yes, but—"

That was all Beth needed to hear. She turned and ran down the aisle. She kept running until she got to the back of the train.

"Miss, I'm afraid you can't..." Bill was right on her heels.

Beth paid no attention. She unlatched a door that shut off the compartment to another train car. It opened with a hiss.

"I must insist!" Bill seemed to be gaining on her and Beth could only hope all the running hadn't attracted the men's attention.

Beth ran until she saw the sign that said *Emergency Access Slide door to the right*. She threw the lever to the right and the door rolled open.

There! Beth could see a second sign that warned *Emergency Exit. Danger! Do not use while train is moving.*

"Ma'am!" Bill had finally caught up to her and put a hand on her shoulder. As she turned, she peered around him and could see the men looking in each train compartment. They were getting closer, and it was only a matter of time before they looked toward the back of the train and spotted her.

Beth threw off the man's hand and put a finger in his face. "You listen to me. I'm in danger. I'm being stalked by men who want to kill me, and I don't have time to stop and report it to the police. See, there they are!"

Bill's eyes grew large as he processed her quick words. He whirled around to see the men, and Beth quickly threw open the second exit door. She could only see the track, and it was a long way down. She stuck her head out and noticed a small ledge that she could shimmy over and step off onto the platform. What if she slipped? Had she read somewhere that the rails were electrically charged? She shuddered. She didn't want to find out. Then there was the issue of her bulky cast.

Just as Beth threw a leg out, a hand clamped on her shoulder, preventing her movement. Her patience snapped and Beth pulled her knee back and threw a sidekick into Bill's chest.

"Sorry, Bill!" she called out as she watched him fly to the ground, no doubt with the wind knocked out of him. She should help him up, but she had no time for that, and the commotion had been too loud.

Beth cursed and slipped around the corner, feeling thankful that she was wearing tennis shoes with slip-proof rubber soles. She stepped out and fully flattened herself to the train. She put her right palm on the slick metal back of the train. She made the only shape she could with her left hand in a cast—a claw—with her fingers sticking out. She used the pads of her fingers for balance. But she had to move. She knew they were coming.

Beth shifted to gain her balance and put her arms out wide, splaying her right fingers against the cold curved surface, her body hugging it for balance. She moved slowly to the edge until she felt sure she could take a giant step to the platform and use her other foot to boost her. It would be tricky with nothing to hold onto and only one hand to catch her.

She could hear commotion inside the train.

"Where did she go?" came an angry man's voice.

"That way," another man answered. She thought it was Bill. She could only hope he'd pointed in the opposite direction. But she couldn't worry about that now. Beth mustered her courage and without looking down, she took a giant step. Her foot did make it to the platform, but her body was stuck. Her legs were practically in splits as she attempted to rock herself back and forth to get a good hold from her back leg and spring herself forward. Her small backpack purse slung over her back jostled with the movement.

"Hey, woah!" a man in a business suit on the platform spotted her and ran to help. He grabbed her hand with both of his and pulled her so that her body flew toward him. She landed on her stomach with her legs dangling off the ledge and down toward the tracks. She heard a crack as her cast thumped a little too hard, and an ache pulsed down her arm. She didn't have time to worry about that.

Beth moved her feet until she found a groove in the wall, put her foot in it, and pushed herself up. With the man's help, this time she managed to get her whole body onto the stand.

"Are you okay?" the man asked, looking concerned.

Beth stood and attempted to brush a few black lines that had stained her t-shirt. Grease. It was the least of her worries. She glanced back to see one of the men poke his head out of the train exit door she'd left open.

"There!" he yelled and pointed.

"Yes. Thank you!" Beth quickly said to the man as she inched away. Beth turned and sprinted for the stairs that led out of the train depot. It was only a matter of time before the men got off the train. Their legs were a lot longer than Beth's. They might have no trouble jumping from the train.

All Beth had on her side was speed and a bit of a head start. But Beth didn't know Chicago, and she had no idea where to go once she hit the street. All she knew was that she had to get away.

She wouldn't survive if she was captured. Of that, she could be sure.

12

WILTON

Watching through Sikes' office window, Stephen could see Alyah react as a tall, built, uniformed man walked into the US Marshal office and went straight for her. Alyah extended her hand and the man took it, using his other hand to clasp her elbow. The muscles in the man's arm and his forearm against Alyah's petite one seemed to engulf her.

"Kansas City Chief of Police," Sikes explained, following Stephen's gaze. "Lynn Sauder."

"Lynn?" Stephen snorted. Something in his gut churned over the interaction with Alyah. Even in his tipsy state, he could see there was something familiar in their greeting. He pushed it away and tried to focus. "We all agree there's no way Alyah tipped off Langsten, right?"

"Yes," Mak said immediately.

Sikes looked less than convinced.

Stephen raised his eyebrows at Sikes.

Sikes shrugged. "Stranger things have happened."

"I've been falsely accused by this office myself, and it did not feel good. Why don't we give her the benefit of the doubt this time until we have a reason to suspect otherwise?" Stephen snapped.

Sikes sighed and his eyebrows knit together. "I don't think she would play double agent. I've known her longer than I've known you. But she's been up there in Washington, DC. Politics can change people."

"That's making some unkind assumptions," Stephen growled.

They watched as Chief Lynn Sauder turned his gaze to Sikes' office. Sikes waved to the man to come in. The chief walked quickly toward them. He pulled open the glass door to Sikes' office, interrupting their conversation.

"Chief Sauder, come on in. You know Mak Cunningham, and this is Stephen Wilton. They're heading up this case." The office door swung shut behind the chief.

Chief Sauder extended his hand to Mak. "Good to see you again, Mak."

Mak took his hand and nodded.

Sauder didn't clasp Mak's elbow the way he did Alyah's, Stephen thought to himself. Sauder turned and reached out to shake Stephen's hand, then addressed them all.

"In addition to the updates on warrants, APBs, and BOLOs we've issued, I have news I needed to deliver in person."

Sikes nodded. "Go on."

"There's been an incident," Sauder announced.

"There always is," Stephen mumbled, sizing up Sauder. He really didn't like the look of this guy with his dark hair, intense dark eyes, and muscular build.

"Obediah Pottstaff is dead," Sauder blurted.

Dead? Did he just say Pottstaff is dead? Blast the lingering alcohol in Stephen's system. Though he wasn't that affected, some things sounded foggy. His brain was taking longer to catch up.

"Dead? How?" Mak asked.

"Cardiac arrest, at first glance, but we are having the coroner confirm the cause of death," Sauder said.

"This seems like suspicious timing," Mak mused. "What are the other possible causes of death?"

The chief paused, looking regretful. "We're looking into that as well. Sometimes the simplest answer is the correct one. It's likely a stress-induced heart attack."

"We've seen people killed in a way that makes the death look natural, accidental, like it's a heart attack," Mak challenged.

"We believe in not making assumptions at our precinct. No speculating." Sauder held up his palms. "Let's wait and see what the coroner has to say."

"Was Pottstaff allowed to see anybody?" Sikes sounded incredulous.

"Just his attorney," Sauder confirmed.

"Well, an attorney isn't going to murder a client!" Mak said.

"Again," Sauder advised. "We don't want to make any assumptions. He's not the most reputable attorney. Still, he's innocent until proven guilty," Sauder mentioned in a low voice.

Stephen took a big swig to finish off his coffee.

"We'll leave that investigation to Sauder's office," Sikes decided. "I need you two to focus on the senator. That's your one job. Find Senator Langsten and bring him in."

Alyah stuck her head in the office. "Pardon the interruption. I just wanted to check if we have a tip line set up anywhere?"

Stephen would have to be an idiot to not notice the way Sauder's eyes softened when Alyah appeared.

"No, not yet. At least, not on my end. I can get on that right away," Sauder said, pulling out his phone.

"Thanks," Alyah smiled kindly back at him.

The exchange made Stephen's insides flip. He didn't want to admit he felt the kind of instant jealousy he had no right feeling.

"You leave tonight," Sikes commanded. "I want you to go interview Mrs. Langsten."

Mak turned to go, followed by Sauder. Before Stephen could make it to the door, he heard Sikes' voice behind him. "Wilton, hang back."

Stephen's heart dropped. His behavior today had been erratic and unpredictable. He should have known Sikes wouldn't let it go. To his credit, Sikes waited until they were alone in the room.

"Wilton?" Sikes stood in front of Stephen and crossed his arms over his chest.

"Yeah?"

"When is the last time you saw that counselor?" Sikes asked.

Stephen blinked. "It was back when I was placed on leave."

Sikes nodded. "Should I be concerned?"

"About?" Stephen could only guess what behavior Sikes was seeing.

"The day drinking is a problem, Wilton. It's not something I'll tolerate on the job." Sikes eyes pinned Stephen with a knowing look.

"It won't be a habit." Stephen felt ashamed. He shoved his hand through his hair, knowing it untamed his messy waves. "There have been a lot of changes that have left me feeling—"

"Unrest?" Sikes asked.

"To say the least," Stephen admitted. He thought about his quick-trigger anger, his extreme feelings of protectiveness, and mixed into all of that, he was surprised by the lingering feelings of grief.

"I need to insist that you stay in contact with your counselor." Sikes worked his jaw.

"Will do." Stephen saluted Sikes and left the room. Internally, he shook his head. Saluting wasn't a typical behavior for him. Sikes was right. He needed to talk to someone. Sooner rather than later.

13

———

ALYAH

Alyah sat in an oversized chair in the conference room, sipping on a hot cup of coffee, staring at nothing. She was surprised that she already needed to take this little break. This day had been so busy with all the twists that she'd had a hard time keeping up. It had been stressful, but it had also been something else. Exhilarating. She'd felt purpose in her work for the first time in a long time. It had felt so much different from her job in Washington, DC. Here, she felt like she was part of a team, fighting to take down evil. It felt good. She'd been able to pause the fears that she'd felt since she'd escaped Langsten.

All that and it was barely noon. She shook her head in wonder. Mak and Stephen had left to go interview Mrs. Langsten. They were likely heading to the jet at this very moment. Things certainly moved fast in this office. But then, they couldn't give Langsten any extra time to get away.

Alyah knew she would have no choice but to explain her extended absence to her boss soon. She just wasn't ready right now. She wasn't even sure what she would say. Her future was so unclear at this point with all her plans re-routed.

Despite her satisfaction over the morning, there had been one uncomfortable moment. Now that she was sitting, letting her brain detangle the chaos that she had thrived on, she knew she needed to process it.

Chief Lynn Sauder had shown up. Alyah hadn't seen or heard from him for years. They'd met when she'd first taken the job as a District Attorney in Kansas City. A case where he had to testify for the state, putting him in her path. After the case ended, they had a brief relationship. Alyah had been the one to call it off. She tried to remember what exactly had gone wrong. But the answer was, nothing. Alyah had been new in her position and the career warranted long hours. She couldn't put her finger on any specific action but had gotten the overall impression that he was pushy and impatient. But that might just be his personality. She was sure that it served him well in his position as chief of police.

But the way he had grasped her elbow... It had been so personal. It felt almost like he was claiming her. She shuddered at the thought. He was so unlike Stephen.

With that, Alyah sighed. She'd never been one to find a man to fill her loneliness. In fact, she'd never really felt lonely. Even in those times growing up when her mother was enmeshed in a relationship with a new boyfriend or surviving the devastation of the break-up or when Carley was sneaking out the window to go to a party or meet boys. During those times, though Alyah had been utterly alone, she'd never felt like it. She always felt relieved. Like she could breathe and be herself.

Books were her drug. Her way of escaping. Then she'd chosen school. She'd excelled at education. She thrived off positive comments from teachers. She'd found herself and defined who she was by her intellect and later, her work ethic and drive.

She'd accomplished so much at such a young age. Given her childhood, some would call her an overcomer. Was she lonely? No. But she'd found it was a little empty to not have anyone to share her success with. Her career kept her so busy, making friends had been hard, causing her only to get close to the people she worked with. People who understood her, like Mak Cunningham. Females in law enforcement were rare. Mak had become an ally.

But the relationship between her and Stephen Wilton remained to be seen. Would he allow her to be his friend? If so, would that be enough for her?

14

WILTON

Considering that Stephen was still living out of a duffle bag in a hotel room, it was no surprise it only took him minutes to get ready to leave. So, he'd taken the time to call his counselor like he'd promised Sikes. Not that he'd wanted to. It was more like a checkmark on a to-do list. A way to honestly answer next time that he *had* talked to his counselor, if it came up again.

He was shocked to find her between clients. He must have been holding in more than he thought, but in a rare moment of word vomit, Stephen summed up his attendance at a recent funeral, that yet another relationship had ended, and someone who he cared deeply for had come back into his life. The counselor had gone silent for a half minute, then thrown a term out that he'd never heard before.

Based on what you're telling me today, along with our past conversations, I'm wondering if you're experiencing anxious attachment, she'd said slowly.

I'm not an anxious person, Stephen had scoffed.

Anxious attachment can be the result of some trauma that occurs. For example, your brother's death. Stephen had told her about that in a previous session. *Your parents had each other, which likely left you with no one to help you through the grieving process,* she surmised.

That's not true, Stephen denied. *I had a great childhood. My parents loved me and were attentive.*

That's good, the counselor stated. *Though it's common for even the best parents to turn inward while coping with loss and comforting each other. You might have seemed fine to them, while they were lost in their own feelings. Meanwhile, you never learned what to do with yours.*

At Stephen's petulant silence, the counselor went on. *Sometimes we engage in risky behaviors as we attempt to cope with complicated feelings...*

Stephen had laughed. *I'm pretty in control of my emotions.*

You've never used alcohol or drugs to numb pain? the counselor asked.

No. Stephen thought about his stupid decision to drink while he was on the clock today. But he didn't do that often.

Food, shopping, or sex? she pressed.

He never had time to shop. But sex... *I mean, I would love to be in a relationship someday, but I can't ever seem to find a woman who wants to stick around.*

Bingo, she said. *People with anxious attachment styles can jump into relationships, attach too quickly without laying the foundation for a solid relationship, and then fear abandonment to the point of accidentally pushing their partner away.*

Oh. That did sound like him. *What do I do?*

Work on you. Find ways to increase your self-esteem and self-awareness. Find hobbies or sports you can do in your personal time that fulfill you. Learn to love yourself before you try another relationship. Be mindful of instances that seem to be a trigger. It seems attending that funeral brought up some unresolved issues. Recognizing situations that might trigger you is important so that you can find

*ways to appropriately cope. You can even use those hobbies as outlets
to help you redirect that negative energy.*

He'd researched anxious attachment style until they'd
boarded the plane.

Now, he glanced over at Mak, who sat with earbuds in,
watching a movie that made her smile from time to time.
Stephen wasn't in the mood for comedy. He wasn't in the
mood for anything. They hadn't been able to book a flight on
such short notice, so they were traveling on the US Marshal
jet. The jet resembled a commercial airliner with its rows of
bucket seats. He could have sat anywhere but chose to sit
across the aisle from Mak. A lot of good it did him. Mak
didn't seem to want to talk about the case at all, which was
the only thing Stephen wanted to focus on.

Stephen had waited until they were in the air before he
connected to WiFi and began searching for everything
published on the internet about Senator Joseph Langsten.
Stephen's stomach twisted as he viewed picture after picture
of the man with his family in various stages of running for
US Senator. The smile on the man's face was so charismatic.
So deceiving. Yet, just by looking at him, Stephen wouldn't
have assumed Senator Langsten was capable of such
atrocities.

At first, Stephen just intended to internet stalk the
senator to get an idea of what kind of man he was. But the
more he looked through family pictures, the more he noticed
differences in the backgrounds of where the pictures were
shot. He took a screenshot of each different home or land-
scape and saved it to a folder on his desktop.

Stephen glanced at Mak who let out a soft laugh, her eyes
still on her screen. He sighed and crossed the aisle, taking
the seat next to her.

Mak glanced at him and paused the movie she was watching. She popped out an earbud. "What's up?"

"I've been doing a little research on Langsten," Stephen began. He pulled up a picture from his file and made it large on his screen. The picture showed Joseph Langsten with his arm around an attractive woman with dark blond hair pulled back into an elegant hairstyle. On either side of them stood two girls who resembled their mother. They looked like twins, with the exception of an obvious height difference. All wore smiles.

"Ah what a beautiful, happy family," Mak's voice held a note of sarcasm, but her brow furrowed, and she got serious. "You think they know who he really is?"

"Hard to say," Stephen answered. He enlarged the photo even more. Behind them was a two-story home that looked like an updated Southern plantation-style home. It was white with black pillars in the front. He pointed to the home. "This is what caught my eye."

"Okay," Mak said, giving him her whole attention.

"If these are all places Langsten has fond memories in—"

"He might have gone to one of them to hide out?" Mak finished.

Stephen nodded. "He could have multiple homes or places where he vacations. I would bet you money he's in one of those places."

"You sure? What if he went underground?" Mak asked.

"Underground?" Stephen smirked. "That's exactly what he did. He's also *in the wind*, if you want to keep going with the cliches."

"No, I mean, what if he's hiding literally underground like the women they abduct?" Mak pushed.

"I'm no profiler, but he doesn't seem like a guy who'd want to get caught so close to the scene of the crime. Nor could I see him toughing it in such a rough spot. No." Stephen shook his head. "I don't think he'd be caught anywhere near his victims."

"A guy like that has probably put so much distance between himself and his crimes that he believes his own lies," Mak snorted.

Stephen turned his attention back to the pictures and opened them one by one. They studied the backgrounds.

"Let's send those pictures to Sikes and have the research team look into Langsten's current properties. We should also compare the age of the girls then and now to determine how long ago it was. But I think you're onto something with the sentimental angle—" Mak stopped and started abruptly. "Not that I think a man like that would be sentimental."

"True," Stephen agreed. Mak's next question made Stephen pause.

"You doing okay?" Mak watched as Stephen slowly closed the laptop. "I mean, with Alyah being back?"

Stephen looked away. How did he want to answer that? The truth was, no matter how hard he tried to distract himself, keep himself busy, or zone into this case, his mind returned to Alyah. But it wasn't for the reason anyone might suspect. Seeing her just brought back the pain he'd felt and reminded him of the bad choices he made with women.

"There was a time when seeing her again would have been exciting. I would have been happy to have her back, even for the short time I would get with her." Stephen paused.

"But now?" Mak asked quietly.

Stephen sighed. "Now, I just want to be alone. I don't want to get tangled up in anything right now. I want to focus on this case and focus on me."

Mak's eyebrows rose. "Mature, Wilton."

Stephen's mind went to the funeral he'd attended twenty-four hours ago. "I keep thinking about Davey's funeral. There were only six people there, and that included me and the clergy man. I don't want to isolate or anything. Davey gave his life for me and I want to live a life worthy of that…"

Mak remained silent, waiting for him to finish his thoughts.

"I want more than six people at my funeral. I want to leave behind a legacy. To know I affected people in a positive way, helped them, and inspired them in some way." He shook his head. "Not sure. I just think there's more to life than looking for the perfect future family. I have Anna. She's my family. In the meantime, I think I need to live for me, in the moment of today."

Mak nodded thoughtfully. "Admirable. Remember, you can still do all those things no matter what stage of life you are in."

"I just need to be comfortable with being alone," Stephen said. Because he never really had been.

"Alone isn't the end of the world," Mak said as she put her earbuds back in her ears and turned back to the movie screen.

"Right." Stephen smiled and scooted back across the aisle. He opened his laptop back up and did another search. "Jackpot."

Senator Joseph Langsten had a website. There were even more pictures under his "About" tab. Stephen zoned into the pictures, canceling out the noise in his head. This man on the screen before him was the only thing Stephen was going to let himself think about until he found him.

As Stephen studied a picture of Langsten sitting proudly on a horse in front of a ranch-style home, he remembered the vow he'd made. Staring hard at the photo, Stephen narrowed his eyes.

When I find you, Stephen thought, focusing all his attention on the murderer on the screen, *I'm going to kill you—for Davey, for Trevan, and for my brother.*

15

———————

ALYAH

Alyah was getting ready to leave for lunch. She was looking around for one of the US Marshals who had escorted her here this morning. She could call something in, but she really wanted to get out of the office. Before she could disappear through the door, Sikes waved her into his office. He motioned for her to shut the door behind her.

Alyah obeyed and sank into one of Sikes' plush leather chairs on the other side of his desk. The chairs were a match to the comfortable seats in the conference room. Alyah shifted to prepare for what looked like might be a long talk, her gaze quizzical.

"Alyah, I need you to tell me as much as you can about how you came across the information from Langsten's office," Sikes stated directly.

"Sikes, you know I'm bound by client confidentiality—"

"Hang confidentiality!" Sikes raised his voice.

Alyah's stomach turned. She thought about why she'd chosen this path. In college, she had worked as an intern for the Attorney General's office, and it had been a vast difference from her first job in a criminal law practice. Alyah wanted to be on the right side of the law. While it was true Alyah still tried many criminal cases, her job as a District Attorney was to seek justice, evaluate evidence, and protect the rights of the accused in every case. To skirt her rules went all through her. She needed to be careful here.

"With all due respect, Sikes, I feel like you're asking me this for a reason." Alyah laced her fingers together and held them in her lap. Courage in court was one thing. Navigating authorities who didn't understand ethics and the rights of people accused of being criminals was tough. In the real world, despite the front she put on, Alyah actually shied away from confrontation.

Sikes sat back and studied her for a minute. His frown was fierce. He appeared to be deciding what to say.

"Ah hell, Alyah!" He scrubbed a hand down his face over his stubble that he typically wore these days. "We think there's a mole—"

"A mole?" she exclaimed.

"Someone who tipped off Langsten and caused him to run."

Understanding hit Alyah like a slap in the face. "You think that person is me."

Sikes grunted. "I don't, exactly. But the question has been raised."

"I see." Her voice went cold. "Well, you are correct that I'm the one who made him run, but not in the way you suspect."

"Continue." Sikes leaned forward.

Alyah hadn't wanted to admit it, but she was cornered. "As you know, I was working on a different case with Senator Langsten—the details of which I will not divulge. He trusted me implicitly, until he didn't."

"What made him stop?"

"During the course of me researching and going through

files, I found the manifest. It was late when I stumbled upon it. He was gone. At a dinner meeting, I think. When I found the names and bank accounts all in one spreadsheet, I stopped what I was doing and gasped. Then I took out a thumb drive and copied the files.

"I've been around criminals before. I've even defended them in court. But none have terrified me the way Langsten does. I couldn't control the fear in my body language. Looking back, I think the next couple of interactions with Senator Langsten made it obvious. My hands would shake, so I'd hide them behind my back. I spoke without taking a breath a few times. I avoided eye contact. It was enough that he asked me if I was okay."

"Still, that's not definitive—"

"There's more," Alyah admitted. "I think there might have been cameras in his office. I should have considered that. I think my behavior triggered him to look back to the day of my discovery."

"Huh," Sikes grunted.

"Just under a week ago—the same day I showed up here —I went in early to Langsten's office, planning to look around more. I overheard a conversation between Langsten and a voice I didn't recognize. Langsten said I knew the truth and they needed to eliminate me."

Sikes let out a low whistle.

"I ran. I didn't even stop to pack. I just drove to the airport and got on the first plane to Kansas City. The senator requested we meet in a different location that morning. I asked to push back the meeting by an hour to buy more time. I was likely in the air when I was supposed to meet him. I'm sure when I no-showed, Langsten knew he'd been found out," Alyah concluded.

"Holy Lord!" Why didn't you tell us that? We need to get

you out of here and to safety." Sikes looked like he was going to pick up the phone.

"That's why. Right there. I don't want to be put in protection. I can do more good here, helping the team." Alyah unfolded her hands and straightened her spine.

"You're in a lot of danger," Sikes breathed.

"I know, and two US Marshals posted at my house will help with that." Alyah tapped a foot.

"Unless Langsten finds out where you live," Sikes argued.

"What's he going to do, smoke me out?" Alyah laughed, but it sputtered to a stop when she realized her joke was in poor taste, remembering suddenly that Anthony Gerritt had burned Stephen's house down. In fact, as far as Alyah knew, Stephen still hadn't bought a new one.

"It's happened before," Sikes said needlessly.

Alyah nodded. "But I'm firm on this. I'll stay at my place, and I thank you for the protective detail."

"Okay," Sikes relented but didn't look happy. "One more thing. I, ah, got a call from Wilton who was concerned about you going out in public without protection. Given this most recent discovery, I need to agree. No outings by yourself until we take down Langsten."

"I can limit the amount of time I spend in public, but I'm not going to be able to send a US Marshal to the grocery store," Alyah protested lightly.

"Order groceries online," Sikes advised.

Alyah nodded slowly, trying to wrap her brain around the rules of confinement.

"I would like you to work with Chief Sauder. Pottstaff's murder connects back to this case. He's investigating it. So, you might find yourself working with him more," Sikes informed her.

Alyah stood and thought briefly about Sauder. "That shouldn't be a problem."

"Okay, dismissed," Sikes said.

Alyah clasped her hands, suddenly feeling insecure. "Can we agree not to tell Stephen Wilton about what happened with the senator? I'd rather he didn't know."

"He worries—"

"I'm not Stephen's concern."

"He thinks otherwise."

"I doubt it," Alyah said with a sad smile.

But as she left the room, Alyah wondered why Stephen was concerned enough to call Sikes. It was professional courtesy, wasn't it? Sure, he'd had feelings in the beginning, but she'd broken his heart. He'd moved on. Hadn't he?

16

———

MAK

Upon arriving at the nice two-story white brick home in a gated neighborhood on Capitol Hill the next morning, Mak asked, "What's the plan, Wilton?"

"Get in and get as much information as we can to find the senator." He opened the door to the rental car, intending to step out.

"That's it?" Mak had asked incredulously. "From the man who always has a plan?"

"What would you like to do?" Wilton asked.

"We could play good cop, bad cop. I can be good and question the wife. You can be bad because you already have this thing going on." Mak waved a hand up and down Wilton, indicating the dark mood he was in. "You can search the house."

"We're not cops." Wilton stepped out into the sunlight and shut the car door.

Mak hurried after him. "No, but it still works, right?"

"Yeah," Wilton agreed as he strode to the front door. "We need to take our time once we're in there. I don't want to miss anything."

Mak quietly knocked on the door.

Wilton gave her a pointed stare. "We have a warrant to go in and search Senator Joseph Langsten's home. We don't have to be so polite."

Mak shrugged. "I want to know what Langsten's wife knows, give her the benefit of the doubt, and let her come clean. I keep thinking this would go a whole lot easier if she just told us what she knows."

"She's a politician's wife," Wilton argued. "The likelihood of her cooperation is small."

"You're stereotyping," Mak told him.

Mak thought Wilton would have preferred they kick the door in, rather than knock. Somehow, their roles were reversed in this case. Mak was usually the impatient one, the marshal to rush in, but as she heard Wilton's barely concealed huff of air from where he stood, she knew this case meant more to him than it did to Mak. For Wilton, this was personal. They were looking for the man who had killed his brother.

Just as Mak raised her hand to knock again, the door opened.

An average height woman with dark blond hair with streaks of gray stood in the open doorway.

Her blue eyes narrowed with suspicion. "Yes?"

Both Mak and Wilton flashed their badges.

"Mrs. Langsten?" Mak asked with a cordial smile.

The woman nodded once. She would have been pretty if her features weren't so pinched together in a mask of coldness.

"I'm US Marshal Mak Cunningham." Mak reached out a hand and Mrs. Langsten reluctantly placed her hand in Mak's to shake. Her grip was firm.

"I'm US Marshal Stephen Wilton." Stephen mirrored

Mak's reach for a handshake. Mrs. Langsten clasped his, but she looked weary as she gazed from Mak to Wilton.

"Have you found my husband?" she asked.

"Can we talk inside?" Mak requested.

Mrs. Langsten put a hand up to stop them. "No, I think you're close enough. I don't have to let you in unless you have a—"

Mak produced the warrant and let it dangle open before Mrs. Langsten could finish her sentence. Mrs. Langsten clicked her tongue, and what appeared to be disappointment registered in her eyes.

"And if I refuse?" Mrs. Langsten put her hands behind her back, fire in her eyes.

"We'll have no choice but to arrest you for obstruction of justice." Wilton met her fiery gaze with one of his own.

Mrs. Langsten swung her front door wide enough for Mak and Wilton to enter her home.

Mak blinked a few times and remembered not to swing her jaw open as she walked into the home. From the outside, it looked like a modest, two-story home. Once inside, Mak could see that this home had been updated, and the interior designer had utilized every square inch to maximize the space. A floor to ceiling bookshelf lined an entire wall in the living room with rows of books and not a speck of dust anywhere to be seen. A big screen TV hung in a white floating entertainment center on the wall adjacent to the books. On the dark hardwood floor was a muted gray rug with maroon colors woven in, sitting under a white leather sofa. Two matching Lazy Boy recliners boxed in the living room but looked like they'd never been sat on. A black spiral staircase led upward in the back of the room. This room looked pristine and untouched. Mak knew the cleanliness would make it easier for Wilton to find answers as he searched this place.

"I've talked to the police and the FBI already. I'm not sure why I have to tell my story a third time." Diane Langsten crossed her arms across her chest.

But Mak answered kindly. "We are all taking your husband's disappearance very seriously. While we are all working together, we, the police, and the FBI are all looking for different things that will lead us to your husband. I'd like to ask you some questions while my partner looks around."

Reluctantly, Diane had led Mak to her dining room. While this room felt no warmer than the living room had, it certainly was big enough to accommodate a large dinner party. The stuffed black leather seats at the dining table were comfortable, at least. Mak stared at the greenery decorating the center of the table.

"We know this is hard for you, Mrs. Langsten—"

"You may call me Diane," she corrected coldly.

"Diane, I need to ask you some questions about the day your husband went missing," Mak made her voice soft.

Diane nodded her head and took a deep breath in, then let her features soften. It felt like Mak was watching a school play. She thought Diane was putting on a show of being brave that came off as disingenuous. Then Mak supposed it was probably Diane's years of being a politician's wife that made it look like Diane was working to put on the *right* emotions. Mak didn't buy how quickly Diane's attitude had changed.

"Joseph got up around midnight—I know because I'm such a light sleeper. He said he couldn't sleep, and he was going downstairs for a glass of water. He does that sometimes, so I went back to sleep. He wasn't in bed when I woke up the next morning. So, I put on my dressing robe and went downstairs." Diane let a tear fall and then dabbed at it.

"Take your time," Mak encouraged.

Diane nodded. "That's when I found a note on the table."

"A ransom note?" Mak asked.

"No," Diane said, quickly dismissing the question.

"So, he wasn't abducted?" Mak confirmed.

An emotion flashed in Diane's eyes. It was brief but Mak caught it before she masked it. Anger. "No."

"Can you show me the letter?" Mak asked.

"No." Diane shook her head.

Mak stared at her with silent surprise and disappointment. She had hoped Diane would comply with her questions.

Diane was the first one to break the awkward silence that had fallen. "Well, it was a letter written to me, you see," her voice sounded haughty as if she was explaining something that should have been obvious to a person of lesser intelligence.

"I do, but I need you to understand that my partner will find the letter. But your refusal means I have to remove you from the house for obstruction of justice," Mak informed her. "The letter might be crucial in our investigation."

Diane lifted her chin in refusal and obstinately remained silent.

"Found the letter," Wilton called from a different room.

The mask fell again, and this time Diane let her irritation settle on her face and in her voice. "Good. Maybe it will prove that my husband is an innocent victim here, and you're wasting taxpayers' dollars treating him like he's a suspect. Honestly, what kind of a justice system do we have when a man has to flee for his own protection and becomes the brunt of some investigation? What do you really think you're going to find?"

Wilton chose that moment to appear. "Well, I've found his laptop, but I need access to a locked door down the hall. I presume that's Senator Langsten's office?" In his hand, he held two clear bags. One held the laptop. The other held a Glock 19.

"You can't take the gun. It's mine," Diane informed him.

"Is it registered to you?" Wilton asked.

"Yes, and legally, I can conceal carry. It never leaves my home, which is how I'll defend myself since my husband is not here." Diane stood when Mak came around the table to escort Diane out of the home.

"You have a permit to carry?" Wilton checked.

"Yes," Diane's chin jutted out in defiance.

"I need to confirm this," Wilton said. He put the note on the table for Mak to read. Before he turned and went out the door, he asked. "Do you have a key to the office door?"

"No, I've lost it," Diane lied.

Stephen rolled his eyes. "It's okay, I can pick the lock. I was just hoping you would cooperate with our investigation."

"Diane, at this time, I'll need to detain you temporarily outside your home. I believe you're obstructing our search," Mak stated as her eyes perused the letter on the table. Mak scanned it quickly, her heart racing.

Dear Diane,

I'm going away for a little while. I don't want you to worry about me. It has come to my attention that I'm being watched. Our finances are being monitored. Please be cognizant of your spending. I no longer trust the DA working on my case, and you shouldn't either. I will be firing her. I'm not sure who she's working with or why, but I think I'm in danger. I need to put distance between us. It's for your protection, as well as mine. Don't come looking for me. Don't talk to anyone. Trust no one. I'll return as soon as I'm free.

Love,

Joseph

Diane looked at Mak with triumph in her eyes. "Maybe

now you'll figure out who is responsible for my husband's disappearance," Diane said, ice lining her words.

But Mak just worked her mind over all the possibilities. Now they knew for sure that Alyah *had* spooked the senator. But not in the way they all thought. Maybe Alyah hadn't been as sneaky about taking the information as she had tried to be. Maybe there were cameras all over the senator's office where Alyah had been working. This confirmed what Wilton had been trying to convince them since Alyah's return.

Alyah *was* in danger.

17

BETH

Beth burst out of the train station, squinting in the sunlight, and looked down the street. She noticed several yellow cars heading her way. She was surprised the city still had cabs. Quickly, Beth stepped forward and put a hand up. A cab stopped. *Wow, that was way too easy.* Beth got in.

"Where to?" the driver asked. He looked bored as his eyes roamed over the busy streets congested with traffic, and back to her. His eyes fell on her cast.

"O'Hare airport. As quick as you can, please. I have a flight to catch," Beth didn't know where that answer had come from, but she was thankful for it. She was just reacting now. She had to keep moving forward. She had to outrun these guys.

"Hope you have plenty of time before that flight leaves because traffic is awful today!" the driver complained.

Beth looked over her shoulder just in time to see the two angry men burst out onto the sidewalk. She let out a squeak and ducked down. "It's fine! Just go!"

"Okay," the driver said in an unsure voice, but Beth could feel the car start rolling into the pandemonium of cars. Beth slumped down further in the seat. It was a good ten minutes before Beth sat back up into the seat and chanced a look around her. She peered into cars to the sides and behind them.

"We were at least a mile away before they got their own car," the cabbie's voice was monotone. "They won't catch us in this traffic. But I've kept an eye out for you."

"Oh, thank you." Beth waved a hand as if the driver hadn't just busted her trying to run from two men. "Crazy ex-husband and friend."

"Say no more," the driver said.

She didn't. Instead, her mind drifted to the time when she was pregnant with Lacy, attending school in the city. Beth remembered having to catch public transportation to get to school. She'd hated it. If she was even a minute late, the bus left without her.

She'd been so relieved the first day back at her old school. Now that she had time to breathe, she leaned her head against the cool window of the cab while she remembered that day.

Nineteen Years Ago…

Beth walked up the steps to her former school, feeling nervous but happy at the same time. She opened the front door and was greeted with the same stagnant smell of must, gym socks, and body odor that she remembered from when she went to school there before. She took a step forward, immediately colliding with a force that pushed her body back so hard, she hit the wall. The air rushed out of her as a human in motion slammed into her.

"Ugh!" Beth exhaled all the breath out of her stomach. Her irritation faded as she looked into the appealing eyes of pure trouble. With dark, straight hair and an impish smile, Greg Wilton grinned at her as he took a step back.

"Beth Donovan! You're back?" He looked sheepish. "Sorry for slamming into you."

Beth pushed off the wall and straightened her pleated skirt.

A gangly boy with limp brown-blond hair ran up and picked up a football. "You missed," Davey Stinnert announced.

"Davey, look who it is." Greg pushed Davey's shoulder.

"Beth Donovan! Hey, welcome back," Davey grinned, his crooked teeth overcrowding his mouth. "I'm helping him try out for the football team."

Beth watched as Davey attempted to palm the football but dropped it. She stared suspiciously at Greg. She'd known him since the second grade, but Greg had grown up a little since she'd been gone. His brown hair hung a touch long and straight, the jersey he wore with the school colors on it had filled out quite a bit since the last time she'd seen him. His eyes sparkled with amusement. She knew boys like him. They were up to no good. She wouldn't make the same mistake she made before.

"I need to get to class," Beth tried to push past them.

"Where are you going? Maybe we can help." Davey obnoxiously snatched the school schedule out of Beth's hands.

Before Beth could answer, a loud shriek sounded down the hallway, causing the heads of multiple teenagers milling about at their lockers to lift in surprise. Her best friend, Shania Woodstone, was running down the hallway with her arms out wide.

Beth laughed. She'd always loved Shania's ability to be carefree and not worry about what people thought of her. It helped that Shania was easily the prettiest girl in school with her long, straight brown hair, and expressive brown eyes. Beth allowed Shania to scoop her up in a hug and swing her body around.

Once Beth's feet were firmly on the ground, Shania looked at Greg, whose mouth was hanging open in surprise, and Davey, who was watching everything.

"Shoo, boys." Shania made a sweeping motion with her hands. "I got this."

Obediently, Greg and Davey walked away.

"Where's your first class?" Shania said, grabbing Beth's schedule back from Davey's hands as he walked by. She peered at it. "Oh! We have our first class together!" Shania linked arms with Beth and walked down the hallway with her old best friend.

Beth felt relief wash over her. It looked like they would pick up right where they left off. Surprising, considering that Beth had stopped talking to Shania after she moved away. She had actually been worried Shania would be mad at her. Maybe they would move right past it all.

"So," Shania said as they rounded a corner and went down a new hallway. "You gonna tell me why you stopped talking to me after you moved away? Lose your phone or something?"

Beth sighed. Then again, maybe not.

18

WILTON

Diane Langsten sat in the back of a police car, and Stephen knew she was watching who went in and out of the house for the search. After Wilton found the gun, he called in back up from the Police Department of Washington, DC. Then Stephen and Mak escorted Diane out of her place to the back of a police car where there were locked doors and bars for transporting criminals.

He heard Mak assure Diane that this would be temporary, as long as everything checked out. By locking the office door and refusing to produce a key, Diane was intentionally obstructing justice. Stephen thought it showed that Diane was purposely misleading their efforts. It was enough to remove her from the scene.

Diane had argued that she had spousal privilege and wasn't obligated to tell them anything incriminating about her husband and wouldn't say anything further until her lawyer arrived. That's when they had escorted her out. She was of no help in the house while they searched.

Since then, Stephen, Mak, and several police officers, along with a detective, combed through Senator Langsten's home. Time was essential here and they didn't have much of it, but Stephen refused to rush this search. He and an officer were meticulously combing through Langsten's files. Stephen had briefed the man on what they were looking for—evidence that connected Langsten to a drug and sex trafficking ring, bank accounts, car loans, home loans, hotel rental records, recreational vacation homes, or receipts that showed any trips Langsten had taken or would take in the future.

Mak was leading up the search for any other weapons and electronics in the home. Stephen knew Mak was hoping Diane would *magically* remember more information about where her husband might have gone since Diane had nothing but time to think in the back of that police car. Stephen was sure Diane was done talking, but he loved Mak's optimism.

Stephen found a file titled *Rentals* and pulled it from the cabinet. There was a stack of loans and paperwork detailing ownership for several Airbnb homes in Joseph and Diane Langsten's names.

"He owns several Airbnb rentals," Stephen mused aloud.

The officer stopped his perusal of what looked like bank statements and met Stephen's eye. He waved a few pieces of paper around. "No promises, but this looks like offshore bank account records."

"Really?" Stephen took them from the officer and looked them over, his heart speeding up. "No way would we get that lucky! Who prints this stuff out?"

"Apparently, an older senator. Maybe he did it so his wife could find what she needed if anything ever happened to him?" the officer suggested.

Stephen nodded. "Yeah, maybe. Look at the dates on this."

"1995," the officer answered. "We were printing out everything back then."

Stephen chuckled. "But why not burn all this stuff before

Langsten fled? Was he really that arrogant that he didn't think we'd come and search his home?"

"Is he a narcissist?" the officer offered with a shrug. "They don't think the rules apply to them. They think they aren't going to get caught and if they do, they can think their way out of it."

"Likely," Stephen kept digging. He picked out a file labeled *College*. Before he could open it, a glossy five-inch by eleven-inch photo floated to the ground, landing face down. Stephen picked it up. As he studied it, his blood ran cold. A young version of Joseph Langsten stood next to Micky Upton, who looked to be the same age. There were two other men in the photo, all of them smiling big while proudly holding a very large fish, clearly excited about their conquest.

So, Langsten and Upton were fishing buddies back in college. Stephen didn't recognize the other two men, but he hadn't immediately recognized Upton either. His knowledge of politicians was limited. Lucky for him, Alyah would likely name these guys on sight. That is, if his assumption was correct—that they'd all gone into politics or business together in some capacity. Stephen placed the photo in a clear evidence bag, but not before snapping a picture of it to keep on his phone.

Stephen held up the picture toward the officer. "Do you know these men? Other than Langsten, of course."

The officer came closer, squinted a bit, and shook his head. "No, none of the others are familiar. Should I?"

"Not necessarily. I just thought since you worked here in Washington, these guys might be someone you knew— maybe they're in office?"

The officer peered harder and shook his head again. "No. Sorry."

"What about that background?" Stephen mused aloud. There was a large blue lake behind them with snowy mountains far off in the distance. Stephen might have assumed it was winter, but the men had on flannel shirts with sleeves rolled up. Stephen knew some places got snow in the mountains in the summer.

"Let me see it again," the officer said. Stephen handed him the evidence bag with the photo. The officer lifted it out with his gloved hands and studied it more closely. "Colorado, maybe? My grandparents had a summer home there, and we would go see them during school break. Looks like Colorado to me."

Stephen nodded. "Good guess." But where in Colorado?

The officer put the photo back in the evidence bag and handed it to Stephen, who surveyed the evidence they had gathered. There was so much here. Solid leads that the Police Department of Washington, DC, would take, scan, and share with the marshals and FBI to continue building their case against Langsten.

But they needed to find Langsten first. That was Stephen's only priority. Find Langsten.

So far, Stephen was failing.

19

MAK

Mak wasn't succeeding at finding additional evidence. The frustration she felt with investigating reminded her why she wasn't a cop or with the FBI. She enjoyed her job when she already had a lead on where the criminal was and all she had to do was go pick him or her up and transport them to a jail cell.

She could see Wilton from her place in the living room. As she suspected, he seemed in his glory, geeking out over all those details Mak tended to miss. With any luck, Wilton would find a lead for them that would take them to their next destination.

As if sensing her eyes on him, Wilton looked up and waved Mak into the room. Mak walked in and scanned over the evidence bags full of papers from the files. He quickly went through what they had found, stopping on a photo he'd bagged.

Mak raised an eyebrow, waiting for the significance. Wilton shoved the picture closer to her, and Mak leaned in until she saw the resemblances. She gasped when it hit her.

"That's Langsten and Upton! Woah, they go way back, don't they!"

Wilton nodded.

"Wonder who the other guys are?" Mak murmured.

"Me too. But if they were with these guys, they can't be good."

"That's speculation, Wilton," Mak cut in, lowering her voice and channeling her brief interaction with Chief Sauder. "They can't be guilty by association. Plus, this was a million years ago. Who's to say these guys stayed with Langsten and Upton?" Mak challenged.

"My gut says it," Wilton shot back. "Bet Alyah would know them. If they're still in politics, that is."

Mak shrugged. "They could be in politics, in business... they could be evil henchmen—"

"Bodyguards," Stephen corrected with a smile.

"Oops, too much Disney lately." Mak grinned back.

Stephen smirked but turned back to study the picture.

"Point is, they could be working for Langsten and Upton, or they could be respectable men who parted ways from them," Mak stated. "Like a fork in the road moment."

"Fork in the road moment?" Stephen quirked an eyebrow.

"Yeah, you know, they parted ways after seeing a different vision than the bad guys," Mak explained.

"Man, sometimes I swear you watch too much TV." Stephen shook his head.

Mak shrugged. "Who has time for TV?"

"We could ask Diane if she can ID them," Stephen stated, looking out the window as he ticked his head toward the police car in front of the house.

"You didn't think she would talk to us," Mak said wearily. "The more I think about it, the more I think you might be right. And we just made it worse by putting her in a cop car on her nice pristine driveway in front of her perfect house in her luxurious neighborhood basically humiliating her in front of her neighbors."

"Or you've scared the pants off her, and she'll tell us everything," Stephen countered.

"Only one way to find out." Mak spun on her heel. She threw open the front door and found a man in a nice suit with a frozen hand raised, poised to knock on the door.

"Hello?" Mak asked.

"Who are you?" he asked rudely.

Mak sighed, grabbed her badge and flashed it at him. "Your turn. Same question."

The man fished out a business card. "Theodore Green the third from Green, Stateman, and York Law Offices. You have unlawfully detained my client, Mrs. Diane Langsten." Theodore pointed irritably at the police car.

"There's nothing unlawful about it," Mak informed the man. "We have a warrant. Mrs. Langsten was getting in the way of our search. We removed her from the premises by escorting her to a car. There's no difference between that and a holding cell. Though we would be happy to take her down to the jail for questioning, if you prefer."

Theodore seemed to be weighing her words. "Are you saying you're about to question her?"

"We are."

"That's fine now that I'm here. Proceed." Theodore put out a sweeping hand, as if arrogantly granting her the authority.

Mak rolled her eyes, then gave him a withering look before bounding down to the car. Theodore fell in step right on Mak's heels, a little too close for her to be comfortable. She opened the door for Diane.

"About time," Diane snapped.

Mak offered her hand to the woman, but Diane pointedly refused it and helped herself out of the car. Mak put a hand on Diane's arm, lightly detaining the woman as Mak guided her back to the house.

"We are going back into the house where my partner and I are going to ask you questions based on what we found. Your lawyer will accompany us. Depending on what we uncover, we'll determine if you are free to stay in your home or if you need to take a ride to the station. Do you understand?"

"Am I under arrest?" Diane tried to yank her arm away, but Mak held firm.

"No, not at this time," Mak said, steering her back into the house and toward the dining room table.

"Then why are you treating me like a criminal?" Diane snapped. She and her lawyer took a seat across the large, wooden table from Mak. Stephen strode to them and took a seat beside Mak. He flipped out his badge and introduced himself to the lawyer.

"As I've said before, Diane," Mak started, her voice the epitome of patience. "When we served you a warrant, it was your job to comply. When we felt you had become an obstacle, we removed you to do our jobs."

"I see," Diane replied icily. "And just what is it you think my husband has done?"

Mak's eyes went large. "Did you not read the warrant? It's all there. Senator Joseph Langsten is wanted for murder, involvement in a drug and sex trafficking ring, and possible money laundering."

Wilton kept his face neutral. Mak had thrown out the last charge to gauge Diane's reaction, and she loved that Wilton quietly went with it. Besides, they did suspect Langsten of that. They just didn't have proof right now.

"What are you—" Diane started.

Theodore placed a hand on Diane's arm. "I'd advise you

not to respond to that. I think these officers are baiting you, Diane."

Wilton pulled his badge out again. "We're US Marshals. We're here to apprehend your husband, Mrs. Langsten. Our goal is to ask questions that will lead us to him." Wilton left his badge on the table and pulled stapled papers out of his back pocket. He unfolded them and tapped on the paragraph at the top. "And this warrant explains why."

Theodore slid the warrant closer and put on a pair of reading glasses. With his head bowed down, they could see his wiry gray hair was thinning on top. Mak kept her eyes on the lawyer.

When he finished, Theodore took off his glasses, folded them back into his suit pocket, and leaned over to Diane. They proceeded to have a whispered conversation.

Mak interrupted them, her patience finally slipping. "Are you about done? We need to ask these questions and figure out the next steps."

Irritably, Diane straightened and folded her hands in front of her. "I have nothing to say about the whereabouts of my husband or in regard to his so-called involvement with any crimes."

"Oh, you sure that's the answer you want to go with, Diane?" Mak asked. "Because it's one thing to not know or be involved with the criminal activities of your husband. It's another to stand in the way of justice—"

Diane opened her mouth but clenched her jaw shut when Theodore raised his hand as if to put a stop to this. "Intimidation will get you nowhere—Mak, was it?" asked Theodore.

He knew exactly who she was. Theodore was playing his own role of attempting to demean her.

Mak nodded briefly.

"My client is willing to cooperate. Mrs. Langsten does have

spousal protection under the fifth amendment. This means you cannot force her to testify against her husband. Nor can you make her disclose any information communicated between her and Senator Langsten. Despite that, Mrs. Langsten is willing to answer some of your questions. You know the rules. You ask questions and she will answer them to the best of her ability and knowledge." Theodore turned to Diane. "Sound good?"

Diane nodded tightly.

"Great," Wilton grabbed a small stack of papers he'd sat on the chair next to him. He began laying out the paperwork that showed property loans paperclipped to pictures one might list on a rental website. One after another, side by side, Wilton fanned them out so everyone could see them. There were four total, all in different towns, registered as Airbnb homes. Mak watched Diane as her eyes studied the paperwork.

"Those are my properties!" Diane stated in surprise as it clicked.

"*Your* properties?" Wilton asked.

"Yes. I'm a real estate agent and I own several Airbnbs that I rent out throughout the year," Diane stated.

"Are these your only properties?" Wilton asked.

"No," Diane corrected. "I have two that aren't listed here, and we sold this one." She pointed to the home on the end, so Wilton pulled that information away.

"Where would we find the paperwork for the other two properties?" Wilton asked.

"I keep electronic files now. If you would kindly bring me my computer, I can help you navigate to find everything." Diane's finger's laced, and she turned her hands inside out and stretched them. Then she shrugged. "Arthritis."

"Right, let me grab the laptop," Wilton stated. "Remind me where you keep that one?"

Diane's cheeks turned pink.

Interesting reaction, Mak thought.

Diane cleared her throat. "In the closet of my bedroom is a small dresser. It's in the top drawer, at the bottom, underneath the clothes."

Wilton went to grab it.

"Were you trying to hide it from us, Diane?" Mak couldn't help but call the senator's wife on her shady reaction.

"You don't have to answer that," Theodore commanded, giving Mak a glare.

Mak smiled brightly. She couldn't wait to get her hands on that laptop.

Wilton returned and popped open the computer. "Password?"

"Please, allow me," Diane requested with an outstretched hand.

"That's okay. This laptop is now property of the United States justice department. We would have eventually asked for your password anyway." Wilton positioned his fingers on the keyboard.

"Maybe I could write it down for you," Diane suggested, her voice little more than a whisper.

Now, both Mak and Wilton stared at her, curiosity piqued.

"May I?" Diane reached for a pen and notepad she had in the middle of a decorative vase on the table. She wrote two words, tore the note off, folded it, and passed it to Mak and Wilton.

Mak reached it first and unfolded the paper. The words shocked her. Especially coming from someone who seemed as prim and proper as Mrs. Langsten. Mak glanced up at Wilton, whose face remained schooled with no expression. But Wilton typed in the combined words: KinkyBits.

Mak tried not to make a judgement or connect meaning to Diane's knowledge of what her husband had been up to for all these years based on that password. But Mak couldn't help but wonder if Diane knew more than she was saying. Was it possible to be married to someone so heinous and have no idea what he was up to?

The laptop came to life.

"Direct me to all your properties, please," Wilton commanded.

Diane did just that. Not only did she show them the properties, she gave him a tutorial on how to find the trail of who had rented what in the past year, the times the properties were vacant, and if any properties were vacant now. Mak had to admit that Diane was certainly cooperating now.

"Do you own any other properties besides these Airbnbs?" Wilton asked.

"Do you mean second homes? No." Diane shook her head.

"Second homes, vacation homes, time shares, any other places where you and your husband spend time?" Mak clarified.

Diane shook her head again. "No, when we go on vacation—which we haven't done in years—we like to go to Aruba."

"Do you own property there?" Wilton asked.

"No," Diane responded.

"Any one particular property you frequent?" Mak tilted her head to the side.

"Yes, I'll write that down for you as well." Diane took her original paper back and wrote the words: Carnal King's Colony.

"Okay," Mak drew the word out, breaking the strained silence. "Can I just ask the question that might blow this case wide open?"

Wilton looked slightly horrified.

"Diane, are you surprised by the charges against your husband?" Mak asked.

"Yes!" Diane's eyes widened. "There's no way my husband is capable of murder and trafficking."

"Okay, but are you in a loving marriage—a safe one?" Mak tried again.

"Yes," Diane nodded once to close the subject.

"I'm asking this because your husband—a man who runs a sex trafficking ring—"

"Allegedly," Theodore interrupted.

"Likes to stay in a place called Carnal King's Colony and makes your password *KinkyBits*. I think we might be able to draw some correlation—"

"No, you can't, and let me warn you, you are getting close to crossing a line here, Marshal Mak. What two consenting adults—a husband and wife, no less—do in their personal life will not convict them in a court of law," Theodore snapped. "Perhaps we should wrap up this line of questioning."

"Fine." Mak gritted her teeth. She leaned forward and stared into Diane's eyes. "Here's a good question. Do you have any knowledge, now or in the past, of your husband's involvement with murder, trafficking of any kind, or money laundering?"

"No!" Diane snapped as her lawyer put a finger up to indicate she stay silent.

"Just tell me this, Mrs. Langsten. Is there anywhere else you or your husband would go to spend time over the years? Anywhere that has sentimental meaning to either of you?" Wilton asked to bring them back on track.

"No, I can't think of anywhere," Diane stopped talking. Then she looked like she had an epiphany. "Our twin daughters are grown up now, but they bought houses near each other so our grandkids could grow up playing together."

"Where is that?" Wilton asked.

"Butte, Montana," Diane told him. "I don't think my husband would go there though."

"Why not?" Mak wondered.

"Because they haven't spoken to him in over three years."

"Why not?" Wilton pushed.

"That's a family matter I would prefer not to discuss," Diane clamped her mouth shut.

Reluctantly, Mak slid the paper back to Diane. "Please write down names, phone numbers, and addresses."

They watched as she did as instructed.

"Okay," Wilton breathed. "One more thing and we'll go." Wilton pulled out the picture he had bagged of the four men with a fish and pushed it across the table.

Mak watched as recognition flashed in Diane's eyes, and a small smile flashed across her lips.

"He was so young there." Diane gazed lovingly at the picture. She pressed her fingers over her husband's face.

"Do you know all the men in the photo?" Wilton asked.

"This man," Diane said, pointing to the man on the end, "was Joseph's brother, Robert. He died in a car crash. The others, no. I'm sorry. I don't know them."

"Do you know where this photo was taken?" Wilton followed up.

"Yes, that's Joseph's childhood home. His parents sold it years before they passed. But it holds a lot of good memories." Diane's face was wistful with past recollections.

"Okay, well, thank you for your time and cooperation, Mrs. Langsten. We will take the evidence we found, and you are free to resume your life here. Please don't leave town, and plan to make yourself available in case we have any more questions," Wilton said as he stood.

Mak followed Wilton's actions. She offered her hand, then she pulled out a card with her phone number on it. "In case you figure out where your husband is and decide to share that information with us."

Diane took the card. She stood and reluctantly shook Mak's hand, then Wilton's.

"Please run all future questions through my office." Theodore handed a card to Mak.

Mak took it and put it in her pocket. She left the house with questions still burning in her brain. Questions that had been shut down. How safe was Diane in that marriage, and was that a hint of fear in her eyes when Mak had asked about it?

As Mak was buckling her seatbelt, she smirked at Wilton. "Dibbs on searching the sex club in Aruba."

"Mak!" Wilton exhaled sharply. "You can't go prying into people's sex lives."

"I think it's relevant." Mak shrugged as she started the car, but her conscience pricked her. "You're probably right though, joking about it is in poor taste. Short of asking Diane to blink twice if she's okay, I had no idea what else to do!"

"Well, let me assure you, that wasn't it." Wilton stared straight ahead.

"But do you think she's safe, though?" Mak pushed.

Wilton shook his head. "I don't know. Maybe that laptop will give us some indication."

They drove a few minutes before Wilton looked up from his phone. "Have you seen the APB for the car Langsten's was driving?"

"Umm, white Cadillac Escalade Sport?" Mak asked.

"Yeah." Wilton cursed as he called Sikes. Wilton barely let Sikes answer before he started talking. "I saw the Escalade in the Langsten's garage. That's not what the senator is driving right now."

Sikes let out his own string of curses. They could hear him typing loudly on a keyboard while mumbling to himself. "How about a black 2025 BMW M5? Was that in the garage?"

"No, I didn't see that car. Is that Diane's?" Wilton asked.

"It is. Well, good catch. Gotta go re-route this. There's no telling how far he's gotten without eyes on him!"

"That's if he didn't already ditch his car," Wilton warned.

"True. Don't worry, we'll get this guy." Sikes hung up.

Mak looked at Wilton. "You're worried, aren't you?"

"For him." Wilton smiled.

Mak grinned back, but something tugged at the back of her brain. Wilton was always intense, and this case was personal for him. But was it the way Wilton smiled, or the crazy gleam in his eye that told her she would need to keep an eye on him? She shook her head. She hoped she was wrong.

20

BETH

The cab driver pulled into O'Hare airport and slowed to inch behind a line of other drivers. Beth was tapping the fingers of her good hand on her leg as they inched to a stop.

"What terminal?" the driver asked.

"The first one you come to," Beth answered but ignored the quizzical look the driver gave her. She didn't need to explain that she had not purchased a ticket, nor did she know where she was going. She figured if she made decisions as she went, there would be no time for anyone to find trails leading to her.

"Thank you!" Beth had cash ready and thrust it at the driver.

"There's an app—" he protested as he eyed the bills.

"No time." Beth shoved the wad of cash into his hands.

"This is too much!" he yelled, but Beth was already out of the car. A blast of wind picked up her hair and swirled it into her face. Impatiently, she pushed it away.

Backpack purse securely on her back, Beth glanced over her shoulder and did a scan as she quickened her pace and pushed through the door of the airport. The terminal closest to her with the shortest line was American Airlines. The scrolling billboard said, "Albuquerque, New Mexico."

"New Mexico, it is," Beth mumbled and got in the line.

As she waited, she took off her ballcap and untied her ponytail holder with one hand. She took off her jacket and awkwardly tied it around her waist. Maybe, if she made her appearance different, it might slow them down if they found her here. She was taking a chance that they didn't know she had a cast on her arm since she'd had it covered up the whole time they'd been following her.

The line advanced and Beth's gaze kept straying to the door of the airport. She scanned the crowd constantly. With every minute, she grew more fidgety and nervous. Finally, it was her turn.

"ID, please?" the bored woman at the counter requested.

Beth placed her license on the counter. "I need to buy a ticket."

The woman's eyes narrowed. "This flight is pretty full. Do you have a preference on where you want to sit?"

"No, I'm completely open." Beth smiled, hoping she looked sincere.

The woman typed away. "Your lucky day. We had a cancellation, and your seat is near the front on an aisle."

That will get me off the plane quicker, Beth thought. "Thank you!"

"Are you checking any bags?"

"No."

The woman named the price and Beth dug into her cash folder. She pulled out several hundred-dollar bills and a fifty when the woman held up a hand. "We don't accept cash."

Beth's heart sank. "No!" She couldn't leave a trail. That's how people got found. She'd seen it in the movies.

"Sorry, we don't have registers up here. We accept debit

and all major credit cards," the woman looked at her expectantly.

Beth tried to calculate the risk, but the fear in her mind was shutting her brain down. She tried to form another plan, but where else could she go? With the admission of defeat, Beth pulled a debit card out of her wallet and handed it to the airport agent.

"Okay, here you go."

Beth glanced at the ticket, checking the takeoff time. Less than an hour before boarding. "Enjoy your flight," the woman said as she handed Beth an airline ticket before she yelled, "Next!"

As she turned, she caught sight of two men moving quickly down the hallway. It was them! Her breath caught in her chest and her mind screamed one word at her, *Run!*

But she didn't run. If there was a sure way to gain attention, it was by running. Instead, Beth made herself slow down and saunter to the nearest ladies' room. Once she was there, she sprinted for the handicap stall and pulled down the baby changing table inside. She changed into a different shirt, slowing down enough to not hit her cast on the wall. She went through every piece of clothing, checked every pocket in her backpack, and patted down the clothes she was wearing. She even took off her shoes and socks. Then she threw her oversized jacket in the trashcan.

"How do they keep finding me?" she whispered. The answer came to her with a start. Hadn't she played her own games with her US Marshal ex-boyfriend by installing a tracking app on his phone and linking it with hers? She took out her phone and scanned her apps but saw nothing. She turned her phone over a few times and wondered if there was a remote way to ping towers and find locations that she knew nothing about.

I have no other choice, Beth thought remorsefully. She did a quick search on how to wipe a phone clean and followed the steps. Once she was sure it had worked, she dropped the phone into the trash can. Her stomach felt like it hit the bottom along with her communication device. Like she was officially wiping herself off the planet. Once she walked out of this bathroom, her old life would be gone.

Beth left the stall and went to wash her uncasted hand, which was shaking violently. She glanced over at the woman next to her, who was wearing a bucket hat and mindlessly washing her own hands.

"I love that hat!" Beth let her voice tilt up an octave.

"This one?" the woman's eyes snapped up to hers in surprise. "I've had it forever."

"Well-worn and loved means comfortable," Beth smiled. "I've always wondered what a hat like that would look like on me."

"You want to try it on?" the woman took it off her head and tentatively held it out to Beth.

"Could I?" Beth took it and plopped it on her head. "Oh, it's so cute!"

"It does look good on you," the woman said, still looking perplexed.

"What if I throw my hair up in a bun, like this?" Beth took off the hat, set it on the counter and tipped her head upside down. She took the hair tie from her wrist and wrapped it around her hair in an extra messy bun on account of the one-handed work. She put the hat back on over it and was satisfied to see it changed her appearance just a little more.

"Yeah, that works too. Listen, I gotta catch a flight—"

"Sorry, I know. Me too. Can I give you fifty dollars for this hat?" Beth asked.

"It's not worth fifty dollars," the woman protested.

"It is to me," Beth said as she pulled out her wallet and produced a fifty-dollar bill. "Please?"

"Okay, if you really want it." The woman agreed with a shrug.

"Thank you," Beth smiled happily. "Where are you traveling?"

"New Mexico," the woman said as she walked toward the exit.

Beth fell in line with her, thankful the woman was taller than her and blocked her from view. "No way! Me too. Small world." Beth positioned her body so she was next to the woman, as if they were friends and traveling together. She caught sight of the men leaning against the wall right outside the hall from the ladies' room. She quickly turned her head away from them and kept walking with her new *friend*.

Beth held her breath and told herself not to look back again as she walked. But when she was far enough away that she could find a seat at the terminal, she chanced a glance to find the men still standing by the ladies' room door. She found a seat that looked out the window facing the planes outside that put her back toward the room. She checked the time. She had less than fifteen minutes until they boarded.

With any luck, she'd be on the plane while these men still waited on her to leave the bathroom. Which only reminded her that she had just trashed any hope of reaching out to the outside world—to the people who loved her. She couldn't change her mind and call Stephen Wilton to come pick her up and take her to safety. Beth's eyebrows rose as the thought surfaced. She wondered if that had been her plan B all along.

As Beth looked out the window at what was starting to become an overcast day, she realized something else. She had been horrible to Stephen. She had put her expectations that he would save her on him without trusting him enough to inform him of what exactly she needed him to save her from.

Beth's stomach started to ache. The list of apologies she owed were starting to mount. Would she live through this to tell Stephen she was sorry? And what about her relationship with Lacy? She had never told Lacy the truth about who she was. Nor had she tried to form a new bond with her. As she waited for boarding to begin, Beth wondered if the secret that she was Lacy's mom would die with her.

21

ALYAH

Alyah had been manning the tipline. At least, she had been the liaison between Chief Sauder's police department and the marshals. They sifted through the tips and passed on anything they deemed credible.

Senator Langsten was seen driving down the highway.

Senator Langsten was seen having lunch at a diner.

Senator Langsten was spotted in a strip club. That one made Alyah snort and immediately disregard the note. Then she thought about it. Why wouldn't he go to a strip club? Hadn't Langsten convinced everyone that he was a fine, upstanding representative when really, he was a deviant criminal? It was all an act. Who knew who the man really was? Alyah kept the note and passed the tip on. They were running down all possibilities. But the tips had become fewer at this point. Maybe she would suggest they run another news interview to generate new leads.

Alyah felt discontent. This wasn't the best use of her knowledge. She had a feeling the US Marshals weren't sure where else to put her. It was like they were giving her busy work. When Alyah had gotten to the end of her small to-do list, she got up and went into Sikes' office.

"Alyah," Sikes acknowledged.

"Hello," Alyah greeted as she sat down. Then she leaned forward. "What am I doing, Sikes?"

"What do you mean?"

"You have me doing busy work. I can do so much more," Alyah asserted.

Sikes nodded slowly, looking like his mind was processing something. "Close the door."

Alyah stretched behind her to the door and swung it shut.

"What are your intentions for the future with your career?" Sikes asked.

Alyah wasn't surprised by his directness, but she didn't know the answer. She'd been contemplating that herself but had not come to any conclusions. She opened her mouth and closed it.

"Yes, I'm asking for a reason. You may or may not know that we haven't filled the District Attorney position here yet. Hell, we didn't even appoint an interim since you left," annoyance lined his tone.

Alyah's eyes widened. "Then how…?"

"Attorney General Alex Kross took on the extra workload."

"Oh!" was all Alyah could say. That must have been a lot of work.

"Truth is, Kross just put in his resignation. Not only will we have your old DA position open, we'll also need to replace the Attorney General." Sikes let the implication of that hang.

"And you are telling me this because you think I'm qualified to apply?" Alyah wondered. She would have never considered such a move.

Sikes nodded.

Alyah sat back. She hadn't checked openings because she

wasn't sure what she was going to do. She hadn't even called her Attorney General yet. She'd just taken a leave, citing it as an emergency.

"In the meantime," Sikes continued, "we need someone to take the evidence we have and make logical sense of it. To tell the story of the crime so it's airtight for court."

"So, you need someone to do my old job?" Alyah smiled knowingly.

Sikes nodded. "In an unofficial capacity."

"I see."

"Perhaps," Sikes said with a shrug, "we'll use you in a consultant capacity. That is, unless you decide to make a change and come back to us."

Alyah let the words hang there. Then she thanked Sikes. Her mind was a whir. She already knew what direction she was leaning, what her gut was telling her. But she needed to think it through.

"Alyah," Sikes called before she disappeared through the door.

She turned back to him.

"Chief Sauder will be here this afternoon to brief us on the evidence we have against Mickey Upton and Boyd Allister. Should be an open and shut case."

"Should be?" Alyah leveled him with a look. Nothing was ever that easy.

Sikes tapped his watch. "Three thirty."

"I'll be there. Thank you." Alyah knew it was all about to take a turn.

22

BETH

Beth sat on the packed plane in awe that she was able to get a seat on this flight. More than that miracle was the one where she had boarded unnoticed. She must have been right about her phone. She'd overheard the flight attendants talking to each other. They were still boarding, but it looked like it would be an easy flight. That was a small mercy considering that Beth would still have a lengthy layover after this. Still, Beth was starting to feel small inklings of something that had always eluded her—hope.

Beth noticed the woman sitting next to her was an elderly woman who looked kind. She was playing with her cell phone.

"Excuse me, ma'am?"

"Yes?" the woman asked. She looked pointedly at Beth's cast like she might ask what happened but thought better of it.

"I lost my cell phone, and I need to call my carrier to have it shut off. Do you care if I use your phone before we take off?" Beth smiled shyly.

"Oh! You poor thing! Of course." She handed her phone to Beth.

Beth quickly called her cell carrier and shut off her phone. As she handed the woman back her phone, Beth thanked her. Maybe that would signify to the men that her phone was no longer trackable, but Beth didn't want anyone to find it and use it. She really had no other option.

As the plane took off, Beth was surprised by how tired she felt. But then, she couldn't remember the last time she had slept. Certainly not in her car. Lately, memories of her past flooded back to her each time she closed her eyes. Today was no different. She'd worked her whole life to forget. She thought if she kept moving, pressing forward, and staying ahead, she wouldn't have time to think about *that* night. The night when everything changed in an irrevocable way.

She wasn't sure if it was the adrenaline dump or the situation she was in right now, but her mind kept returning to that night. She closed her eyes and took deep calming breaths. But try as she might, she could not keep the memory from flooding back to her.

Nineteen Years Ago…

Beth bit her nails as she stood next to her best friend and waited for Jacob Greenly to return. He'd been gone for quite a while. Beth stifled a sigh. What she wouldn't do to go back and unmeet Jacob. But then, she wouldn't have Lacy. She just wished she could break the power he had over her. He was her first love. The father of her baby.

But she'd promised her parents she'd never tell him that. It was part of the deal she'd made them to come back. Beth had missed her friends so much, she would have promised anything to get back here. But now that she was back, seeing him, it was so hard not to tell him the truth.

Jacob finally returned with two red solo cups and a matching shade of lipstick on his cheek. Beth's stomach turned when she saw the remnants of the lipstick smeared on his cheek. That wasn't hers. Jacob handed Beth a cup, leaned down, and attempted to pull her into a hug. Beth shoved him away so hard, Jacob's alcohol sloshed over onto his shirt.

"Hey!" Jacob protested in surprise. "What the hell?"

"Are you kidding me right now?" Beth snapped. "You have lipstick on your cheek."

Jacob grinned. "That's yours, baby!"

"I'm not wearing lipstick, you idiot." Beth attempted to turn away, but Jacob put his hand on her arm. "Get your hand off me."

Jacob jerked his hand away like he'd been burned.

"Shania?" Beth turned to find her friend in conversation with Trevan Collins, the hunky football linebacker who'd made the varsity football team. It was unthinkable for someone his age.

"It was nothing, Beth. Come on, you gotta believe me," Jacob whined.

She didn't. Before Beth could answer, she heard raised voices near her and turned to find Greg Wilton had walked up and wasn't happy about Trevan talking to Shania.

Beth rolled her eyes but couldn't look away as the shouting became shoving and Trevan flew backward into a wobbly card table with alcohol sitting on top. Beth gasped.

"Let's take this outside," someone said.

Mindlessly, Beth followed Shania and the boys outside, vaguely aware of the small crowd that followed them. She watched in horror as Greg threw the first punch, resulting in Trevan tackling Greg to the ground.

The crowd started to chant—fight, fight, fight!

"Listen, Beth," Jacob put a hand on her shoulder.

Beth whirled around to face him. "Put a hand on me one more time and I'll break it off. I don't know why I thought we could take up where we left off. I don't need you!"

Greg and Trevan were rolling around taking shots at each other.

What were they even fighting about? Her gaze landed on her best friend as Shania tried to break up the boys.

"Fine," Jacob raised his voice so Beth couldn't ignore him. "Some girl kissed me on the cheek as I walked through the room. That's where the lipstick came from. I didn't even know her." His voice was pleading, as if begging her to forgive him.

"Please, you were gone forever. I know all about you," Beth spat.

"No, it's not like that. You're the only one for me!" Jacob sounded frantic.

"You'll probably knock her up too." The words popped out of her mouth before she could think about it, and she immediately wished she could recall them.

Jacob froze, his eyes searching hers. He'd gone instantly pale. "What?"

Sirens sounded in the distance and someone shouted, "Police!"

But Beth was locked in a stare-down with Jacob.

"You're pregnant?" he whispered, horror spreading over his face.

"No," Beth snapped. "Not anymore."

"You—"

"Shania?" Beth's gaze shot to her friend who staggered to the boys.

"Okay, I'll go home with both of you," Shania said with a big dopey grin on her face.

"Woah, how much did she have to drink?" Jacob muttered.

That's when Beth noticed Shania bobbing closer to the cliff. The Cliff was what they called the old rock quarry that wasn't in use anymore. At least eighty feet deep with no water in the bottom, no one would survive that fall. It's why they usually stayed in the old shack at the top of the hill.

"Shania!" Beth lunged forward. Everything began to move in slow motion, but Beth knew it had probably all happened in a split second. Because as Beth moved, her legs felt too heavy to lift, and Shania lost her balance. Beth reached out her hand, but Shania was

too far out of her grasp. Then Shania was gone, leaving Beth grasping at the air.

Beth fell to her knees, the realization slamming into her and leaving her unable to breathe, gasping for breath that had whooshed out of her lungs. Shania was gone. No, not gone. She was dead.

Beth inhaled deeply, trying to catch her breath. She jerked, her whole body shocking awake, and opened her eyes.

"There, there, dear," the elderly woman in the seat beside her was looking at her with concern, patting Beth's shoulder.

Beth's cheeks felt wet. She wiped them and wondered if she had been crying. Embarrassed, Beth sat up straighter in her seat. She accepted the Kleenex the woman held out to her and blew her nose. After that night, it was as if Beth had jumped tracks and had been living someone else's life. The wrong life. And she'd never gotten it back on the right track.

23

———

WILTON

Stephen stared out the window of the US Marshal jet that was currently en route to Aruba. Despite Mak's jokes about volunteering for the Carnal King's Colony, Sikes had assigned it to Stephen—alone. Stephen was officially out of rookie status, which meant Sikes had decided Stephen was perfectly capable of handling himself on this one. Stephen knew sending him was just a precaution because Sikes didn't think the senator was in Aruba, and he wasn't worried about sending backup with Stephen.

"Why me?" Stephen had protested.

Sikes had speared him through FaceTime with a stern gaze. "Do I really have to spell it out?"

"Yes," Stephen stated. He felt a little objectified before he even heard the answer.

"You're single. You can go there and fit in easily, do a little recon, get eyes on the senator—"

"If he's even there," Stephen protested. "You know he's not likely to go to any of these locations. He has to know that these are the exact places we would look for him first. He's not going to go anywhere this obvious."

"And I'm not sure if I should be offended by your reasoning or thankful, Sikes," Mak interjected with a pout.

"Be thankful. Men hitting on you tends to blow your cover," Sikes quipped.

Stephen snorted at the truth of it.

Mak whipped her head to him and narrowed her eyes.

"Not to mention, you won't have time for any sight-seeing," Sikes said, then got serious again. "You'll be there a day, two tops, and then you're back on the plane home. Got it, Wilton?"

"Yes, sir," Stephen agreed.

"Plus, it will give you a chance to do what you love best, Mak—drive," Sikes smirked. "You'll be checking out the Airbnbs."

"I feel like you're getting too much enjoyment out of this," Mak grumbled.

What Sikes wasn't saying was that time was of the essence. As in, they didn't have any of it to spare. Once they had all the addresses of the Langsten's Arbnb properties, the marshal headquarters were able to put together a map of all the homes. It turned out, the locations were all within easy driving distance of each other. Sikes had assigned that task to Mak.

Now, as Stephen disembarked the jet into a warm, tropical night, he wished he'd thought to wear something other than jeans. Then he gulped. Would there be a dress code at this club, or lack thereof? Obviously, there was no way to anticipate every twist and turn this job threw at him, but as much as possible, Stephen liked to know what he was walking into.

After a short shuttle ride to what turned out to be a gated resort community, Stephen grabbed his overnight bag, gave the driver a tip, and walked into the posh lobby. The octagon-shaped room was open so Stephen could see straight out to the ocean. He could hear the waves crashing on the shore. The marble floors under his feet looked immaculate in white and gray swirl. Pops of plants Stephen had never seen, which he assumed were indigenous to Aruba, decorated the high-end tables sitting next to leather chairs.

The lobby was practically empty. Stephen assumed it was because he had arrived late. Still, he bet this club would become far more active.

"I can help you over here, sir," a kind, female voice called out.

Stephen turned and followed the voice. A young woman wearing a classy black cocktail dress looked at him expectantly. Her name tag said *Leisa*. Her thick dark hair was pulled up in a high ponytail and curls cascaded down her back.

"How can I help you?" Leisa smiled pleasantly.

"I need to check in. I'm Stephen Wilton," Stephen gave her his name and most charming smile. He would have loved to use a fake name, but there had been no time to generate a fake ID.

"Ah yes." Leisa winked as she started typing on her computer. "I bet that's your real name, too."

Stephen's eyes widened until he noticed she was teasing him. Her tone was fun and light, and Mak might even have said the woman was flirting. Stephen decided to use that to his advantage. He leaned forward.

"Is that the required uniform here?" he asked.

Leisa looked up with a smile. "We're required to wear black."

"Well, you take black to the next level." Stephen allowed his eyes to rove over her, trying to play the part of a single guy looking for a good time.

Leisa leaned forward and lowered her voice. "Flirting will get you exactly what you're looking for. I'm off in seven minutes. I can give you a tour and then show you where the *activities* are for the night."

Stephen's stomach turned. Though he was curious, he wasn't interested in any of this. He was just here to do his job.

"Great," he said and turned his charming smile up a notch as he glanced around the empty lobby. "I was a little worried about how dead this place was. I heard this was a good time, but so far I have my doubts."

"Oh, you're a first timer?" Leisa looked up again with mischief in her eyes. She put two keys in an envelope and handed it to him. "We'll go easy on you."

She was cute with her laid-back personality and polished appearance, Stephen would give her that. He just hoped he could pull this off—whatever *this* was.

"Tell you what," Leisa purred. "I'm going to go to the ladies' room. You wait right here, and I'll give you a tour when I get back."

"Deal." Stephen listened to her black stilettos disappear down the hallway and then went around the check-in desk. He immediately typed in *Joseph Langsten*. He found a record, but it dated back six months ago. "Would Langsten really give a real name?" he mumbled.

Stephen's fingers flew over the keyboard searching every variation he could think of until he felt a hand on his back. Surprised, he whipped around to find Leisa behind him.

"Find what you're looking for, Mr. Wilton?" There was a smug smile on her face, but Leisa's eyes had turned a shade darker, a clear sign of irritation.

"Sorry." Stephen put his hands up guiltily. "You caught me. I was looking to see if there are any celebrities here tonight."

"Are you a reporter who works for one of those tabloids? Because it could cost me my job if one of my guests ends up in *Star Inquire* tomorrow." Leisa put her hands on her hips.

"No. I just heard this is where the biggest names hang out." Stephen pretended to look embarrassed.

"Well, us being friends depends on you staying on the other side of this desk," Leisa stated.

Stephen walked back around and tried to look sheepish. "Did I lose my chance at a tour?"

Leisa studied him. "I oughta say *yes*. But I'm required to give them, so let's go, stalker."

"I'm not a—" Stephen stopped himself with a laugh. "Okay, maybe a little. I heard that senators even come here sometimes. Have you ever met one?"

"A senator?" Leisa raised a brow. "That's what you're into?"

"I mean, power and money, who isn't?" Stephen smiled. It really was too bad he was working and had sworn off women. He was enjoying her easy banter.

"Fair," she agreed. "Yes, I've met a senator or two in my day. As you can see, this is the path down to the beach. The dark blue cabanas are ours. Don't wander past the privacy fences on either side or you'll jump resorts. Clothing is optional on the beach, but we do ask that guests wear clothes inside the restaurant and commons areas."

"Ah." Stephen nodded as if these were normal, everyday rules. He followed Leisa down the hallway where she pointed out the pool and bar areas, also clothing optional, but closed for the night.

Leisa led him down a few more halls, up a set of stairs, and to room 222. "This is your room. Would you like to set your stuff down?"

"Sure," Stephen agreed. He put his key in the slot and opened the door. He tossed his bag in and quickly shut the door before Leisa could get the wrong idea and invite herself inside. Inwardly, Stephen shook his head. The universe was clearly testing the strength of his decision to swear off women for the time being.

"Alright, you ready for tonight's activity?" Leisa asked as she led him down several more hallways and up a few flights of stairs. The higher they climbed, the louder the beat of the music got.

"Can you tell me what to expect?" Stephen asked, legitimately nervous.

"Well, it's a rooftop party with lots of alcohol that has been going on for about an hour now. Anything goes. You'll see it all. You choose what, if anything, you participate in," Leisa explained. "Consent is important here."

"And this is where *all* the guests hang out?" Stephen asked.

Leisa shrugged. "This is where they start out for the evening."

"Right," Stephen said.

The scene that unfolded before Stephen might have been shocking had he not tempered his expectations. The rooftop was surprisingly glamorous with a bar in the corner, a DJ spinning in the opposite corner, and a large hot tub and infinity pool right down the middle. Soft, glowing lights lit up the space from under the leather benches that lined the walls. What really caught Stephen's attention was the view of the ocean, just over the top of the privacy wall. They were close enough to hear the crash of waves over the thump of the beat. A full moon lit the sky overhead.

He sighed inwardly, thinking about how to play this. He tried to look bored, as if clubs like this were his norm. Like he wasn't looking for someone specific. In truth, he was anything but bored. His adrenaline was high—he was on guard and his heart was racing.

"See anything you like?" Leisa purred near him as she put

her arm through his like she was claiming him, closing the gap between their bodies. "Or, anyone...?"

Stephen used the opportunity to slowly look around the rooftop, working to focus on faces, not on stages of undress or explicit acts happening all around them. Thanks to the open layout, he could see much of the roof, but didn't want to miss it if Langsten was here.

He scanned the faces of people in the pool and hot tub as well. The clean smell of chlorine lingered among various perfumes and colognes. No one looked familiar yet. In fact, few appeared to be in the same age-range as the senator at all. He thought this might have been due to the Botox, fillers, and facelifts prevalent among the crowd.

"How about a drink?" he asked as he trailed his fingers along the inside of Leisa's arms and linked fingers with her. For better or worse, he had decided that she would be his guide for the night.

"Good place to start." Leisa smiled and led him to the bar.

"Seven and seven, please," Stephen requested. "What are you having?"

"White wine, please," Leisa said to the bartender.

Stephen pulled out his wallet.

Leisa waved a hand. "Put it on your room." Her long manicured fingernail tapped Stephen's back pocket, reminding him where he'd put his card earlier.

Stephen obeyed and pulled his room key out.

"Start a tab?" the bartender yelled over the thumping music.

Stephen nodded and pulled Leisa to the side to wait on drinks. As he stood there, he let his eyes wander over the party from this vantage point. He really had hoped he would be able to quickly spot or determine if Langsten was here, but he could see he was going to have to move around a bit more to see everyone in attendance. Then there was the chance that if Langsten was here, he might keep a low profile in his room. Stephen vaguely wondered how chatty Leisa got after a few drinks. Maybe that would help him out here.

He turned to find her staring up at him expectantly.

"A bit of a voyeur aren't you, Mr. Wilton?" Leisa teased, that pretty smile barely pulling up the corner of her lips.

"Isn't everybody?" Stephen shot back with a wink.

Leisa shrugged. "Some of us like a little more action."

Stephen closed the small gap between them and leaned down to whisper in her ear. "What kind of action?"

Leisa turned to him, her chest brushing against his and looked up at him as she whispered her preferences in his ear. Stephen was thankful for the dark night because he was sure his face heated up. He was even more grateful when the bartender gave them their drinks. He grabbed his and handed Leisa hers.

"Let's walk," Stephen suggested. With Leisa on his arm, Stephen turned down multiple dance requests and a couple propositions. He was having a hard time ignoring the way Leisa liked to mindlessly trail her fingers up and down his arm. Her touch affected him more than he let on. Finally, he grasped her hand in his, linking their fingers together in hopes that would stop her sensual touches. It worked until her thumb began rubbing slow circles around his palm.

After three walks around the entire rooftop, Stephen was convinced that the senator was not there. Several more drinks led to Stephen's discovery that Leisa could hold her liquor and her gossip. Leisa must have noticed his disappointment.

"You seem stressed," she purred. "Let me make it all better." She led him to an empty seat in the corner of the room and pushed Stephen to sit down. Stephen allowed it. With the exception of Leisa, who had certainly spent quality time with him, it had been a disappointing night. But as she knelt on the leather bench beside Stephen and lowered her lips to his, he had to admit, in this moment, he wanted her. Maybe not her, exactly, but the distraction she promised.

Stephen deepened the kiss and surprised her by pulling her onto his lap. As she straddled him, the skirt of her cocktail dress rose indecently high. Stephen let his hands drift to her outer thighs and lightly rubbed up and down her legs until he felt goosebumps erupt over her skin.

The song changed to something slow and heavy, and the air suddenly seemed thick with the promise of anything he desired. As she kissed him back, Stephen let his fingers drift under her dress. Leisa gasped and smiled onto his lips, which were still pressed on hers. She responded by unbuttoning the top buttons of his dress shirt. As she moved against him, she put one hand down his shirt and caressed his bare chest.

"Let's take this to my room," Stephen whispered on her lips.

"Why?" Leisa asked. "Look around you. No one cares what we do here."

Stephen opened his eyes and could see other couples doing exactly what he and Leisa were doing. Various couples of men, women, and multiple people all enjoying a guilt free night of exhibitionism. The magic dissipated for Stephen and he halted his movement.

"I can't," Stephen said.

Leisa went still. "You sure?" she asked gently.

"Yes." Stephen's mind went back to that conversation with the counselor. *Sometimes we engage in risky behaviors just to cope with complicated, unresolved feelings...* He'd laughed at the counselor. But here he was doing exactly that. Gently, Stephen moved Leisa off his lap. "I'm sorry."

Disappointment settled in her eyes. "Me, too."

It wasn't long before she caught the eye of another man who fit the cliché of the tall, dark, and handsome category.

He sauntered over with confidence and ease. His tailored jacket was high quality, and he wore it, along with his tight-fitting jeans, well. He immediately hugged Leisa and whispered something in her ear that made her giggle.

"Stephen, this is Jerry. He asked if he could join us for the rest of the evening?" Leisa tried one more time.

"Thank you, but no," Stephen said quickly with a kind smile. "I'm actually feeling a little jet-lagged and think I'm done for the evening. Enjoy."

It was well past midnight, and only when Stephen reached his room did he let out a sigh of relief. He flipped on the lights and let out a low whistle. He hated to think what the US Marshals were paying for this room. The room was white with grey and blue accents and a black and white swirled marble floor. There was a black leather couch, a matching chair, and a small TV on the wall in a sitting room. A king-sized bed sat on a platform floor, slightly elevating it and setting it apart from the rest of the open layout room. Everything was pristine and comfortable.

But what really drew his eye was the view he spied through the balcony door. He opened it and let himself out. He had an ocean view and a hot tub. He shook his head. Less than ten minutes ago, Stephen had asked someone, a perfect stranger, to come to his room. His mind went to Alyah, who was never too far from his thoughts these days. What had he been thinking?

"Don't mind if I do," Stephen mumbled as he viewed the hot tub. He turned off the lights in his room, ditched his clothes, eased himself into the hot water, and turned on the jets. He felt the tension in his muscles relax under the hot water and the sound of waves crashing on the ocean. The night was cool enough to make the hot water feel comfortable.

Stephen wasn't sure how long he sat there thinking.

Contemplating his behavior, the next steps in the case, and wondering why he didn't do things like this—sit in a hot tub—more often. Take more time for himself. He was disappointed he hadn't seen the senator and frustrated by his own behavior. He'd almost made a mistake but felt glad to be alone again.

Huh, he thought, *that's a new feeling.* Stephen typically hated being alone. Tonight, he found he didn't mind it nearly as much as he used to. In fact, in this moment, Stephen found he quite preferred it.

24

BETH

Beth walked out of the Albuquerque airport feeling grateful. Despite a very long layover filled with her looking over her shoulder the whole time, Beth had finally arrived, and she was alive. She had nothing but the backpack purse on her back, the cast on her arm, and the few clothes she brought.

New Mexico was warm, even in the night sky. In fact, Beth felt downright hot the minute she stepped outside. Still, there was something promising about the change of scenery. She'd never been to New Mexico. She had no ties here. She could truly start all over. No one would ever find her. Would they?

A shuttle for the Marriott was pulling up to the curb. Beth wandered closer to the stop. A plan was forming in her mind. While she didn't have unlimited funds, and she would have to find something more permanent, not to mention a job, she could afford a nice hotel for a night or two while she rested, took a shower, and figured out her next move.

Beth wasn't concerned that she had no idea if the Marriott had availability. For now, that wasn't an issue. She just needed to keep moving. She boarded the shuttle and took a seat, surprised that the driver didn't ask for some sort of confirmation.

As it turned out, the hotel did have availability. She stopped at the gift store and bought a t-shirt and a pair of pajama pants. A short time later, Beth surveyed the room, delighted to find it had a big jacuzzi tub.

Beth started the hot water and shirked her clothes. Her eyes fell on her cast. She couldn't get it wet. She gazed at the bag holding her gift shop purchases. She dumped the items on her bed and wrapped the bag around the bulky, dried plaster. She felt thankful that her right hand was dominant as she tied the two handles of the bag at the top one handed.

She let the tub fill a bit more before grabbing the little shampoos and soap and hopping in. The hot water soothed muscles Beth hadn't even known were sore—likely from being on guard and ready to spring into action. She turned off the water, cleaned off, then laid her head back on the headrest, stretching out her body.

She turned on the jets and let her eyes close, enjoying the sting of the hot spray as it massaged her body from every angle. As Beth let herself be lulled away, her mind began to remember what happened after she lost Shania.

Nineteen Years Ago...

Beth sat in a dark, cold jail cell with three boys who were not her best friend. None of these boys knew her secrets from the second grade. Her eyes closed as tears streamed steadily down her face, as if they would never stop. Shania was dead and Beth was utterly alone. She'd never felt more heartbroken and more afraid in her entire life. Given that she'd been through a teenage pregnancy and childbirth, that was saying something.

She felt Jacob's hand slip around her shoulder, and without a thought to their earlier argument, Beth laid a head against Jacob's shoulder where it had always fit so well. She let him hold her until she realized that he was just a stupid boy who didn't really care about her. The likelihood that they would reunite over Lacy and end up together was zero.

Beth opened her swollen eyes and pushed his arm off her. She leaned as far away as she could—into the corner. The sudden lack of body heat chilled her. Why was it so cold in here? Her nostrils picked up on another smell. Urine. She gagged a little at the thought.

Jacob moved closer, pinning Beth with his large shoulder. He was broad for his age. They sat like that, shoulder to shoulder, until Jacob poked Beth's side.

"Hey!" Beth hissed.

"Were you serious?" Jacob whispered, his eyes searching hers, panic evident in his white face. "Were you—" His hand made a round half circle over his stomach.

"Ugh! None of that matters anymore, Jacob!" Beth pushed him. She could see Greg, Davey, and Trevan sitting on a bench across from them, now eyeing her and Jacob with open, undisguised interest.

"It matters! You moved away without saying good-bye. For a year! You didn't answer any of my texts, or Shania's. I know. I asked her. Is that why? Did you—" Jacob stopped talking abruptly.

All attention in the cell was now on Jacob as he seemed to be thinking intently about something.

"Drop it, Jacob! Shania is dead. Don't you get that? That's all that matters right now!" Beth started crying again.

"My mom saw your mom in the grocery store the other day." Jacob was now ignoring Beth's tears. "You have a new baby sister. She's an infant. My mom didn't remember your mom being pregnant. Ohmigod!" Jacob doubled over, his breaths coming in short, sharp pants.

"Hey, are you okay, man?" Greg asked. "You hyperventilating?"

"I can't—" Jacob gasped. "I can't get in trouble again."

"What?" Beth heard how sharp her voice came out.

"He's going to make me join the military," Jacob groaned.

"No one can make you join," Davey's voice sounded indignant. "Aren't you like seventeen?"

Jacob looked up, fear in his eyes. "You ever seen my dad?"

"That's what you're afraid of right now—getting in trouble?" Beth asked dully. "You're sitting in a jail cell."

"I'm not built for the military. I don't—I can't do it!" Jacob heaved.

"Hey!" Trevan raised his voice and yelled out. "Can we get a trashcan in here?"

"Shut up, kid!" came a gruff voice.

"Don't we each get a phone call?" Greg smarted off. "We've been in here for over an hour!"

"Who you gonna call? Your parents?" They heard a sarcastic snicker. "You'll get a call when I say you get a call." Officer Pottstaff came into view.

The five of them turned to stare at the man in the uniform.

Casually, Pottstaff leaned against the wall outside the cell. He folded his arms over his slightly bulging belly. "You have a few options. I'd choose wisely if I were you. This is an all or nothing deal. You all choose the same thing, or I'll choose for you." Pottstaff grinned, pure evil exuding from his pores.

"Should we wait until our lawyers get here?" Greg asked. He appeared to be the smart one of the boys.

"You get a lawyer and all deals are off. You'll be lucky to ever see freedom again." Pottstaff picked his teeth.

"We didn't murder anyone. Shania tumbled over the cliff on her own. It was an accident!" Davey shouted.

"Hmm, that's not what I saw," Pottstaff drawled.

Horrified, they all stared mutely at him.

"Ready to listen?" he asked.

They nodded their heads.

"Okay, either I charge and book you all for murder. Or you work for me." Pottstaff stared into each of their eyes.

"What does work for you mean?" Beth asked.

Pottstaff rubbed the scruff on his chin. "Here's an example. Sometimes I need carriers. Kids who will pick up and deliver things into the high school and back out. I'd need you to be stealthy because if you got caught, you'd be on your own."

"What things?" Trevan's voice sounded like a growl. Like he knew the answer to his question.

Pottstaff wagged a finger at him. "I won't divulge everything until I know if you are all with me."

"We need to discuss this amongst ourselves." Beth sat up straighter.

All eyes turned to look at Beth.

Beth shrugged. "What? You said you need us all to agree. Let us talk about it. Alone."

"Okay," Pottstaff pushed off the wall. "Don't take too long. Your parents are going to be mighty worried." He walked down the hall.

"My dad can't know about this—any of this!" Jacob looked at Beth when he said that. "If he finds out, forget the military. My dad will kill me."

Beth couldn't breathe. Anxiety left her with a pain so acute in her chest, for a minute, she wondered if she was having a heart attack. *No,* she told herself, *it was an attack alright, but not that kind.* She had these more frequently when she was a child.

Tears came to her eyes and she let them fall. She'd cried for that little sixteen-year-old who felt at the mercy of corrupt authority. For that same girl who'd grown up doing someone else's dirty crimes. For the broken relationship with her daughter. For Beth, the adult, who might always be on the run and looking over her shoulder for the rest of her life.

She got out of the tub, drained it, found a bathrobe, and wrapped herself in it. She lay down on the bed and let her eyes close again. This time, she'd sleep forever, and hope that she never woke to this nightmare that was her reality.

25

ALYAH

The rain started as a light patter on the roof of the US Marshal building where Alyah sat still working. They had set her up temporarily in Stephen Wilton's cubicle. While she had felt strange about being in his space, she also felt a little closer to him here. On his desk was a picture of him smiling with his parents. Another picture showed him with his daughter, Anna. Anna was sitting on Stephen's shoulders wearing a karate uniform. She was laughing and the joy on Stephen's face took Alyah's breath away. She'd never seen that level of happiness from him.

Alyah shifted her gaze to the floor-to-ceiling windows as the rain fell harder. She blinked a few times. Her eyes were burning from staring at the computer so long. She looked away and noticed how dark it was in the office. Where was everyone?

Alyah shut down her computer and reached for her phone. The silence surrounding her was eerie. She walked out into the main office.

"Hello?" she called out. She slowly felt along the wall until her hand made contact with a light switch. She flicked it, but nothing happened. No light flooded the office like she had expected. She flattened her back against the wall, adrenaline flooding her. Had the electricity gone out?

The storm had picked up outside, but Alyah hadn't noticed any lightning or big trees swaying. For minutes she was frozen to the spot. Where was her protective detail? Weren't they supposed to check with her before they left for the evening?

A loud crash sounded from the opposite side of the building. Was that coming from Sikes' office? Alyah gasped and launched into motion. She ran. It was a straight shot from where she was to the door. Sweat rolled down her spine, her heart raced, and her legs moved of their own volition.

She could see the front door and thought she had made it when a blackness obscured her vision. Her body crashed into a wall of human muscle. Alyah screamed as strong arms closed around her. She thrashed and tried to move. In desperation, she stomped her heel into the big, immovable foot next to hers.

"Alyah! Stop. It's okay," a man grunted.

Alyah stilled. She knew that voice. She looked up and squinted into the darkness.

"Sauder? What are you—"

"Sikes texted me and asked me to come escort you home. Your detail got their wires crossed and are waiting for you back there."

Alyah blinked, processing his words. "What time is it?"

"Just after eight," Sauder answered.

Alyah gave him a push and stepped back, out of his arms. "Was that you? I heard a loud crash. Did you drop something when you came in?"

"No," Sauder looked confused. "I just walked in here."

Alyah's pulse picked up. She lowered her voice. "The

lights won't turn on and that crash came from over there." She pointed toward Sikes' office.

Sauder's jaw clenched and he searched her eyes. Did he think she was lying? He grabbed her hand with one of his and drew his gun with the other.

"What are you doing?" Alyah gasped.

"We're going to clear the office, but I'm not leaving you alone."

Alyah gulped. She wanted to resist, but Sauder gripped her hand tighter, pushing her behind him with his arm and holding her there. Sauder was thorough. He went from room to room, but they found no one in the office.

Once outside, the rain pelted them as Sauder asked, "Do you have a key to the front doors? With the electricity down, I was able to walk right in."

"Oh!" Alyah exclaimed in surprise. She had her set of car keys, but not ones for the building. "Let me text Sikes."

"Come on. You can do that in my car," Sauder commanded.

Alyah hesitated. Something about his pushy tone irritated her. "I have my car here. I'll text from there."

"I can't let you drive home without protection—"

"It's fine," Alyah told him. She should feel grateful to him. "Just follow me to my house. The marshals are there, correct?"

Sauder nodded, his dark eyes considering. He stared long enough to make Alyah feel uncomfortable. Her hair now dripped into her face.

"I'll take off as soon as I make contact with Sikes. Thanks for your help. And the escort home." Alyah turned to her car. Once inside, she turned on the heat and the seat warmers, shivering in her wet clothes. But she wondered if it was the rain, the crash in the office, or her interaction with Sauder that made her shiver.

She explained all that happened to Sikes, who promised to send someone to check the office. Once she verified that Sikes had, in fact, sent Sauder to aide her in getting home, Alyah felt her shoulders relax.

See, she chided herself, *there was nothing to worry about.*

Long after she arrived home, waved goodbye to Sauder, and took a shower, her discomfort lingered. She put on a warm pair of sweatpants. What if the threat had been real? She wanted to yell at the agents for leaving her in the office alone. Some protectors they were if they couldn't even stay with their witness. Instead, she opened the bedroom door and walked down the hall to where they were watching TV. They looked up, instantly alert.

"Do you need something?" US Marshal Tim asked.

Yeah, for you to do your job, Alyah wanted to snap. Instead, she requested, "Yes, I need you to show me some self-defense moves. How to get out of a hold if someone grabs me."

"Sure." Both marshals stood up and pushed furniture out of the way to clear a spot in the living room. Once they had a big enough space, they took her through a series of basic moves designed to free her if someone got past her detail. *Or if they forgot about her again...*

She wasn't content to learn one time. She would practice until she was proficient. Because Alyah was tired of feeling afraid.

26

MAK

The first Airbnb had been a complete bust. It was a pretty neighborhood in Great Falls Park. To her surprise, Diane was working with her. As a courtesy, Mak agreed to wait until the family staying in the home had loaded up their vehicle, complete with two kids and a dog, to go out for the day after Diane had messaged the family to explain Mak's presence should they return while she was still there. There had been no signs of the senator or the BMW.

Mak went to the second location and repeated the process.

Now she was driving to the picturesque Harper's Ferry. As much as she enjoyed recreational driving—racing—it was the thrill of the chase she loved, not the monotony of the road. And though the Airbnbs were close together, that still meant an hour of driving between locations. Mak groaned aloud and cursed Sikes for not sending her to Aruba where at least she'd have a minute of sunlight and be able to see the ocean.

Mak turned up the music in her car and tried singing along for a bit before she finally snapped off the radio and decided to try sitting in silence. After intensive therapy at an alternate healing clinic, Mak had taken up meditation. Not that she was good at it. She still hated silence, and her thoughts binged around her head like an active game of beer pong. But she was challenging herself more and more to try.

Her phone rang and she answered with relief. It was John.

"Perfect timing!" Mak cried as she popped in an earbud.

"Why?" John's voice sounded cautious. "What am I getting myself into?"

"Nothing," Mak answered. "Just bored to tears driving to Nowhereville, USA."

"Sounds just awful," John deadpanned.

"It is." Mak put on her blinker and turned into a colonial neighborhood with mature trees and cobblestone exteriors. She was likely going to have to sit and watch this house for a while.

"Hey, I called because I have news," John announced.

"Great! I could use some good news," Mak said as she slowed her vehicle and let her eyes scan the area.

"Well, I didn't say it was *good* news, exactly," John hedged.

"Oh?" Mak responded but she felt distracted as she slowed her car a few houses from the Airbnb she was set to watch. This one was empty, and Diane had given Mak the code to go on in. Then she would drive another hour to her next destination.

"Yeah, I had an interview with—"

"A new client. Yeah, I remember," Mak cut in, her focus on the home.

"Not a client. Mak, are you with me or do I need to let you go for now?" John asked.

Something felt off about this location. It was nearing noon and everything was still, but it didn't feel peaceful, it felt ominous. Mak's gut churned. There was nothing to indicate a problem, and yet, Mak felt her senses heighten. She rolled down her window and smelled fragrant fresh-cut grass. The overcast day hid the sunlight that kept trying to break through. A woman in leggings and a t-shirt walked a large poodle. It looked too perfect. A calm before the storm.

"Mak, are you there?" John's voice broke into her musings.

"Sorry, John. You were saying you interviewed with—" Mak stopped talking abruptly. She looked in her rearview mirror and spotted a black BMW M5 cruising toward the house. Her pulse quickened and she slumped down in the seat and pulled her phone up to make it look like she was playing on it.

"Mak—"

"I have to go, John. Sorry." Mak hung up quickly and called Sikes.

"Mak, tell me you have something," Sikes commanded.

"2025 black BMW M5 just rolled past me at the location of the third Airbnb. The one at Harper's Ferry." Mak rattled off the address. "He just pulled in. I'm going in but I'll need backup. Just in case."

"On it." Sikes hung up.

Mak waited, still fiddling with her phone as a decoy to watch what the driver of the car planned to do. The car slowed and pulled into the driveway. She double checked the license plates. When Mak was sure it was Langsten's car and he was about to exit it, she opened her car door and pulled her gun, keeping it low—aimed at the ground—as she jogged closer.

Just as she closed in and was about to reach the driver's door handle, Langsten threw the car in reverse, peeling out in his attempt to get away quick. Mak could see the senator behind the wheel. As Langsten threw the car into drive and hit the gas, Mak aimed for a tire and fired. The shot missed the tire and pinged against the wheel, and the car was still accelerating away. Mak knew she couldn't keep firing in a residential neighborhood.

She ran back to her car, turned it on, and hit the gas, weary of anyone out walking a dog at this time of day. At a stop sign heading out of the neighborhood, Mak spotted the taillights of the BMW. He had a lead on her, but Mak was confident she could close the gap.

"Siri, call Sikes cell," Mak yelled. She listened as the cell rang once.

"Go," Sikes answered.

"In pursuit. Leaving the neighborhood. Where's my backup?" she shouted.

The BMW was moving fast, so Mak accelerated.

"Heading to the address you gave."

"Okay, I turned left out of the neighborhood, and I'm on some old country road." Mak followed the road as it twisted and turned, losing sight of Langsten's car when she went up a hill. She could see reduced speed signs. He had the advantage. It appeared he knew these roads and she did not. Still, Mak pushed the pedal as far as she could go. "I'm on Farm Road 87."

"On it. You might need to—"

"No!" Mak swore violently as she rounded a curve and saw a straightaway where a couple miles ahead of her, the BMW had sailed right over railroad tracks just before the arms had begun to lower.

Mak had two choices. She could speed up, crash through the arms, and play chicken with the incoming train. Or... Mak sped up to the train crossing line and then slammed on her brakes. Judging the speed and size of the train, Mak would never make it.

"No!" she howled again.

"You lost him?" Sikes guessed.

"Yes. Damn train cut me off." Mak sat in her car, watching the train go by and dropped her head to the steering wheel. "We were so close!"

"Standby." Sikes' line went quiet for a minute before he was back. "Okay, we've alerted the PD there, and they're sending out patrol cars to comb the area. When you're able, re-route to the police station and introduce yourself to the chief. If they find Langsten, I want him in our custody. You'll need to bring him in."

"Yes, boss." Mak hung up the phone, allowing herself to wallow in her feelings of self-loathing over her missed opportunity. Seeing no other cars behind her, she backed up and turned around on that desolate farm road. Then she drove toward the police station.

When she arrived, she texted Wilton, refusing to admit that instead of attempting to shoot his tire, she should have run to her car to immediately began pursuit, effectively closing the gap to follow the senator more closely. This one choice had led to the senator slipping away.

Mak had no one to blame but herself.

27

———————

BETH

Beth had to admit life in a hotel so far had been glamorous. Beth actually found herself relaxing some. She managed to catch up on her sleep. She lounged around watching her favorite shows. She'd even gone downstairs when the cleaning crew showed up. Of course she wanted a clean room. Who wouldn't?

Trying not to look over her shoulder the entire time but failing, Beth checked out the complimentary breakfast. Her stomach grumbled in response to the smells of bacon, eggs, and fresh-made waffles. She scanned the dining room. She found a few families there, but no danger. So, with her good hand, she poured batter into a waffle iron and made a big plate consisting of one of everything. By the time she flipped the iron, there was little room left on her plate. She speared the waffle, plopped it on her plate, and poured strawberry syrup on top. Then she found a seat in the corner by herself.

She went back for coffee, and as she turned back to her seat, she saw that the hotel had a hair salon. Her heart beat faster as she consumed her breakfast. That was going to be the answer to blending in here. Beth had never changed her hair. She loved the cut and natural black color, but she didn't have a choice. Her daughter's hair color was blond. Beth smiled absently when she remembered thinking Lacy's hair would probably turn darker to resemble Beth's, but it never did. Jacob had been blond.

Jacob had never gotten to meet Lacy, and it was Beth's biggest regret of her life. Bigger than all the bad things she did put together, though she regretted those too. The last day Beth ever saw Jacob had became a vivid memory. If she had only reacted differently, would he still be alive?

Eighteen Years Ago…

Jacob followed Beth down the emptying hallway after the final bell rang. Beth quickened her pace, trying to avoid him, but Jacob easily caught her. She stopped at her locker and grabbed her backpack. If any teacher ever stopped her to search her backpack… Beth didn't want to know what would happen. Though, maybe that would be better than the hell she was living in now.

"Come on," Jacob pushed. "Just let me see her."

"Oh my gosh, you have to let this go." Beth hoisted her backpack on her shoulders. She slammed her locker and turned to face him. She looked around but saw no one. "My parents legally adopted her, okay. Do you know what that means? It means she's their daughter now."

Beth was lying, but she was desperate.

"I have a right to see her," Jacob argued.

"No, you don't. You have no rights to her," Beth shot back. "Why do you even care? You're almost eighteen. Go! Live your life already."

"This isn't a life, Beth. Don't you get it? They own us. You all have a purpose—a reason to keep going. Someone you're keeping safe. I have nobody. I just thought…" Jacob's voice cracked. "I just thought if I could see her, I'd have a purpose too. A reason for me to keep going, to keep fighting through the hard days, you know?" Tears clouded Jacob's vision.

Beth softened and put a hand on Jacob's cheek. "I promised my parents I would never tell anyone. It's the only reason they allowed me to move back. I'm sorry. I can't." Beth turned away before she changed her mind. Who knew this would affect Jacob so much—the baby, their lifestyle, the daunting fear that someday, one or all of them would get caught. Not Beth.

That's why no one was more shocked than she was when Jacob put a gun to his head later that night. Though she wasn't there, in her dreams, Beth sometimes still heard a gunshot with the echo of his words.

"I just thought if I could see her, I'd have a purpose too. A reason to keep going, to keep fighting through the hard days…"

Beth gasped as she came back to the present and noticed she'd only eaten half of her food. She wasn't hungry anymore. Her cheeks were wet with tears she didn't even know she'd cried. What was wrong with her? It was like her past was seeping into her current life, and her emotions kept running down her face.

She'd make an appointment at the salon later. For now, the need to get back to her room, crawl into bed, and go back to sleep overwhelmed her. So that's exactly what she did.

28

WILTON

Stephen had slept hard the night before. He'd kept his balcony door open. The nice, temperate breeze and the sound of the crashing waves had serenaded him into a deep sleep. He woke to the sunrise over the ocean, feeling wide awake and more energized than he had in years.

He threw on a pair of shorts, a t-shirt, and tennis shoes (having limited selection based on what he'd been traveling with) and went downstairs in search of breakfast. When he found he was too early for the buffets to be open, he went out to the beach, sat in a lounge chair, and watched the waves break.

It didn't take long for the morning sun to climb and heat Stephen up. He walked down to the shore and dipped a toe in the cold saltwater. He inhaled a deep breath. When was the last time he'd been in an ocean, let alone in a large body of water? He waded out and stood up in it, letting the water lap up to his waist in awe over this opportunity to reconnect with nature. Stephen couldn't recall the moment when he had disconnected. Though he would guess it was when he'd become a US Marshal. Maybe even before that.

After wading around enough to cool down, Stephen found a cabana with beach towels, grabbed one, and headed back to a lounger. He dozed as he allowed his body to dry off. When he came to, there was a gentle murmur of voices around the beach and the sounds of activity as people bustled around. The guests had awakened.

"Can I get you a drink, sir?" a server asked Stephen.

Stephen considered, then shook his head. "Are the buffets open?"

"Yes, sir," the man confirmed.

"Great!" Stephen hopped up to find food, or at the very least, coffee. He was hungrier than he expected and piled food high on his plate. He was at the buffet for a second round when a man bumped into him, causing Stephen to drop everything. The loud sound of his breaking dishware rose above all the voices.

Annoyed, Stephen turned to clean the mess.

"I am so sorry!" a man with a slight Texas accent said. "Here, let me help with that—"

Before Stephen could answer, a server was at his side. "I will clean this, sir! You go eat more food."

"Are you sure? I can help you…"

The server tsked his tongue and waved Stephen away.

Stephen turned back to the man who was now hovering by his elbow.

"Sorry about that, son," the man drawled. "That was so clumsy of me!"

"No problem," Stephen said as he reached for another plate.

"Senator! Where are we sitting?" a man approached the Texan.

Stephen paused as his eyes flicked to the friend. The man who had knocked into him was a senator. Maybe there was a group of them here? Stephen straightened, plate in hand, only to find both men staring at him.

"What?" Stephen looked down to see if he had food on his shirt.

"I knocked this poor guy's breakfast to the floor, Melvin. I doubt he'd do us any favors…" the Texas senator was saying.

Had Stephen missed something?

Melvin answered his friend, but his response was directed toward Stephen as a way of explanation. "Grant here just informed us we are down by one today for a pickleball tournament."

Grant looked Stephen up and down.

Stephen felt an uncomfortable sweat break out on the back of his neck. *Is pickleball code for something else around here?* he thought.

"What do you think, man? Do you play pickleball?" Grant asked.

Stephen shook his head. "I never have. I don't even know the rules."

"Well, the rules are easy. If we old guys can do it, you can too. You just look like you have way more stamina than us," Grant stated.

"Stamina and muscles. You work out, son?" Melvin asked.

"Some," Stephen answered, feeling weary.

"We could use some new blood," Grant said with an open smile on his face as if he made some decision.

Stephen looked from Grant to Melvin as he considered. He knew enough about pickleball to ask, "What happened to your fourth person?"

"Sick," Melvin said.

"Self-induced flu," Grant corrected.

"Are you all senators?" Stephen chanced to ask.

Senator Grant laughed. "Why, you think that would make us more competitive?"

"Something like that," Stephen smiled back, despite himself. What were the chances that Langsten might be among this small group? He couldn't figure out a way to casually ask. Joining them might be the only way to know for sure.

"You play on the beach?" Stephen asked, looking toward the sand where other patrons lounged. He thought Leisa's description of *clothing optional* was accurate. No one on the beach was wearing any.

"No, we belong to a racquet club here in Aruba. They host pickleball tournaments. Ours starts in..." Grant paused and checked his waterproof Rolex Sea-Dweller watch. "Forty-five minutes."

"Is it clothing optional there as well?" Stephen tried to ask as delicately as possible.

Grant and Melvin laughed out loud. Grant slapped Stephen's back. "Shirt, shorts, and shoes are all mandatory there. It's a respectable establishment."

Stephen sagged with relief. "Okay, I'm in."

"Great!" Grant nodded. "Fill a plate and come eat breakfast with us. You can meet Terry. He's the third on our team. We'll tell you the rules. Also, you should know we do like to win."

Stephen followed them. Maybe this would be a way to get more information and figure out if they were connected to Langsten.

They were not. It turned out they didn't even know Langsten. Stephen didn't know why he thought every senator in office would know each other. In truth, they might know of each other, but sometimes only by reputation.

What had surprised him more than anything was how quickly he learned pickleball and how good at it he was. Stephen had always been athletic, but he had gravitated to baseball in high school. The hours flew by with them winning several matches. The older senators had actually given Stephen a nice challenge. It had felt good to work up a sweat and use his body for something other than running after criminals for a change.

When they had finished and were on their way back to the resort, Grant asked Stephen what he did for a living. Stephen debated about how honest he should be and could not come up with a reason not to tell them.

"I'm a US Marshal," Stephen admitted.

"Well, look at that!" Melvin cried out. "We've had an esteemed law man in our midst this whole time and didn't know it."

Grant chuckled, as did Terry, who had joined at the end of breakfast. "Good thing we're all honest senators, right guys?"

Everyone nodded.

Stephen smirked and knew better than to ask if their wives all knew they were here. It wasn't a judgment he needed to make. He was here for one reason alone—Senator Langsten. And Stephen was convinced that Langsten was not here.

Once back at the resort, Grant broke away from his friends, holding up a finger to indicate they wait, and took Stephen out of listening range.

"Listen, I'm in the market for a private detail," the senator began.

"Oh, US Marshals only provide protection for state witnesses in criminal trials—"

"Right," Grant chuckled. "I'm not looking for US Marshal protection, I'm looking to employ an individual or a team who follows me around and protects me. It's private sector. Like the president, but not as high stress."

"You live the kind of life that needs protection, sir?" Stephen asked.

"Every man in office needs protection. The arrogant ones won't consider it," Grant stated.

"I see. And you think I would be a good candidate for this job based on...?" Stephen let his question dangle.

"Your stamina and physique, not to mention you've been in law enforcement for how long?" Grant asked.

"A year as a US Marshal and seven years as a detective before that," Stephen answered, again surprised he was being so honest.

Grant nodded. "Well, I'm not hiring you on the spot, I'm letting you know that I'm in the market for someone with your skillset." He produced a business card from the pocket of his shorts.

"You carry business cards in your athletic wear?" Stephen smiled.

"Yes. In my field, you carry one in your underwear, if need be." Grant laughed.

"Good to know." Stephen took the card and hoped that wasn't where it had been prior to the man's pocket. Before he could commit to any future plans, his cell phone chimed with a notification. "Excuse me, I need to check this."

"Sure. It was good to meet you, son. Why don't you text me your number?" Grant suggested.

"Okay," Stephen considered it as he accepted the hand Senator Grant had extended. Stephen was surprised to realize he might entertain an offer from the senator. He fingered the business card as he went up to his room.

Mak: *Found the senator and lost him. Patrol cars are searching the area as we speak.*

Wilton: *Okay, I'll route to the plane. This place is weird.*

Mak: *Said no single guy ever...*

Wilton: *Trust me, oddest vacation I've ever been on.*

Mak: *Can't wait to hear about it. I'll drop you a pin. Safe travels.*

He scanned Mak's text, which confirmed what Stephen already knew. Senator Langsten wasn't in Aruba. He was in Harper's Ferry and Annapolis where Mak was. Or he had been. Looked like Langsten was on the run again.

Stephen took time to shower and was contemplating the lunch buffet when he got a text from the US Marshal pilot telling him when the jet would touch down to collect him and take him to meet up with Mak. He quickly shoveled some food in his mouth and took a few snacks to eat on the way to the airport.

Stephen grabbed his duffle bag and headed out. Only, his thoughts weren't fixed on Senator Langsten this time, they were on Senator Grant. What would it be like to work in the private sector as a bodyguard to an older senator? Stephen had to admit the thought of a job like that was oddly appealing.

29

MAK

The Harper's Ferry police force was utter pandemonium as Mak stepped into the station. They seemed extremely busy for such a small town. Phones were ringing all over the large, open room. There were several desks with computers, and officers were checking people in and taking testimonies.

Mak blinked a few times and wondered if perhaps this town was bigger than she had initially assumed. That, or they had one major catastrophe on their hands. Someone was crying loudly, and Mak could hear the loud honking sound of a nose blowing. She approached a receptionist whose desk was at the front of the room.

"Hi, I'm US Marshal Mak—"

"Cunningham!"

Mak's head jerked up in surprise at the sound of a man's voice bellowing her name. A large man, easily six-foot-five-inches tall with dark skin and a no-nonsense attitude stood in the doorway of an office with a nameplate that said, "Chief Justess." Mak smirked at the name and how closely it resembled the word *justice*, which was appropriate, given his line of work. She wondered if he'd had any other choice than to work this kind of job with a name like that.

"Excuse me," Mak said to the woman at the desk and obeyed the chief, who was beckoning her to come on back.

He started talking almost before Mak walked through the door. "Had a conversation with your boss while you were on your way over here. Go ahead and show me your badge—as a formality—but I got the rundown and know who you are." The man swiveled his computer screen to reveal Mak's background and the picture from when she was a rookie US Marshal. Oddly, she hadn't really changed a whole lot.

"Impressive," Mak mumbled. "I go by Mak."

The chief nodded. "I run a tight ship around here and don't have time to mess around. See that lobby?"

Mak nodded and opened her mouth to speak, but the chief cut her off.

"Bus accident. A load of middle school kids and parents were on a field trip when a car decided not to stop at a red light. In the middle of what has become the busiest day we've had in my station, I get a call that we have a fugitive on the run in my town, and you need backup."

Mak considered apologizing but didn't have time to speak.

"So, I sent out three of my finest. They split the town into sections and are combing every hiding place they can think of, as well as having conversations with our most notorious gossips, to spot your criminal's vehicle. If he's in this town, we'll find him." The chief crossed his arms over his chest and regarded Mak. "But if you don't mind me asking, when did Senator Langsten become a criminal?"

Finally sure that the man was done talking and it was her turn to speak, Mak answered. "We have evidence that he's involved in murder, and we put a warrant out for his arrest in conjunction with a sex and drug trafficking ring a day ago."

Chief Justess whistled lowly. "You think you know your representatives… Well, if the man is still in this town, we'll sure find him."

"Any chance I could jump in a car and ride along, Chief? I really can't afford to lose this guy." *Especially since I let him get away the first time,* Mak thought to herself. She didn't often make mistakes, but when she did, they were big ones. She gritted her teeth as she berated herself.

"Call me Justess. And yeah, I'll have an officer swing back by the office and pick you up." He nodded.

Mak thanked him and made her way back outside. She didn't have to wait long until a squad car showed up. Before she could reach for the passenger side door, it swung open.

"US Marshal Cunningham?" A female police officer with a soft twang in her voice smiled from the driver's seat.

Mak showed the officer her badge. "It's Mak."

"Hop in. Things are gettin' exciting around here! I'm Marina." The woman tapped the name etched on her brown and black uniform.

Mak jumped in quickly and shut the door. "First name or last name?"

"Last, of course." Officer Marina threw the car in drive.

Mak inhaled quickly and bit back the urge to explain she wasn't the best passenger. If there were two people in a car, Mak preferred to be the one driving. But she couldn't exactly take over a policewoman's squad car.

"All units be advised. Black BMW has been spotted on State Street in the fifteen hundred district at the abandoned warehouse on State and Elm. Proceed with caution."

"Woo!" Marina let out a loud whoop and made a U-turn. Mak found herself grinning in response. Exciting day indeed.

"You gonna turn on your sirens?" Mak asked, feeling caught up in the excitement of it all. Never mind the fact that this was actually *her* mission.

Marina looked horrified. "And what, give him a chance to run? No way!"

Mak laughed and admitted, "We don't have sirens on the Range Rovers we drive. I've always wanted to play with one."

"Well, today is not that day, my friend." Marina pushed the gas pedal down and Mak swore the car jumped forward. Mak had never been a police officer. That was more Stephen's past life. But if she had, she decided this station would be her perfect fit.

In less than ten minutes, Marina whipped the car into the parking lot of a big, red brick building behind a black BMW, effectively blocking the BMW from leaving. Before they could get out of the car, two more squad cars showed up and parked on either side of the senator's car.

"See?" Marina winked. "No lights."

Both Mak and Marina got out of the car and drew their weapons.

Two officers—both stocky men—got out of their respective vehicles and pressed in like they were all in a huddle.

"There are three entrances into the building," Marina said in a hushed voice. "Ralph, you take the south entrance. Billett, you take the west side. Mak and I will go in this door. Once you're in position, text me. Wait for my *Go* text back. We'll burst in at the same time."

The men nodded and trotted off.

"You guys use text instead of radios?" Mak whispered, feeling a little disappointed.

Marina gave her a *duh* look. "Radios are too loud. We use modern technology to our advantage."

A minute later one text popped up. Then another. Mak watched Officer Marina's screen light up.

Ralph: *In position*

Billet: *Ready when you are*

Marina: *Go!*

Marina stowed her phone in her back pocket, then put her hand on the knob and threw open the door.

A man stood in a corner by himself. The sheer expanse of the large, empty warehouse made him look small. Mak thought he looked suspicious standing there by himself.

"Freeze!" Mak yelled. "Put your hands in the air!"

Mak could see, even as the man moved slowly, that his body style and build wasn't quite right. But it wasn't until he had fully turned, hands held high in the air, that Mak understood why.

"That's not the senator," Mak mumbled.

"No, duh!" Marina shot back, with a light lift to her voice. Loudly, she called out. "What are you doing here? This is private property and you're trespassing."

The man took a step forward.

"Stay right where you are. We'll come to you," Marina warned him.

Convinced that this man wasn't who they were looking for, Mak scanned the rest of the room. There were no upper levels and not much to see except dust and cobwebs dangling from the corners—save one lone door that broke up the monotony of the red brick wall. Mak ran toward it and quickly opened the door, pointing her gun inside and sweeping the small room.

It was a bathroom, and it was not the cleanest. Mak breathed through her mouth as she quickly scanned the interior.

"Clear," she called out.

Mak wasn't sure what she expected from the man whose back was literally against the wall, but casual was not it. His hands were in his pockets and there was a relaxed look on his plain face. His big nose made his face more interesting, but everything else about him seemed average, down to his long, mousy brown hair.

"Hands up where we can see them," Mak commanded quickly.

Guns drawn, the four of them pressed forward. All attention focused on this man who was still standing in the corner, raising his hands to the sky, his eyes wide and bulging.

"Woah!" he uttered. "Are you serious? Is this for real?"

"We're looking for a man named Joseph Langsten," Marina's voice boomed with authority.

"Don't know 'im." Now, there was a shake in the man's voice.

"He's the owner of that BMW outside," Mak clarified.

"Did you see the man who drives the BMW?" Officer Billett asked, his voice laced with curiosity.

"Oh! That guy?" The man reached down toward his pockets.

All officers exclaimed loudly, but Officer Ralph yelled loudest, "Keep your hands where we can see them!"

The man quickly lifted his hands back up.

"I was just going to show you the keys. It's my BMW now." Despite his situation, the man smiled excitedly.

"The owner of the BMW gave you his car keys?" Mak clarified. "So, you *did* see Joseph Langsten?"

"Yeah," the man bobbed his head. "He gave me the car and five hundred dollars to stand here for an hour."

"What the...?" Billett left the question dangling.

"And why didn't you take the car, the money, and run?" Marina asked.

"He promised me another five hundred if I texted him when I left," the man explained.

"How was he planning on giving you money?" Mak asked.

"Venmo. I gave him my Venmo handle."

"What's your name?" Mak asked.

"Brandt. Brandt Davis."

"Alright, Brandt. Trust me when I say you'll never see that money." Mak assured him.

Brandt shrugged. "It was worth a shot."

"Did you see which way the man went?" Marina asked.

"No, he took my car keys and ran." Brandt said.

"So, you traded cars?" Mak stated. "What were you driving?"

"2022 Tacoma. It's blue," he told her. "Navy blue."

"Okay, you're coming with us." Billett grabbed his arm and began reciting his Miranda rights.

"Hey, wait! I didn't do anything wrong!" Brandt protested.

"You were aiding and abetting a fugitive. You need to come with us. We're taking the BMW from you, and you need to file a stolen vehicle complaint," Marina said as they all walked the man out of the warehouse.

Mak stepped forward. "I'm going to remove the keys, Brandt." Mak slowly reached toward him. "Do you have anything else in your pocket I need to know about?"

"Yeah, I have a pocketknife," Brandt admitted.

Once Mak had the keys to the BMW in hand, she opened the car and looked around. It was spotless, and she guessed it wouldn't give them any clues. Not that she should be surprised. A criminal of the senator's caliber knew how to wipe down a car he was leaving behind.

"Here," Marina was at Mak's side with a pair of gloves. "I'll meet you back at the station."

"Thanks," Mak said as she put the gloves on and sat behind the wheel of the car owned by the man she planned to take down. She shut the car door and tried to think like the senator, but didn't think she would ever completely surmise what the mind of a deviant man might conjure up.

Her hand reached toward the ignition, when she stopped abruptly. She had a sudden flash back to a race where Anthony Gerritt had rigged Mak's car to catch fire.

Mak snatched her hand back and got out of the vehicle. She flagged Officer Marina down just before her car left the parking lot.

"I'd feel a lot more comfortable having your ATF team come check out this car before we even try to start it. Way I figure, a guy who leaves behind a car, can't be trusted to not have rigged it first," Mak said as she got back in the passenger seat of Marina's car.

"Right," Marina said as she shook her head and pulled out of the parking lot. She grinned at Mak. "Way to think like a criminal."

Mak shrugged. "I just know the way these guys operate, and I'd rather be safe."

"Why do I get the feeling you know this from personal experience?" Marina asked as she scrutinized Mak's face.

"Because I do. These guys tried to blow me up—twice. Nearly succeeded both times," Mak explained.

Marina nodded. "I'll send in a K-9 with the order to pick up the car."

"Good call," Mak agreed.

Dodged a bullet there, she thought, *or an explosion.*

30

ALYAH

The meeting took place that afternoon at the police station on account of the evidence board Chief Sauder's team had put together and to train the rookies just joining the force. It was a two birds, one stone situation. They were bringing Alyah in on what evidence they had so she could best prosecute the criminals when they wrapped up the case.

When Alyah had convinced Sikes that she was not some double agent, it had been a huge relief. Now, she sat taking notes as Chief Sauder explained the criminal involvement and evidence to the sex trafficking ring they theorized had been running for at least twenty years. Alyah's heart had sunk at that knowledge.

"Senator Joseph Langsten." Sauder pointed to a picture of Langsten still at the top of the board, positioning him as the ringleader. The picture had been taken a year ago, his face aged, his hair silvery and shorter than he wore it when he was younger. He was still handsome and more distinguished. He almost looked like a cult leader. Beside the professional photo was the picture of Langsten from eighteen years ago, holding a gun to Greg Wilton's head with a timestamp, minutes before he pulled the trigger. The background of the picture was fuzzy.

"Langsten was the mayor when he murdered Greg Wilton. Due to the wrongful conviction of David Stinnert, Langsten got away with murder this entire time. This photographic evidence just surfaced a little over a month ago." Sauder took a swig from a water bottle and swept his hand toward Alyah. "Thanks to Ms. Smith, we were able to not only clearly identify the man in this photo but acquire additional evidence that proves his involvement with a drug and sex trafficking ring this entire time. We now believe that this ring originated with Senator Langsten."

Sauder used a laser pointer to highlight the pictures underneath Langsten's. "Anthony Gerritt, Micky Upton, and Boyd Allister are Langsten's known leaders in the Midwest region—"

Alyah shuddered and raised her hand. "Does this mean there are more leaders in other regions?"

Sauder nodded. Murmuring ran through the room, and he held up his hand. "We are tasked with focusing on the Midwest. Know that this case has become big enough for the FBI to join forces with PD in other counties and is running down the leaders in rural cities across the US."

Alyah's eyes widened, but she agreed with Sauder's point. They needed to focus on their task. Her goal was getting all the information she needed to put these guys behind bars and keep them there.

"We have three witnesses who can ID Gerritt, Upton, and Allister as their captors. They are guilty of dressing the women In golden dresses, putting them in a golden cage, taking pictures, and posting them for sale on the black market," Sauder stated.

There were several gasps and more murmuring around the room.

"Where are those witnesses now?" Alyah asked.

"Witness protection," Sikes answered.

Sauder went on. "That brings us to this man."

Alyah studied the photo where the laser pointer rested on the second row of photos. It pointed to a man who wore a Sherriff's uniform, complete with a badge, grinning at the camera. There was a watermark under the picture with the word *deceased* woven through.

"Sherriff Obediah Pottstaff was arrested for the murder of Anthony Gerritt, who had agreed to inform on the ring. Thanks to Gerritt, we saved three women in transit, but he was killed before he could give us any more information."

"Do we have evidence that Pottstaff killed Gerritt?" Alyah asked.

Sauder nodded. "We do. The bullets matched a gun we found in Pottstaff's home—an unregistered piece. Pottstaff was also charged with the murder of Trevan Collins, after the knife used to kill Collins was found buried on Pottstaff's property. Which leads us to the mules."

"Wait, before we move on, Pottstaff is dead now, correct?" Alyah checked.

Sauder paused a beat. It was long enough that Alyah thought about repeating her question. "Yes," he finally said. "We believe he was given cyanide after he was incarcerated and died in jail before we could transport him to prison to wait for his sentence."

The hands of three rookies shot up.

"The murder of Obediah Pottstaff is still under investigation, and I can answer questions about that after this meeting." Saunder looked at each of his rookie officers.

Alyah opened and shut her mouth. *I wonder why he's not going deeper into that,* she thought.

"We have a second witness who gave us an interesting testimony about these five people." Sauder pinpointed the same picture from above, the one of Langsten pointing his gun at Greg Wilton. The image was cleaned up, and there were three teenagers in the background looking frightened.

"Who are they?" Alyah asked, pen poised to write their names. She knew of Beth Donovan. In fact, she'd heard the scuttle around the office that Stephen had started seeing Beth after Alyah went back to Washington, DC. Alyah didn't fault him for that. She had clearly broken things off. She'd given him no hope of a relationship in the future. What interested her more was Beth's connection to this case.

"Trevan Collins, David Stinnert, and Beth Donovan." Sauder highlighted each one as he named them. "Beth Donovan, the second witness, is the only one of a group of five teenagers who is still alive today to tell the story of how they were used as drug mules back then by Pottstaff and Upton."

"Who were the other two?" Alyah wondered.

"Greg Wilton, who you know about, and a boy named Jacob Greenly, who died by suicide." Sauder was consulting his notes.

"I see... and where is Beth Donovan now?" Alyah asked. A big part of her job was to work with witnesses and prep them to testify.

"We don't know. She refused protection and took off with plans to protect herself. Her whereabouts are unknown," Sikes answered.

Alyah wanted to ask why Beth was allowed to take off. Was she cleared from any involvement in this ring? Instead, Alyah asked, "What did her testimony say?"

"She said Pottstaff took advantage of the accidental death of their friend, accusing them of murder, and coerced them into running drugs and money for him throughout high school."

Alyah whistled. "We'll need to get her on the stand."

Sauder nodded. "I have a feeling there's a lot we don't

know about Beth's story. I'd filet an officer who let someone so valuable go before the case was over."

Alyah watched Sauder's eyes turn darker with anger. She understood what he was implying.

Stephen Wilton had let Beth Donovan leave. Though she could understand Sauder's frustration, one look at his face told her Sauder was beyond that. He was furious. But she didn't know if he was furious with Beth's release or with Stephen's decision to let it happen.

As she looked at Sauder's face, Alyah felt the shudder run the length of her spine. Sauder's evident anger was a sight to behold.

31

─────

ALYAH

Alyah waited until they were back at the US Marshal office and followed Sikes to his office. She sat across from him and looked over her notes. One job of the District Attorney was to advocate for witnesses and prep them to share their testimony. But she couldn't help but feel there was more to the story than what they had told her.

"Tell me about Beth and Lacy Donovan." Alyah held a pen in her hand.

"You'll have to be more specific," Sikes stated.

"I find it interesting that two of our witnesses are related to each other, but play different roles in this case," Alyah pointed out.

Sikes' eyebrows rose. "Well, it was Beth Donovan who called Stephen Wilton to tell him her sister, Lacy, had gone missing. We were following Anthony Gerritt at the time. We had no idea she was connected to him, let alone that Lacy was one of his victims."

"So, why did Beth call Stephen?" Alyah asked.

"They went to high school together. Dated his brother," Sikes answered.

"Beth dated Greg Wilton, who was killed by Senator Langsten, not David Stinnert, and she's the one who pulled Stephen in to work this whole case. Why would she do that?" Pen forgotten, Alyah mused aloud, trying to think like the potential witness.

"You'll have to ask her. If we ever find her again." Sikes sighed.

"Yeah." Alyah was trying to understand why Stephen would let a witness go to fend for herself when he was so adamant that Alyah have protection. Then again, maybe that was why he was taking such a strong stance. Maybe he regretted his actions.

"Have you thought about our conversation yesterday— about running for Attorney General?" Sikes changed the topic and Alyah let him for now.

Had she thought about it? Yes, of course she had. But that brought up the memory of when she ran for District Attorney. She'd graduated from KU School of Law and was working for a criminal law office when she got a tip that Kansas City was looking for a District Attorney. She had been interested. But the tip had come from someone she'd tried to forget—to leave behind. He was the epitome of what Alyah wanted to fight against. He was a criminal. He was also the man who'd financed the college bills her scholarships didn't cover, helping her get through college.

Scott Milternett was her mother's boyfriend for several years when Alyah was growing up. He was the only one who she and Carley connected with. Milternett was more like a father-figure than any other boyfriend in the long revolving door of significant others her mother had. He genuinely seemed to care about them as was evident from the money he sent, not only for birthdays, but randomly for ten years after he and her mother broke up. Carley had squandered her money, but Alyah had saved hers for college.

In the beginning, Alyah hadn't thought accepting money from him was a problem. Then, as she got older, she discovered who he was. Milternett was an organized crime boss in charge of the Kansas City area. He belonged to a crime syndicate.

That was when Alyah had put her foot down. No more money and no more gifts. Her moral code was too important. It was why she'd started on a path to becoming a lawyer. Not to mention, she was about to graduate as a valedictorian, and she had been awarded a full ride to the KU School of Law. Uncle Scott, as she and Carley had called him back then, hadn't taken *no* for an answer.

For years, Milternett continued to send her money and Alyah would write *Return to Sender* on the envelope and send it back without opening it. She could not be associated with a well-known criminal, no matter the good relationship they'd always had.

Alyah vividly remembered the conversation she'd had when Milternett called her to tell her about the job opening for District Attorney in Kansas City.

"Thank you so much for this information, Scott. Whether I decide to run for District Attorney or not, I need to stand on my own. It's time we go our separate ways." It had taken all her courage. She had to take a stand because she wanted to run for the position, but she could not be backed by him or his people. She shuddered at the message that would send.

"Don't shut me out, Alyah," Milternett had insisted. "I can get you in office. I have connections."

She knew all about his connections and knew if she gave in to him, even a tiny bit, she would end up working for him and his criminal organization instead of the state.

"No," she'd said boldly and directly. "I will run on integrity. There can be no hint of grey morality. It's my strong conviction to put criminals away," Alyah had asserted.

Milternett had fought her every step of her campaign. To the point that Alyah had to hire a campaign manager and small team to run down every contribution toward her efforts to be sure they knew exactly who supported her. She would be doing no unethical favors for anyone once she got in office. She'd stuck to that. It was how she developed her direct, no-nonsense approach that had served her so well in her career.

She hadn't heard from Milternett in years, and she wondered how he would react to seeing *Alyah Smith for Attorney General* signs and billboards around town.

"Have I thought about running for Attorney General?" Alyah repeated Sikes' question. *Yes, too much.* "I have."

"Good," Sikes responded. "We could use someone like you at the top."

Alyah thanked him and excused herself. She needed to go back through the information she'd extracted from Senator Langsten's office so she had everything together and was ready to start the prosecution proceedings the minute Stephen and Mak apprehended him.

But try as she might, Alyah's mind kept returning to Milternett. The question nagged at her. Was she where she was today because of her connection to the criminal? No one had uncovered that bit of information when she ran for office before. Was it only a matter of time before they did if she ran this time?

32

WILTON

Dark shadows of the evening were starting to form when Stephen got off the jet. He checked his watch. It was around seven-thirty. He grabbed an Uber. He knew Mak had a Range Rover, and they would work together from there on. The police department was only fifteen minutes down the road. Mak said this was a small town, and from what Stephen could see she was right. So, the big city senator had been hiding in a small town.

As Stephen pulled into the station, the sky darkened, and droplets of rain began to fall. He hunched his shoulders, knowing his US Marshal t-shirt wouldn't protect him from a downpour. His blond, wavy hair was already reacting to the damp sky. Stephen walked into the police station. His blue eyes immediately fell on the back of Mak's head. Her auburn hair was pulled back into her signature messy ponytail. Dressed similar to Stephen, in jeans and a US Marshal t-shirt, she looked comfortable. She was sitting on a desk surrounded by three other officers, drinking coffee with them. He shook his head. Her ability to make friends in stressful situations was uncanny.

Mak turned her head to see Stephen walking toward them and stood up to greet him. She quickly introduced Stephen to the three other officers and caught him up to speed. At the realization that they had been so close and had even found the senator's car but then lost him, Stephen felt his blood pressure skyrocket.

"It might be good news, Wilton," Mak was saying. "We've got him on the run, and he can't be too far away."

"You're kidding, right?" Stephen breathed his annoyance. "He could be anywhere by now. In fact, what are you doing sitting around?"

"I was waiting for you." Mak stood and took a few steps away from the curious officers. She lowered her voice. "We just got back to the office. We interviewed Brandt, the man we found at the warehouse. They ran background checks and are looking into his story before they confirm that he's not connected to this. They just got the BMW back here and ATF is combing through the vehicle. I looked inside, and the senator didn't leave anything that would indicate where he was going next. Then you showed up."

Stephen nodded. He should have known Mak would never sit around on a case. "Sorry," he said with genuine apology. "I just really want to get this guy, and you were so close. Tell me again how he got away in the first place?"

"Tell you what, why don't we get on the road. You're right, we don't have time to sit around," Mak agreed. "I'll let them know we're leaving and make sure they have my number in case Langsten shows up somewhere in town. They know they need to detain him, if so."

Stephen watched as Mak made her way back to the group, handed them her card, and shook hands with all of them. What was wrong with him? Why had he come in with such an attitude? He wondered if it had anything to do with the quick turnaround trip out of the country. He'd relaxed and caught up on sleep, so he didn't think that was a valid excuse. He knew Mak was a hard worker. He'd even wager that she wanted to find Langsten as much as he did.

"Okay," Mak hit the back of his arm and kept walking. "We're good to go."

They walked to the Range Rover and Mak jumped into the driver's seat. Stephen sighed. Some things would never change. The only time Stephen had driven was when she was healing from a back injury. It was a nice change, but not when Mak was the passenger. She did not sit well in that seat. He got in the passenger side and buckled his seatbelt.

"So, how did Langsten get away? Didn't you say he showed up at one of the houses? If you saw him drive up, why didn't you just apprehend him?" Stephen wondered.

Mak bit her lip, looking sheepish.

Stephen could tell there was something Mak didn't want to say.

Mak's phone rang. The screen lit up the words, *Hubby John*. "I can get that later."

"Okay, so tell me," Stephen pressed.

"I saw him approach in my rearview. I stayed casual, played on my phone, and pretended not to be watching him. He pulled into the driveway. When it looked like he would get out, I pulled my gun and got out first. I jogged toward him, intending to pull him out of the car. He must have seen me. He threw the car in reverse and sped off. By the time I got back to my car, he had a lead on me."

"You have got to be kidding me!" Frustration lit in Stephen. "You were that close to him, and you let him get away?"

"Are you seriously going to get mad at me right now?" Mak glanced at Stephen.

"It's been a long twenty-four hours, Mak. Maybe we could

just have a little quiet time," Stephen commanded in a low voice.

Mak closed her mouth and averted her eyes, keeping them on traffic. She turned the radio on and increased the volume a little.

Stephen knew Mak hated silence, but Stephen hated not getting the fugitive even more. He didn't trust himself to speak. The words that were coming out of his mouth weren't kind or fair. He'd let a criminal get away. One he'd yet to find. And that criminal—Demitri Abbott—still haunted his dreams and made him fear for his little girl's life.

Sometimes when a criminal escaped, they were never located again. Mak might have blown their only chance to capture Langsten. They needed to find him before he disappeared forever. Someone was going to die by the end of this, and Stephen didn't plan on that being him.

The phone rang and interrupted his silence. Mak accepted the call on her car console. It was Sikes. "Hey, Mak. Wilton with you?" he asked by way of greeting.

"I'm here," Stephen spoke up.

"Good, glad I have you both." Sikes cleared his throat. "Wilton, we looked into those pictures you sent over—the ones from Langsten's website. At the time those pictures were taken, the twins were about fifteen years old. They are now twenty-five. It was the home they grew up in. It now belongs to an Earl and Shanna Reeves."

"Shoot. Then that's a dead end," Stephen grumbled.

"What's your next step?" Sikes went on.

"We're moving on, sir. To the next Airbnb. The officers will notify us if they have any activity on their end—if they find the senator or the car. In the meantime, we're going to keep moving," Mak answered. "What else is going on there?"

"Well, the coroner's report came back on Pottstaff. I'm

here with Chief Sauder. You're not going to believe what we found," Sikes' voice held excitement.

"Hey, Sauder here. Pottstaff was poisoned," a deep male voice came over the phone.

Stephen grimaced at the sound of Sauder's voice. There was something about that man that grated on Stephen's nerves. He told himself it went deeper than his interest in Alyah.

"Poisoned!" Mak exclaimed.

"Yep, we think someone slipped him a cyanide pill," Sauder confirmed.

"I knew it!" Mak said.

"Remind me who had access to Pottstaff while he was in your custody?" Stephen didn't try to soften his words, though that day had been hazy for him.

There was a brief pause. *Good*, Stephen hoped he'd offended Sauder.

"As I mentioned the other day, the only person who met with Pottstaff was his attorney. We have cameras throughout the facility. The exception was the room where Pottstaff and his attorney had client confidentiality, and all cameras were turned off. We have no evidence of the attorney slipping a pill to Pottstaff," Sauder summed up.

"We're gonna need the name of that attorney. An angel of death attorney who might be carrying information to and from Langsten," Sikes mused.

"Our office is already on it. The attorney is Kent Clarkway," Sauder stated. "I'd love to see him go down. He's one shady criminal attorney. I've suspected him of getting a little too close to his clients and playing for the other side. We've launched an investigation into his office."

"Without solid evidence, it's doubtful he'll confess," Stephen stated. "It's probably a dead end."

"Unless we find something in his office that proves he

had the pills... We have to have proof before we make an arrest," Sauder explained like they had no experience with the law.

Stephen rolled his eyes. He didn't care for Sauder's know-it-all attitude. "Just keep us posted, please." He hung up the phone and looked at Mak, daring her to challenge him.

In truth, Stephen felt like he could go for a good fight. He smirked, thinking about how he'd love to see Sauder on the receiving end of his fist. Better yet, they needed to find Langsten. Stephen knew that's who he really wanted to fight.

33

———————

MAK

By the time they got to the hotel, it was eight. Mak barely made it through the door before she collapsed on the bed. She'd intended to relax a little, but before she could grab the remote control, she had fallen asleep.

She woke to her cell phone ringing. Disoriented, Mak sat up and looked around. The events of the day came rushing back to her and she looked around for her phone. She spotted it lit up on the floor. She must have dropped it when she fell onto the bed.

She answered on the last ring. "Hello?"

The irritation in John's voice surprised her. "You never called me back, Makayla."

"I'm sorry. I just got back. I fell asleep." Mak shook her head, trying to clear the sleep webs in her brain. Was she making sense?

John let out a loud, audible sigh of frustration. Mak knew it well. But she couldn't think of what she'd done to cause it. *This time...*

"Okay," Mak dragged out the word as she slowly flipped on a light to try to wake her foggy mind. She wasn't completely sure she was in the right state of mind for a serious conversation, but she would try. "It sounds like you're unhappy with me, so let's have it. What's the deal?"

"Makayla, I have been trying to talk to you since you left. I think I'm an understanding and supportive husband—"

"Most definitely!" Mak frowned, wondering where this wind-up was heading.

"Will you please just let me finish?" John asked sharply.

"Yes. Sorry." But Mak didn't know what to be sorry for.

"I understand when you're on the road. I even get it when you have to cut me off because I assume you are on the chase of a bad guy and something urgent has come up. But at the end of the night when you find yourself in a hotel room or a WITSEC room, would it be too much to ask that you call me back so we can talk?" John finally stopped.

"Of course not!" Mak agreed. "I'm sure you don't want excuses, but like I said, I crashed out when I got to my room. I wasn't trying to avoid you."

"I know," he agreed. The fight seemed to leave John's voice. "I'm sure you weren't. I know you have a hard job and it's physically taxing. But those are the times we have to work harder to communicate and connect."

"Agree!" Mak said. "Please, tell me your news."

"I had a phone interview. It's a really big job. They set up another interview, and it looks promising," John finished.

"Babe, that's great! We should have a party when I get home." Mak smiled. She loved parties.

John chuckled. "Only you, Makayla."

"Yep, I'm one of a kind," Mak quipped. "Is Harper in bed?"

"Yes, she apparently crashed out tonight, too. She—"

Mak's phone beeped on her end and lit up with an incoming call. It was Sikes. "John?" Mak interrupted her husband.

"Let me guess, you have to go?" John's voice slid back to the tense tone.

"You know I wouldn't if I didn't have to, babe," Mak said in a soothing tone. "Listen, this case has gotten really intense, and I'm going to try harder. I am. I just need to go now."

"I love you," John said, his voice resigned, giving Mak the impression this conversation wasn't quite over.

"Love you too." Mak made a kissing noise and hung up. She had no choice but to focus on what was in front of her. Lack of focus could compromise them. It could get them killed. She clicked over to Sikes. "What's up?"

"You and Wilton awake?" Sikes answered without preamble.

"I am now," Mak's mind was still on her conversation with John. "Not sure about Wilton."

"That navy-blue Tacoma with the license plate that matches the new BOLO for Langsten was spotted. I'm sending you a pin."

Mak looked at her phone and did a quick GPS search. They were half an hour away. Her heart raced, and the sudden adrenaline woke her up the rest of the way.

"Where is that? A diner?" Mak tried zooming in. If Langsten was at a hotel, they'd have a better chance of catching him. But if he was just getting a quick bite to eat, they needed to hurry.

Mak certainly hoped a couple hours of sleep would be enough for whatever they'd find when they got there.

34

WILTON

Stephen paced around his hotel room. He felt jet-lagged, which was a lot like being hungover. He was exhausted but couldn't sleep. His head was pulsing. The light smell of cigarette smoke told him that though he'd asked for a non-smoking room, it only meant someone wasn't smoking in this room right now.

Nothing felt right with him. He'd changed into a t-shirt and basketball shorts and tried to do a short workout of burpees, pushups, and squats to work through this tired energy, but that had only drained him further. That's when his head had started to ache.

Stephen fiddled with his phone. He called his daughter.

"Hi, daddy!" Anna's voice rang out and he was struck by how her voice seemed to mature with every phone call. His biggest fear was of her growing up without him realizing it had happened.

"Hi, Anna," he greeted. "How's my girl?"

"Good!" she answered.

"What are you up to?" Stephen smiled and felt a little better just hearing her voice.

"Mommy says I can't talk long because I have to go to bed soon," Anna informed him.

Stephen's eyes flicked to the clock in the room, surprised to find it was later than he thought. With the time difference, it would be just after eight back home.

"Okay," Stephen agreed. "How's it going, kiddo?"

After a quick conversation, Paige called Anna to bed. Bedtime was sacred because it had helped with the nightmares Anna used to have. Stephen respectfully honored Paige's rules.

As tired as he was, he could not seem to relax. He opened the last picture in his photo gallery, remembering that he'd snapped the photo from the senator's home.

He enlarged his screen. Staring at a younger version of Joseph Langsten with a smug-looking Mickey Upton by his side pumped new rage through his veins. They'd gotten away with so much for so long.

Diane Langsten had identified the man on the end as Langsten's deceased brother, Robert. But what about the man sandwiched in the middle? Maybe Alyah would know. He checked the time again. *This was important,* Stephen told himself. Who knew when he would have time to talk to her again?

Before he could talk himself out of it, he called her.

Alyah picked up on the first ring. "Stephen?" She sounded breathless.

"Alyah, hi. I have a work-related question for you. Is now an okay time?" Stephen asked.

"Oh," Alyah's voice sounded sad. Was that disappointment? "Um... sure."

"Okay, I'm going to send you a picture I took on my phone of an old photograph I found in Langsten's home. You'll see Langsten and Upton in it. Diane Langsten identified the man on the end as Langsten's deceased brother. I would like to figure out who the other guy in it is." Stephen put the phone on speaker and sent the picture to Alyah.

"Stephen, what makes you think I'll know who the man is?" Alyah asked. She went quiet for a half second. Stephen assumed she was looking at what he'd sent.

"I'm wondering if he's a politician. Someone you came in contact with while you were in Washington, DC?" Stephen let his voice trail.

"Hmm, he doesn't look familiar," Alyah said.

"Damn it!" Stephen blurted.

There was a small pause on Alyah's end before she spoke. "You're going to get this guy, Stephen."

"What if I don't?" Stephen asked, surprising himself by voicing his fear. "I've let someone slip away before. He's still out there somewhere."

"Demitri Abbott," Alyah said quietly. "That one's personal to you."

"And to you," Stephen stated, remembering her sister, Carley. "Every day that he's free is another day my daughter might be in danger. Not to mention—"

"What?" she asked, prodding gently.

"I'm letting you down. I need to bring Carley's killer to justice." Stephen put his hand on the back of his neck, feeling the heat rise to the surface of his skin.

"You will. It's just a matter of time. Both of these cases are highly personal. The stakes are higher for you. But I've watched you do this before. You're a pro," Alyah encouraged. "You'll get them."

Stephen shook his head. "I don't know about that."

Before Alyah could answer, he heard a male voice in the background asking her if she wanted him to come in.

Stephen's gut turned with instant jealousy as he wondered who was talking to her. Had she been out with someone? Had the man been there the whole time she'd been on the phone with Stephen? He felt relieved when she told the man *no thank you.*

Stephen inwardly sighed in relief.

"Night, Chief. Thanks for dinner," Alyah's voice sounded soft, like she had dropped the phone from her mouth. To Stephen she said, "Let me call you back."

Stephen didn't have time to respond before she hung up. True to her word, ten minutes later, Stephen's phone rang.

"Okay, I'm back," Alyah greeted.

"Who was that?" The question popped out before Stephen could stop it.

"Sauder. Chief Sauder from KCPD. You met him the other day..." Alyah's voice held an edge.

"I wasn't aware that Chief Sauder was part of your security detail," Stephen gritted out.

"He's not, Stephen. He took me to dinner. He and I go way back. We were just catching up," Alyah stated.

"What do you mean by *you go way back?*" Stephen persisted.

"He and I dated for a while. It was when I started working as a DA for KC," Alyah answered.

"I see. Is he trying to date you again?" he asked. He knew he had no right to ask that.

"You know what, Stephen? You don't get to do this," Alyah bit out.

"Do what?" Stephen knew exactly what she was going to say, but he wanted to hear her say it.

"You don't get to be cold to me one day, then jealous if I go to dinner with another man. You and I are not together. But because it seems important to you, I'll answer the question you really want to know. It wasn't a date. I'm on day three of having a marshal guard everywhere I go, and because I was with the Chief, I got to go out to dinner like a normal person. Everyone assumed he could keep me safe. Happy?"

Alyah's voice held venom. It reminded him of when they first met. Her temper was impressive.

"Not remotely," Stephen argued. "I'll likely have a talk with Sikes tomorrow. You shouldn't be out in public right now. Your life is in danger. You need to lay low. That was a stupid decision on Sauder's part."

"Fine, Stephen. You do that. Stick your nose in my life just enough to try to control it from a distance and see where that gets you. Just remember that the DA office is still over yours," Alyah snarked.

Stephen was silent as he processed her words, trying to puzzle them out. "Is that some sort of threat?" *Does that mean Alyah is thinking about coming back?* he wondered.

"Just forget it, Stephen. I think I'm done with this conversation. No, I've never seen that man in the photo." Alyah sounded tired.

"Fine," Stephen said but before he could say more, Alyah disconnected. "Well, that couldn't have gone any worse." What had Stephen been thinking? He was letting her go. So, why had he felt so jealous?

He needed to sleep. Maybe a hot shower would help. Stephen made sure the water was extra hot and stayed under it long enough so that his muscles relaxed. He turned off the shower just in time to hear his phone stop ringing. He hopped out and dried off quickly. Then he checked his phone.

Sikes: *Navy-blue Tacoma with the license plates AZW774 spotted outside a diner. Sending you a pin. Go get him.*

35

ALYAH

Alyah hung up the phone with Stephen, her hand still on the door handle. But she paused. Lynn Sauder still stood there, leaning against the wall next to her door. An arrogant smirk lined his handsome face. At least, Alyah used to think he was handsome, back when they first met and she dated him. She remembered him as charming and excited to have just accepted his new promotion. As she looked at him now, she saw none of that. Sure, his dark hair and piercing brown eyes were compelling, and his body had improved over the years, if that was possible, with more lean muscle mass.

But the way he assumed how Alyah was feeling without asking irked her. He'd done it several times at dinner.

"You must be pissed that this dickwad cost you your job in Washington," Sauder had stated.

"Senator Langsten? Well, no—"

"I would be too." He'd nodded and waved a server over. He studied the menu for two seconds and told the server what he wanted.

Alyah blinked, not quite sure she was ready to order. Luckily, she had been to this restaurant before.

"I'll have—"

Sauder had cut her off. "For the lady…"

Alyah was so shocked, she didn't correct him, nor had she remembered what he'd ordered her until it had come out. Duck. Alyah's stomach turned. She'd picked through it and began counting the minutes until Sauder took her home.

After multiple attempts to find a neutral topic, and having Sauder tell her what she must think of this or that, Alyah finally crossed her arms and stopped talking. Sauder was exhausting to be around. He did a lot of winking, too.

"Something in your eye, Chief?" Alyah had finally blurted. Maybe he wasn't aware of how overtly flirtatious he was being. Sauder had just smiled broadly.

In the end, she'd simply asked him to take her home. She had been looking forward to going out, like a normal person. Then, she found she only wanted peace and quiet. Even if that meant she was going home to an armed guard waiting to watch over her.

Now, she felt her annoyance rise another notch as she stood there gazing at Sauder who was casually leaning, practically inside her doorway.

"You don't have to come in," Alyah repeated, feeling frustrated. Why was he still here?

"Seriously, Alyah, I'd feel better if I did a sweep of your house." Sauder made no move to leave.

"It's fine, Chief. There are two US Marshals inside waiting for me." Alyah unlocked the door and pulled it open.

"Call me Lynn, Alyah. I feel like we know each other pretty well by now." Sauder let his eyes lazily roam over her body as he put a large palm out and held the door in place. "How well do you know them? You should have someone in your home you feel comfortable with."

"I do and I am," Alyah answered through gritted teeth. She moved his hand and opened the door further, revealing two US Marshals she'd known for years. "Good night, Chief. Thanks for dinner."

She felt Sauder put a hand on her arm. Alyah's irritation rose. This guy did not take cues very well.

"I had a good time tonight, Alyah. It felt like we were picking up where we left off." He stood there gazing into her eyes.

Alyah was speechless. Was he angling for a goodnight kiss?

"Yeah, I'll see you around." Alyah yanked her arm away and shut the door in his face. The nerve of that guy! She turned to face the two US Marshals who were watching her. An awkward silence fell. Should Alyah explain that wasn't what it looked like? No. Her life was not their business.

She cleared her throat. "Thank you for being here. If you don't mind, it's been a long day and I'm off to bed."

They stood to their feet. Finally, Tim spoke. "We cleared the house and all is secure. We'll arm your security system every night, and we'll take turns sleeping on the couch and the guest room every night. Please let us know if you need anything."

Alyah stared at them. Then she nodded. What she needed was Stephen Wilton. Having two co-workers in her home was beyond uncomfortable. But then she thought about the alternatives—going into WITSEC, or Senator Langsten eliminating her—and she knew she had no choice. She'd rather stay alive. Her discomfort overrode that. Because Alyah knew the first chance he got, Senator Langsten would kill her.

With a sigh, Alyah shut her bedroom door and called Stephen back. Her foolish heart wished this was a romantic phone call. But she doubted they would ever be in that place again.

36

WILTON

All chance of getting sleep that night disappeared as Stephen dressed and met Mak, who was walking out to the Range Rover. They would not be using those hotel rooms tonight after all. It took Stephen and Mak a little over twenty-five minutes to drive to the busy but quaint diner and find the Tacoma.

It was there, parked in the diner parking lot. Stephen could see the excitement in Mak's eyes as she got out of the car and pulled her gun. Stephen recognized the emotion in her eyes because he felt it too. He expected the senator would not go down without a fight.

Quietly, they circled the Tacoma. It was a dark night, making it hard to see in the vehicle. Guns pointed, Stephen threw open the driver's side door and Mak opened the passenger side. Stephen blinked in surprise that one, the car had been left unlocked, and two, the senator was not inside it.

Stephen let out a loud expletive.

Mak was already by his side. "Hey," her voice was calm. "I need you to put your emotions away and reach inside to find that logic of yours. Love your passion, but you can't let your feelings overtake you right now. Let's go scan the diner. Maybe he's having dinner inside."

Right, Stephen thought, *logic*.

The smell of burgers, grease, and French fries immediately assaulted their senses as they went in. They quickly scanned every table. Oblivious to them, diners conversed and laughed loudly, dishes clanked, and forks scraped plates. There were single diners, as well as small families scattered about the large room. Though it seemed late for dinner, Stephen supposed it could be a twenty-four-hour diner.

Stephen felt his heart sink with the realization he immediately vocalized. "He's not here."

"Can I get you two a seat?" A perky hostess with her hair tied up in a high ponytail approached them with menus already in hand. She wore a black and white checkered shirt and bright red lipstick. Her nametag said *Carrie*.

"No, we're not staying," Stephen said quickly. To Mak he said, "I'll check the men's room." He heard Mak speak to the hostess as if trying to explain and soften his abruptness. Stephen kept moving. He wasn't here to make friends.

He found the men's room empty. There were two stalls, and he opened each one to make sure. Just to be thorough, he looked around and knocked on the ladies' room door as well. When no one answered, he went in and checked those stalls. He exited and shook his head in response to Mak's expectant gaze.

"He has to be here, somewhere. That's definitely the car," Mak said.

"Let's search outside." Stephen started toward the door, already thinking about the lightly wooded area surrounding the diner. The truth was, he hadn't paid attention to that because it hadn't been his focus.

"Somebody stole my car!" A loud, angry voice rose above

the low hum of voices in the room. The noise level dropped as all eyes fell on the man who had entered the diner. He was a big man with a ballcap on his head. He puffed up his chest under his t-shirt, planted his boot-clad feet, and stood glaring at the room as if looking for the person who'd done it. Every diner seemed to tune in for the response, the room suddenly as quiet as if someone had paused a TV show.

The pieces clicked into place. Stephen approached and discreetly flashed his badge. "Sir, can you come with us?"

Mak made eye contact with Carrie, the energetic hostess, who was now frozen in shock as if she didn't know what to do. "Can we see your night shift manager, and do you have a break room or an office we can borrow?"

"What's happening?" the man protested, his expression thunderous. "Why am I in trouble? Someone stole *my* car!"

"We think we know who took it. If you will come with us, we'll put out a BOLO and connect you with a cop to take a stolen vehicle report," Stephen said as the hostess led them through the kitchen's double doors.

"Order up!" a cook yelled as he shoved a plate of food on a rack where a server came and snatched it away. His eyes flicked at them and he stared, causing the other workers to pause and look in their direction.

Stephen noticed an assembly line of food and a small vat of brown chili simmering on a stove. Stephen was surprised by how organized the back kitchen appeared to be.

"Here you are," Carrie showed them to a small office.

An older man with a balding head was sitting in the room counting a money drawer and putting bills in a bank bag. He looked up, surprised to see several people outside his office.

"What the hell, Carrie?" The manager gaped. His white t-shirt was tucked in. His stomach hung over his jeans. His jaw was working a piece of gum like he was nervous.

"I'm US Marshal Wilton, and this is Marshal Mak

Cunningham," Stephen began as they both flashed their badges.

The manager's mouth stayed open.

"Can I go back to the front?" Carrie asked.

"Yes," Mak agreed.

"And who's this guy?" the manager pointed to the man who had come in with them.

"I'm Tony, and someone stole my car from your parking lot!" The angry look still rested on Tony's face.

"We needed a place to get this guy's information and call your local PD without interrupting the diners," Stephen explained.

"We would also like to see any footage you have of the parking lot—if you have cameras out there?" Mak requested.

The manager's head bobbed up and down, but he put a finger up as he finished counting the money, then put it in a drawer and locked it away. He turned and motioned for them to step inside. Four people in this tiny office would be cramped, but it would have to work.

Mak turned her attention to the manager, who was showing her the camera footage. Stephen glanced at the video as he called the local police department, grateful that the camera showed a clear view of the parking lot. Stephen introduced himself and rattled off his badge number, making sure his phone was on speaker.

"How can I help?" the dispatcher asked.

"I have a man here named Tony—" Stephen's voice paused as he looked at Tony.

"Gonzales," the man supplied.

"Tony Gonzales left Fort Diner about ten minutes ago and discovered his vehicle had been stolen. We need to put out a BOLO and report that vehicle stolen."

"Okay, Mr. Gonzales, what car were you driving?" the dispatcher asked.

Stephen shoved the phone into Tony's hand and grabbed a Post-it note and pen off the manager's desk.

Tony licked his lips. "It's my wife's—a 2008 Toyota Camry. It's black."

Stephen wrote it down.

"Do you know the license plates, sir?" the dispatcher asked.

"Yes," Tony rattled it off.

Stephen wrote that down as well.

"Confirmed, it's him," Mak said over her shoulder, then turned back to the footage.

"Okay." Stephen took his phone back. "Thanks, Tony, you've been a huge help."

"Wait, what? What do I do now?" Tony whined. "I don't have a car."

"Why don't you get an Uber and head to the police department to finish filling out that report. They'll help you from there." Stephen dismissed him.

Tony took off grumbling something about being *unhelpful*.

Stephen turned back to the phone with urgency in his voice. "Put out an all-points bulletin and be advised that a wanted fugitive, Senator Joseph Langsten, stole that Camry and is still believed to be in your town."

"Okay…" They could hear her clicking on the keyboard. "Got it."

"Do you have officers you can spare tonight? We plan to keep moving on down the highway, but we need to coordinate efforts. Take down this number, and if you spot him, please let us know. I'm also going to give you information for Deputy Director Rob Sikes, who is over the Kansas City US Marshal office. He's coordinating efforts to take this guy down." Stephen spoke fast.

"Got it," the dispatcher said again.

"Great." Stephen hung up. Mak's brown eyes connected

with his as he nodded to her, indicating he had what he needed. Mak thanked the manager and turned away. Without waiting for a verbal acknowledgment, Stephen and Mak headed to the parking lot and got in the Range Rover.

Mak made a phone call before she started her car. Officer Marina answered.

"Hey," Mak began without introduction as she smoothed a stray auburn hair out of her face, "we found the navy-blue Tacoma, license plates AZW774." She listened to her phone for a second. "Yeah, I'm looking at it. I'll drop you a pin. Thanks!"

"Which way?" Stephen asked as Mak hung up and started the car.

"According to the video footage, he turned left out of the diner." Mak backed out, turned her car around and put her left blinker on.

"So, there are two places left on our list to check for the senator. The final Airbnb and his daughters' homes," Stephen tried.

"Which one is the closest?" Mak asked.

"The Airbnb." Stephen was looking at notes in his phone.

"Airbnb it is," Mak said.

Stephen put the address in for the GPS to guide them.

"Call Sikes phone," Mak instructed Siri.

Stephen listened as the phone rang and Sikes picked up. "What do you have?"

They ran through the events at the diner from the abandoned Tacoma to Senator Langsten spotted on camera stealing a black Toyota Camry.

"We put out an APB on Langsten and the Camry," Stephen said.

"Great."

"I called Officer Marina and gave her the location of the stolen Tacoma," Mak put in.

"Okay, where to next?" Sikes asked.

Mak answered. "We're heading to the last Airbnb they own because it's the next stop along the way. The only other places we haven't explored are his daughters' homes—"

"He won't go there," Stephen interrupted impatiently.

"How do you know?" Mak asked a little sharper than she intended.

"His wife said he had a falling out with the twins, and the senator wouldn't likely go there." Stephen's tone was matter of fact. He didn't think they should waste their time.

"Maybe that was Diane's way of discouraging us from going there. Ever think of that? What if that's exactly where he went, and Diane was trying to lead us away, and this whole Airbnb thing has been one wild goose chase led by Diane?" Mak argued.

Sometimes Stephen wondered if Mak argued just for the sake of arguing. "So, you're saying you think Diane is dirty now? That she's helping her husband play us?"

"Anything is possible." Mak tapped her thumbs against the steering wheel.

Sikes stepped in. "Let's not get ahead of ourselves. Making assumptions without evidence can be a dangerous thing."

"True," Mak acknowledged quickly, seeming to take it as a reprimand. "You're right. I'm just so tired. My brain is a little foggy."

Stephen didn't respond. But he thought Mak's overactive imagination might be at play again.

"While I realize the likelihood of Langsten returning to a place where he's familiar is low, we also have to consider that he might not go to any of those places. He could find a hotel to hole up in for the night." Sikes sighed. "I don't envy your jobs tonight."

Mak snorted.

Stephen smirked at the way it seemed to cut the tension in the car.

"Listen, don't chase your tails too long tonight. You need to take care of yourselves and start strong in the morning."

They hung up, and Stephen was quiet as he contemplated Sikes' words. Was he taking good care of himself? He hadn't eaten since he'd left Aruba and was surprised at how hungry he was. This case was consuming him.

Stephen knew one thing for sure. Killing Langsten would avenge his brother and Davey. The sooner he accomplished that, the better. Then he could prioritize himself.

37

MAK

It was quiet as Mak drove, so she flipped on the radio. She turned the knob until she found something acceptable, which ended up on country rock. Mak thought they might call it rockabilly. She opened her mouth to ask but decided against it when she glanced at her partner.

Wilton was broody as he stared out the window. Was it her imagination, or was his mood getting darker the longer they worked this case? She knew this was personal for him. In fact, if she took her eyes off their singular task of finding the senator, she would have felt very overwhelmed. At this very moment, the FBI was likely moving into position to take down all the people on that manifest that Alyah provided. But Mak knew it would all begin with Langston. They needed to move on everyone involved at the same time or risk spooking some of the other people involved in this trafficking ring. Thank God the FBI was huge and had the resources to coordinate that effort.

"You never told me. How was Aruba?" Mak grinned, remembering Wilton's grumbling about how weird it was. Maybe she could shake him out of his mood.

Wilton lifted his eyes to Mak's. "A shit show. You can't unsee that stuff!" he groaned.

"Was it really that bad?" Mak balked.

"I was escorted to a sex party they called an after-hours *activity* where anything goes, and it did. While everyone else watched. Since it was my job to try to find the senator, I probably looked at every person in that place, twice." Wilton shuddered.

Mak laughed. "Still. Gotta love the sun and beach!"

"It was clothing optional on the private beach," Stephen deadpanned.

"You didn't have any fun?" Mak scoffed.

Stephen hesitated but decided not to tell Mak about his time of relaxation, beach time, or pickleball with his new senator friends. He wasn't sure why. He just wanted to keep that for himself. In truth, he felt like he'd been taking advantage—playing on the job. Not to mention, he'd really enjoyed pickleball. Having fun wasn't in the job description.

"No. I've sold my soul to the job. Women only lead me into trouble. Speaking of which, I talked to Alyah earlier, and she didn't recognize the fourth man in the picture from the senator's house," Stephen stated, pushing all the information out in one quick rush.

"I take it from the tone of your voice, that conversation with Alyah didn't go well?" Mak had heard the way Wilton's voice caught when he'd said Alyah's name.

"It did not. It ended in an argument. Again." Wilton looked off into the dark night. The moon was a sliver in the sky. Mak thought he looked tired. But then, it was around eleven at night.

"What are you arguing about now?" Mak asked, well aware of her nosiness.

"Did you know she used to date Chief Sauder?" Wilton turned his angry voice toward Mak.

"No! Really?" Mak had only met Sauder a handful of times working on other cases. "How did that come up?"

"He took her out tonight," Wilton stated. "I heard him walk her to the door."

"Awkward," Mak sang. "And wait. Should Alyah be going out? I thought she had protective detail following her around anytime she was in public."

"See! You get it. Alyah didn't appreciate it when I brought that up. She's the key to taking this whole ring down with that manifest, and when we do it, we might want to get her out of town for a while." Wilton's logic was sound.

Mak nodded. "But what you're really upset about is that she went on a date."

"What? No. I mean. Who has time to date right now?" his voice trailed off.

"You know, John and I met in college. We had this strong connection—a love at first sight kind of thing." Mak smiled at the memory. "But he was staying to get his master's degree, and I was off to US Marshal training. He knew it was my plan when he met me. But the inevitable happened when we graduated."

"What did you do?" Wilton wondered.

"We broke up," Mak stated.

"What? You and John? The man you're married to now?" Wilton's eyes were big.

"I know." Mak shook her head and smiled a cheesy grin. "Crazy that he could let me go like that."

"Let me guess. After spending the weekend apart, John quit school and moved to be closer to your training?" Wilton half joked.

"No. We were apart that whole two years. Well, we talked some and after training, we went on a few dates here and there before I was officially stationed in KC. But the entire time we were apart, we fought. We were not nice to each other. John explained later, after he graduated and eventually followed me to KC, that it was about self-preservation for him. It was way harder than he thought it would be when I left, so he tried pushing me away. It would have worked too—I'm not into toxic relationships—but he showed up with one heckuva apology." Mak's eyes held a happy sparkle.

"Do I even want to know more about this apology?" Wilton asked.

"Oh. It involved him on one knee and a wedding ring. We eloped that weekend. We were married before I even started my job." Mak closed the story.

Wilton's mouth dropped open.

"Yeah, I move fast," Mak quipped.

"I suppose you're going to give me the moral of the story?" Wilton rolled his eyes.

"Nah, you're smart. You'll figure it out. You'll either be with Alyah in the end or you won't, but maybe you should think about why you keep fighting with her," Mak summed up.

"Thanks, mom." Wilton's voice was laced with sarcasm.

Mak shrugged. "Who's in the long-term committed relationship? Just sayin'…"

"For the love of—"

"We're here," Mak interrupted.

Wilton sat up straight.

In the driveway there was a black 2008 Toyota Camry.

Mak jammed on the brakes, pulled the Range Rover to the curb, and quickly cut her lights. There was no way she would let him get away this time. She'd made that mistake last time, and she wouldn't make the same one again.

Mak pulled out her gun and racked it, making sure it was hot. Wilton did the same thing. "Listen, we need to split up." Mak reached behind the seat and grabbed two Kevlar vests. She thrust one at Stephen, then put her vest on. "I'll approach from the left, and you approach from the right. Last time, he was sitting in the car. He waited for me to get close enough, backed up, and hit the gas."

Wilton's eyes hardened in instant anger. Mak wondered how he'd feel if she told him she'd shot at his tire and missed. He opened his mouth to speak, but Mak held up a hand.

"Later," Mak hissed as she turned off her car dome light, threw the door open, and closed it quietly. She dropped into a crouch, thankful she was wearing dark jeans and a black shirt as she jogged across the street. She didn't have to look over her shoulder to know that Wilton was moving in the same stealthy way.

Mak was in a full squat now, lowering herself down below the window of the driver's side of the vehicle. She waited until she knew Wilton was in position on the other side. From where she stood, she could see the side of the house. She scanned it in case the senator was hiding in the bushes. There was nothing but a side yard and a few trees leading behind the house.

Mak turned her attention back to the car. She popped up, her gun pointed, hoping for the element of surprise, but her heart instantly sank. The car was empty.

She heard Wilton utter a whispered expletive on the other side. They locked eyes over the top of the car.

Mak jerked her head toward the house. It was late and if she interrupted a family who was sleeping, resulting in a bad star rating for Diane Langsten, so be it. Wilton followed her lead.

Mak hated knocking on the door. What if Langsten was in there and they tipped him off, giving him a head start out the back door?

"Wait!" Mak's whispered word stopped Wilton. "We need

to clear the outside of the house, and someone needs to be at the back door."

"On it," Wilton said.

"Text me when it's clear and you're in position." Mak backed up and scanned the front of the house. She stood next to the car should Langsten come barreling out. At least Mak would be blocking his ride this time.

Mak's phone lit up.

Wilton: *Outside clear. I'm in position.*

Heart racing with adrenaline but mind clear and calm, Mak marched up to the front door and knocked. She gave three short, quick bursts and took a step or two backward.

Minutes ticked by but there was no response from inside the house. Impatiently, Mak pounded harder on the door. This time, she heard footsteps. Instead of the door opening, a male voice sounded on the inside. Was that the senator?

"Who's there?" he called out.

"US Marshal, open up!" Mak called out. She kept an eye out for any movement at the front of the house.

The door cracked open, and from what she could see of the man, it was not Langsten.

"Can I see some ID?" the man asked. His brown hair was rumpled and his eyes looked sleepy.

Mak pulled out her badge and showed him with her free hand. She tried to peer around the man. Was Langsten in there with a gun on him?

"We have reason to believe a fugitive is hiding in or around this home. Is there anyone else in here with you?" Mak asked with authority in her voice.

"Just my family, and the kids are still sleeping." The man threw open the door. Mak could see a pajama-clad wife holding a baby peeking curiously around the corner.

Mak entered with her gun lowered to the floor. "What's your name?" she asked the man.

"Ethan, and this is my wife, Sandy."

"Okay, Ethan, my partner is at your back door. I'm going to need you to let him in. Then we need to check this house," Mak commanded, her eyes already wandering around the living room she was standing in.

Ethan obeyed and opened the door for Wilton, who quickly pulled out his badge as he entered the house.

"Ethan and Sandy say they're here with their kids," Mak said as she opened a coat closet and peered inside.

"I need you to get your kids and have a seat at the dining room table," Wilton commanded in a calm voice. "This shouldn't take long."

Sandy sat down with the baby as Ethan disappeared with Wilton trailing him. Ethan came out holding a little girl with a young boy zombie walking beside him. The family sat down, tension in their movements, fear in their eyes.

"Living room, clear," Mak called quietly.

Wilton's voice called out from the other side of the house. "Bedroom and bathroom clear."

Mak moved toward the sound of his voice and ducked in a second bedroom opposite the one Wilton was in. She looked behind the door and then the closet. Both were clear. She checked under the bed. "Bedroom clear."

The house was small. She met Wilton in the hallway. There was only one door left. It must be the garage. She indicated he go first and fell in line to back him up as he threw the door open. They burst into the garage, guns pointed, but the garage was also clear.

Mak's confusion must have shown on her face, and she could see the disappointment on Wilton's. They holstered their guns and went back to the family. The wife was wide-eyed and shaking. The husband just sat waiting on the edge of his seat.

Wilton pulled out his phone and showed them a picture of Senator Joseph Langsten being sworn in. "We're sorry for bursting in on you like this. But this man is a wanted criminal. He also owns this home. I'm going to give you my number and if he shows up, I want you to first call nine-one-one. Then I want you to get in touch with me." Wilton held out his hand for the man's phone.

Without question, Ethan handed it to Wilton. Wilton programmed in his number and gave it back.

"Thank you," Wilton said as they turned to leave.

"Wait," Ethan called. "Why did you think he was here?"

"That's the car he stole parked in your driveway," Mak answered. She was actively working on a game plan. It looked like it would be a long night of searching yards and waking up the neighbors. They might as well call for backup.

"The only car in the driveway should be mine," Ethan told them with bewilderment in his tone. "It's a silver Tesla."

Alarm slammed into Mak. "There's no Tesla out there."

Mak, Wilton, and Ethan rushed out to the driveway, seeing the Toyota Camry in place of his Tesla. "My car is gone!" Ethan howled.

"Are you sure you didn't park it down the street?" Wilton asked, looking around.

"I remember where I parked my car! I didn't want to park outside at all, but there was no way to get into the garage! We just got a radio update, which was supposed to make it impossible to be stolen! I had my phone on me all night!"

"Did you turn on the PIN safeguard?" Ethan's wife asked quietly.

Ethan turned pale. "No. I thought the update would be enough."

His wife shook her head in regret.

Wilton took out his phone and opened Google. After a few minutes of reading, he looked up. "Looks like car-hackers can perform relay attacks by tricking a Tesla into detecting your unlocking app on a smartphone. Instead, a hacker's device near the car has relayed the signal from the owner's real key, which could be hundreds of feet away."

"Like someone sleeping in the house with the car in the driveway," Mak mused. "Do you really think Langsten is that techie?"

"Not likely," Wilton replied. "Though, we wouldn't know for sure. My bet is on Langsten having access to a tech person who walked him through it or did it for him."

"Do you have GPS capability to show where your car is now?" Mak asked with a burst of inspiration.

Ethan pulled out his phone and opened his app. He made an exclamation of surprise. Mournfully, he showed them the app. His car was offline.

Wilton scanned the article. "GPS blocker."

Ethan threw his hands up in disgust.

"I'm sure we'll get your car back. The criminal we're tracking has been stealing cars, driving a ways, then ditching them for another vehicle."

"Was the car fully charged?" Mak asked.

Ethan nodded his head.

"This game of leapfrog is getting old," Wilton grumbled as he pulled out his phone to repeat the process of reporting yet another car stolen, and that they found the stolen Toyota Camry. They would call in a new, updated APB after they finished up with Ethan.

"Are we safe here?" Ethan asked. "What if he comes back?"

As Mak stared at the car left in the driveway, she knew Langsten was long gone. Too far ahead for them to catch him tonight. Not to mention, they were almost out of leads. "He won't be back tonight. He got what he came for." Mak instructed Ethan on how to fill out a stolen vehicle report.

They finished with Ethan and called Sikes to update him.

It was well after midnight when they found a new hotel off the highway to stay for the night. Mak was exhausted and fell into her comfortable bed. She hoped Wilton got some sleep, but she was beginning to think he might be an insomniac. When he let himself in his room, he seemed keyed up. She sighed. Having a zombie as a partner tomorrow was not going to be beneficial.

But as she felt herself drift off, she decided she'd worry about that tomorrow.

38

BETH

With aluminum foil wrapped around her hair, Beth sat in the hotel salon under a dome of warm air to help her *process*, as the stylist had said. She'd never spent so much time in the salon in her life. She went in for conservative trims every other month, and she'd be lying if she said she wasn't already grieving the six inches of hair the stylist had happily cut off. She had minutes to stare at the way her hair swung just to her chin before the stylist returned with a bowl of bleach to highlight her black hair to caramel-colored strands and lowlight some auburn red into it. In short, Beth would walk out looking very different, which was exactly what she needed.

The stylist had been quick to point to Beth's cast and ask what happened to her arm as she'd slathered dye on her hair. Beth's salon lady back home had always loved gossip too.

The smell of bleach had singed Beth's nose. "I fell out of a chair."

"Must have been a tall chair." The stylist clicked her tongue.

"When I fell, the chair fell on top of it, along with my

body weight. Broke several bones in my hand." Might as well stay as close to the truth as she could.

The stylist didn't buy it. She leaned close to Beth's ear. "Blink three times if it was really an abusive partner."

Beth had actually smiled at that. The stylist didn't know how close she'd come. Instead, Beth shook her head.

The warm air circulating around her made Beth feel sleepy, though she had slept well the night before. This made her think about prom. Prom had been the last time she'd gone to the salon to try something new. They'd talked her into a perm. She thought she would have nice big waves that she wouldn't have to mess with. Instead, the curls were tight and uncontrollable. Beth had left the salon in tears. The more she'd tried to get the curls to relax, the frizzier her hair got.

Beth's mom had found her in a puddle of tears on the floor when she got home. She patiently picked Beth up, sat her down in front of her vanity, and sprayed water over her messy hair. Then she started pinning it into a cute, messy updo with curls spilling over to one side. Beth knew she hadn't been crying over her hair, but over Jacob. He was supposed to be her prom date. But now he was gone.

Greg Wilton had stepped up. He'd caught her crying into her locker one day over a prom flyer when she thought the bell had rung and everyone was in class. He'd leaned on the locker next to hers.

"You miss him, don't you?" Greg asked.

Beth nodded.

"I miss Shania too," Greg admitted. "Every time something big like prom comes along, I wonder what it would be like if she were here, going with me."

That only made Beth cry harder. "We've lost so much!"

"Yeah, we have. We lost our people. Maybe our soulmates. Our lives are not our own. Sometimes I just want one normal experience to

remember life by. One good memory in the middle of all this bad," Greg said, snatching the flyer from Beth.

Beth was sobbing and trying to pull it together, but she couldn't even see through the torrent. She wiped her nose on the back of her sleeve.

"Should we go together and pretend we're normal teenagers?" Greg asked.

Beth looked up and squinted at him through her tears. It sounded terrible.

"For them. To honor their memories," Greg coaxed.

How could she say no to that? So, Beth nodded in agreement. She bought a dress. A red one that hugged her curves to the waist but floated down to the ground in a full skirt, making her feel like a princess.

Greg was dead a few short months later.

Where she had failed Jacob in his last moments, she had made up for it by indulging Greg's. They had fun that night pretending they were just like everyone else on that dance floor, but they weren't. And they knew better. But that night, Beth and Greg had bonded over the ghosts of their first loves. They made a promise they would always have each other's backs. No matter what. In the end, only one of them kept that promise.

Beth opened her eyes with a start. Her drier had stopped, and the stylist was coming her way. Though her heart was pounding from that memory, Beth had managed to keep her emotions in check.

After washing and drying her hair, Beth could only stare at her own reflection. She'd never looked so different—so good. It was edgy and fun, two things that had never described Beth. She only hoped that her new look didn't get her more attention. She needed to stay unnoticeable. Her life depended on it.

39

WILTON

Stephen woke to Mak pounding on his door the next morning. He felt so groggy and worn down. As he lay there ignoring his insistent partner, he realized how hard they had been pushing themselves. Though from the glance at his cell phone, Mak had let him sleep in a little while. It was just after ten in the morning.

Stephen sighed and got up, made sure he was in appropriate clothing, and opened the door. He squinted at Mak, who was wide awake and looking perky. There was excitement in her eyes and a cup of coffee in her hand, which she offered to Stephen.

"Get a move on, Wilton! We've got a criminal to catch," Mak had entirely too much energy today.

Stephen, on the other hand, felt hungover. He hoped he wasn't coming down with something. "Give me ten minutes." He took the coffee and shut the door in her face.

Exactly ten minutes later, Stephen went across the hall to Mak's room and pounded on the door. Mak yanked the door open, juggling her duffle bag, coffee cup, and phone, which she held in the crook of her neck.

"It'll all work out. I know you'll make the right decision," Mak said. "Hey, gotta run. Love you and love to Harpy."

Stephen watched her, surprised when she managed to loop the duffel strap over her shoulder, pocket her phone, and free her hands, which now cupped only her coffee. He lifted an eyebrow in question before he fell into step with her.

"Oh, John is considering taking on some new client. I guess they're a big deal, and he's really agonizing over it. He's way overanalyzing this if you ask me. What's the big deal? It's either a *yes* or a *no*. Pick one and move on." Mak glanced at Stephen. "Ugh, you do that, too. I forget. John's usually so laid back. I'm not sure why this has been so hard for him."

"Did you ask him why it's a big deal?" Stephen asked.

"Of course." Mak rolled her eyes. "Trust me, it's all he's talked about for the last several phone calls."

"Just remember, there's talking and there's listening, Mak." Stephen pulled the car door open when they got to the Range Rover and threw his overnight bag in the back. Mak did the same.

"What's that supposed to mean?" Mak hopped into the driver's seat.

"It just means, sometimes you hear, but you don't stop to fully comprehend what someone is saying." Stephen put on his seatbelt.

"Wait, that sounds like you're speaking from experience. I listen to you. Are you mad about something? When have I not listened to you?" Mak bristled.

"No, I'm not holding anything against you. It's just an observation. You mean well, but you can be very single focused. Right now, it's on the case. I'm sure John gets it. You're right, it will all work out. Now, where are we going?"

"To pay a surprise visit to the twins in Montana." Mak grinned. "I had an epiphany."

Stephen hoped this was good because he did not think the senator would go see his children right now. "Do tell."

"I think the senator is messing with us. Leaving bread-crumbs for us to follow. Like he wants us to find him. But on his terms. I'm thinking he's trying to lead us into a trap. And he's using Diane to set it up. Think about it. He's shown up at two out of five of the Airbnb's at the time we were going to be there. Diane tells us *don't go see the twins*. I say we do the opposite. Go see them. Worst case scenario, they give us information. Best case, they're harboring their dad."

Stephen thought about it and nodded. "Weird logic, but it might be a solid plan. How do we get there? Montana's about a day and a half drive, and no offense, but I can't be in a car with you that long."

"Offense taken." Mak rolled her eyes. "Headquarters already booked us a flight and a car. The jet is unavailable, so we're back on commercial."

"Good, maybe I can get some more sleep," Stephen mumbled.

"Nobody sleeps on planes, Wilton. They always think they will, but they don't." Mak wagged her finger, looking too much like the know it all she sometimes was.

"Watch me," Stephen replied. On a plane was the one place Stephen had no problem sleeping. He'd taught himself to do that to avoid conversations with strangers. He never understood why people got so chatty on planes.

True to his word, Stephen was fast asleep shortly after takeoff. He woke when he felt Mak poking his side. The flight had been short. Just enough time to give Stephen the energy he needed.

As they disembarked to the cooler air and mountains in

the distance, Stephen felt hopeful. Senator Langsten was here. He could feel it.

40

MAK

The mountains in the distance overshadowed the split-level home with brown siding and shake shingles. Inside the home of Emily Langsten, Mak and Wilton sat in overstuffed recliners across from twin sisters, Emily and Dawn. The sisters were practically identical, though their style seemed different enough. Emily wore jeans and a t-shirt. Her hair was short with beach waves, giving it body. Dawn wore leggings and a tank top. Her hair was pulled up in a ponytail. Mak could see the resemblance between them and their mother, Diane.

The sisters sat on the couch next to each other. Every once in a while, their eyes would stray to the back window that showed a large playset outside where the warm afternoon sun shone brightly overhead and their children played. Mak knew they were checking on the kids.

"So, someone is finally here about our criminal father, huh?" Bitterness lined Emily's words as she crossed her arms.

"Way to jump right into the conversation." Mak sat up

straighter. She loved how direct Emily was. "But I'm a little surprised."

"Don't be," Emily said with an eyeroll. "I've known for—well, all my life."

"Don't mind her," Dawn said, shooting Emily a compassionate look. "Emily was always the more observant one of the two of us. She overheard a conversation when we were younger. We were too scared to say anything for years—"

"And when I did, all hell broke loose," Emily stated. "It was like I painted a target on my back!"

Mak held up a hand. "Can we start at the beginning? As I mentioned when we arrived, your dad is a fugitive. Would it surprise you to know he's wanted for murder and running a drug and sex trafficking ring?"

Emily shook her head adamantly.

Dawn hesitated, looked mournful, then shook her head along with Emily.

"I get the feeling you have information that you've been dying to share but haven't?" Mak surmised.

"Yeah," Emily said. "When I was about ten—or were we eleven?"

"I think eleven," Dawn said. "He was the mayor then."

"He was the mayor?" Wilton repeated, processing her words.

Dawn nodded.

Emily went on. "One night, I overhead my dad talking to a friend. It was late. I couldn't sleep, so I got up for a glass of water. They were talking pretty loud on the front porch. I crept closer to the door and put an ear to it. At first, I couldn't understand what they were saying. But I caught it pretty quick. They were arguing. A man—not my dad—yelled, *'This wasn't part of the plan!'* My dad told him to lower his voice. The man refused. Then he said, *'You killed him in cold blood. You took out a perfectly good carrier with witnesses, for what?*

To assert your power?' My dad laughed. He freaking laughed at the man! Then he said, *'So what? This has all been one big experiment in control. Those kids aren't going to say anything. I just put them back in line. They'll do what I say because they're terrified. And you'll fall in line too. You know why?'* The man said, *'Let me guess. You'll kill me too?'* And my dad said, *'Now you're catching on.'* Then the guy's voice got so low, I had to really strain to hear. He goes, *'I have photographic evidence that will put you away and I'll use it if I need to.'* And my dad said, *'Good thing we're on the same side then.'* Then my mom caught me and grabbed me by the ear—"

"I hated when she would do that!" Dawn interrupted with a shudder.

"She marched me right up to my bedroom and grounded me for eavesdropping. I tried to explain it to her, but she wouldn't listen. Just told me to respect my elders and mind my own business." Emily shook her head.

"When Em told me what she heard, I thought she was making it all up," Dawn said. "We peeked out the window and saw a cop car in the driveway. That didn't make sense. There was no way a cop was accusing my dad of murder and letting him threaten to kill him."

"I started to think I'd dreamed the whole thing up," Emily admitted. "I wrote it down to remember and hid my journal under my mattress."

"After that, we overheard so many things over the years. Things that confirmed what we already knew. He was a terrible person. And he got worse once he got into office." Dawn glanced out to the yard. "We got away as soon as we could."

"How did he get worse?" Wilton asked.

"Well, we know he was cheating on mom," Emily pulled a face. "He'd go on these business trips. He'd get back, then he and mom would argue for hours—"

"Your mom knew?" Mak asked.

"Oh yeah. But she never left him. We always thought she put up with it because she loved being a senator's wife." Dawn rolled her eyes.

"I take it you're not close to your mom, either?" Mak asked.

"We were," Emily said. "We defended her, championed her, felt sorry for her… Until the incident."

"What happened?" Wilton asked.

Dawn looked somber. "She found Emily's journal. She was waiting for her when we got home from softball practice. We were about sixteen at the time. She said she wanted to *talk* to Emily alone."

"She gaslighted me for an hour straight. Tried to convince me the conversation had never happened. I should have just gone along with it and agreed. Instead, I kept arguing," Emily explained. Her eyes wore deep regret in them.

Dawn grabbed Emily's hand. "I'll never forgive myself for not rushing in. I was sitting outside the door. There was a weird energy. I heard a loud smack and Emily screamed. That's when I ran in. There was blood everywhere!"

"What happened?" Mak breathed.

"She backhanded me and the diamond on her wedding ring cut my face open." Emily pulled her hair back to reveal a scar above her cheekbone. "Four stiches."

"Mom told the ER that Emily had walked into a tree branch," Dawn sneered.

"I'm sure they believed that," Mak said sarcastically.

"We figured out something that night," Emily stated.

"What's that?" Wilton asked.

"Mom was as bad as he was. She knew way more than she let on. We definitely couldn't trust her." Dawn looked at Mak and Wilton. "Don't you guys trust her either."

"Your mom is the one who gave us your address. How does she know where you live?" Mak asked.

Emily jerked a thumb at Dawn. "She sends Christmas cards to mom. Thinks she should know she has grandkids."

Dawn shrugged. "What if she changes? Or gets away from dad and needs a place to stay?"

"You're too soft hearted," Emily said. "Mom's guilty by association."

"Dawn, I need to know. When is the last time you saw your dad?" Wilton asked, his voice sounding more on guard.

"When we moved out at eighteen. He came to our college graduation, but Emily told him we didn't want to see them again. I didn't see him then and haven't since." Dawn put her palms up.

"And if your dad showed up, what would you do?" Wilton asked.

"The correct response would be call the cops," Emily said sassily. "But the first thing I would do is go for my gun. I don't trust that man. He's not my dad. He's a powerful, corrupt politician. Family in his vocabulary is a status to make him seem more approachable and trustworthy."

Dawn put a hand on Emily's arm. "We would call the cops. We aren't sixteen anymore. We know we can talk to the authorities without repercussions. We don't need to live in fear."

Mak nodded. "Thank you for telling us your story."

The women nodded.

"One more thing before we leave." Wilton pulled out his phone. He handed it to the women. "Do you know the men in the photo?"

Emily and Dawn peered closely. Emily reached down and enlarged the photo on Wilton's phone. "Just dad. But that's grammy and papa's place. We used to go there for summer vacations."

"It is!" Dawn exclaimed. "I loved that place!"

"It wasn't the same after they passed away." Emily looked sad.

"Wait," Wilton stopped them. "Did your parents keep the place after your grandparents passed?"

The women nodded. "They left it in the will to dad."

"Do you have an address or know how we can find it?" Excitement was evident in Wilton's voice.

"Not since we don't talk to mom. I can't imagine how to get it…" Dawn's voice trailed off.

"What were your grandparent's names?" Wilton asked.

"Dudley and Lorraine Langsten," Emily stated.

Wilton made a note of it. "How old were you when you went?"

"As young as we remember, and we stopped going around fifteen or sixteen, right, Em?" Dawn asked.

"Yeah, we lost them both within a year of each other. Childhood sweethearts," Emily stated wistfully.

"Sorry to hear that," Mak murmured, wondering what Wilton was thinking.

"How old are you now?" he asked.

"Twenty-five," Emily answered.

Wilton seemed to be doing calculations in his head. "Okay, thank you. Can we take your number in case we have more questions?"

"Of course." Emily reached for Wilton's phone and put in her number.

Wilton immediately texted Emily his number.

They thanked the women and shook hands. Once outside, Mak made a call to Sikes. A cool wind whipped from the direction of the mountain. The air smelled fresh and clean. The sun still streamed overhead.

"Can you contact the Police Station in Washington, DC, and have them take Diane Langsten into custody? We have reason to believe she might be an accessory to her husband's crimes," she informed Sikes.

Mak hung up the phone and was about to climb in the Range Rover when Dawn came jogging out, her blond ponytail bouncing. She stopped in front of Mak and Wilton and hesitated. Mak could see the fear in her big blue eyes.

"Are you, uh, going to ask us to testify in court?" Dawn smoothed her palms down the front of her leggings like her hands were sweaty. She looked over her shoulder, and Mak noticed Emily was standing in front of a picture window in the front room, watching them from inside the house.

Mak felt confused. "Well, I'm not sure what they will need as they're putting the case together, why?"

"Emily might seem tough, but those things we talked about were really traumatic for her. She had nightmares for years. She'll probably have one tonight since we brought all this up. Maybe testifying could be a last resort?" Dawn asked.

Wilton stepped forward. "We have some damning evidence against your father. I'm not sure we'll need your testimonies."

"Good." Dawn nodded. There was still fear in her eyes. "You're going to get him, right?"

"Dawn, are you afraid of your dad?" Mak asked.

"Yes. I'm a twenty-five-year-old woman who has always feared him. Now, I guess I fear retaliation. Like, if he knew we talked to you..." Dawn trembled.

"Don't worry," Mak rushed to assure her. "I lost your dad once, and I do not plan to make that mistake again." Mak still regretted not hitting his tire as he drove out of the neighborhood.

"Thank you," Dawn said with a quick wave, and she ran back into the house.

Mak didn't miss the instant anger that crossed Stephen's

face when she told Dawn she wouldn't lose her dad again. She was just being sincere. Was he worried about her making promises she might not be able to keep?

Mak got in the Range Rover. Before she could buckle her seatbelt, Wilton's words, backed by seething rage, paused her actions.

"How, Mak? How did you lose the senator the first time? What are you not telling me?"

41

BETH

Beth was tired of sitting in her room. She stared out the window, looking at the view of mountains in the distance. The sun shone brightly overhead. More than anything, she wanted to be out there. Free to feel the warm sun on her arms and face. To move through life without fear of getting caught and killed.

She wasn't sleeping well. Somehow, being on the run had brought back the fear and anxiety that she'd stuffed way down deep as a kid. Her horrible memories coming back to her in vivid detail told her she could not lock them down anymore, no matter how hard she tried. They were seeping into her dreams now, too.

Last night, she had a nightmare of the night Greg died. She was standing next to Trevan Collins and Davey Stinnert, frozen in horror as Mayor Langsten lifted a gun to Greg's head while Sherriff Pottstaff and Mickey Upton held her and made her watch. Only, when Beth looked again at Greg, it wasn't his face she saw, it was Lacy's. She'd woken sweating and crying.

She got out of bed and sat in the dark, in a chair, looking

out at the moon which illuminated the mountains, and she thought about Greg. About the night he'd gotten himself killed because of Beth. If Greg could see her now, would he do the same thing over again? Would he determine her life had been worth it?

Eighteen Years Ago…

Greg stood pacing like a lion stuck in a circus cage at the park where they had all played together as kids. He'd called a meeting here because he thought if they were in a public place, no one would be stupid enough to try anything. Beth had known deep in her gut that wouldn't stop them. They—the Corrupters—were above the law. They were the law. What chance did a bunch of young, stupid kids have against them?

When Beth had learned about Greg's plan, she'd bolted. She rounded up Trevan and Davey and they'd all sprinted to the park. The Corrupters thought they were meeting with Beth. They'd asked Beth to start bringing them teenage girls, one at a time, so it didn't look suspicious. They said they just wanted to talk to them. But Beth knew better. Greg agreed. He planned to put an end to this once and for all.

"Trust me," he'd assured her. "I have a plan."

Upton, Pottstaff, and Langsten were already there. They were angry. Beth could tell as she came to a stop. Stiff, jerky motions lined their movements. Hands were crossed. Langsten was wearing a gun holster and his hand rested dangerously close to it.

"What the hell is this?" Upton demanded. "We asked for you." He pointed to Beth who felt like heaving on the ground, and she knew it wasn't from her sprint there.

Greg stood up taller. He angled Beth behind him. "We won't be doing your bidding anymore."

Beth heard a gasp beside her and thought it must have been Davey.

"Is that so?" Langsten stepped closer to Greg, now standing right in front of him.

"Yes. I learned something in my advanced government class. What you're doing is called coercion. Only, I've been thinking about it—a lot. We never did anything wrong in the first place. We didn't murder Shania. It was an accident. Not you, not any lawyer, and no jury would ever have convicted us. So, this ends now. You want to get to them," Greg seethed as he pointed to his friends, "you go through me."

"Is that right?" Langsten smiled, baring his teeth, but it really looked like a grimace.

"Look who grew a backbone," Upton, standing at Langsten's right side, snickered.

Trevan, Davey, and Beth stood stock still. Beth's entire body was shaking. She clenched her teeth to keep them from chattering and making noise.

Langsten remained where he was, his posture aggressive and angry. His eyes swept over the three of them. "Does that go for all of you?"

Beth remembered Greg's words to her at prom: *I have your back.* She nodded, terror shooting out of every pore in her body. She didn't dare glance at Trevan or Davey, but she saw them do the same thing out of the corner of her eye.

It was so fast, Beth almost missed it.

Langsten pulled his Glock and pressed it against Greg's head.

Beth cried out and then clamped a hand over her mouth. She didn't want their attention directed to her.

Because she was standing behind Greg, she couldn't see his face. But she'd bet his eyes wore quiet defiance. She'd certainly seen the look many times in the past year.

The blast was deafening as Langsten pulled the trigger. Beth would have screamed but Greg's brain matter had blown out of the back of his head and was all over her face. Beth was mute. The horror turned into numbness as she wiped her eyes and watched Greg fall lifelessly to the ground. Blood poured out of his head, making a deep red halo around his head. Strong arms clamped around her shoulders, holding her in place. Beth could not move.

Langsten looked coldly at Beth, Trevan, and Davey. "Who's next?"

Beth felt her head shaking.

That's when Langsten pointed to Davey.

Davey's eyes bulged.

Langsten took a cloth out of his pocket and wiped down the gun. Then he tossed it to Davey, who caught it on reflex. Then Davey dropped the gun like it had burned him. But not before putting fingerprints all over it.

Langsten's attention remained fixed on Davey. "How could you do this to your best friend?"

"I—I would never. I didn't..." Davey stammered. His face was white.

Langsten clicked his tongue. "I guess that's what happens when you finally get fed up with your closest friend bullying you your whole life."

"No, I—"

"Mr. Stinnert, you will take the fall for this. You'll go to juvie for a few years and get out early for good behavior. If you don't... Well, I know where your mom and sister live." Langsten's grin was predatory.

"You leave them alone," Davey whispered.

Beth could tell Davey's mind was trying to process what they were telling him to do. She felt her stomach turn and was sure she was going to hurl any moment. She could smell the metallic tang each time she breathed through her nose, but she refused to open her mouth for fear of accidentally consuming Greg's blood, which was now drying and feeling sticky on her face.

"Okay," Davey was agreeing. Then he was crying. Suddenly, they were all crying as three powerful, corrupt law officials looked on with satisfaction in their eyes.

"Get this called in," Langsten told Pottstaff. Then he turned to them. "And you guys get out of here. Clean yourselves up. Leave the murder weapon right where it is. The story will tell itself. Let this be a lesson to you. Now is not the time for heroics. Heroes end up dead. Or in jail."

Unbenowst to Beth, Pottstaff had been wearing a body camera, and that's where the dreaded picture had come from. The one that Trevan had stolen from Pottstaff and gave to Stephen.

With that memory playing vividly in her mind, something snapped in Beth. She realized the truth. What good was sitting around feeling sorry for herself doing her? Had she really been completely powerless as a kid? Look at Greg. He put his foot down and stood up to them. Sure, it had gone all wrong. But at least he took a stand to stay and fight for their rights.

The life she'd chosen—a life on the run—was no life at all. Choosing this route meant she would never have anyone in her life. She would never be able to trust friends or family or let them in. Not to mention, she'd left behind the most important person in her life, her daughter. Remorse filled Beth. She should have listened to Stephen. The marshals would have protected her the same way they were protecting Lacy.

The same way Greg had been protecting her by taking that bullet for her the night he died. Now, Beth knew what to do. It was her turn to take a bullet—not literally, if she could help it. Testify. Do the right thing. For once, not go along with the easiest path. She didn't want life to happen to her anymore. It was time to make choices and move her life forward. Not run away and hide. Stand up and fight. Take back her power and help put these guys behind bars, saving Lacy and all the other women they must have taken over the years.

Only, Beth had thrown away her phone and she had no way to contact Lacy, not that Lacy still had her old phone either. Neither did Beth have a way to contact Stephen Wilton. She needed a plan. She was still in danger. At least she looked different. Maybe that would help her move around unnoticed.

After a few more hours of thinking and rethinking, she made a decision. She would go back to the US Marshal office in Kansas City, turn herself in, and testify about everything she knew. The tricky part would be getting back to Kansas City safely. It had been hard to get here, but she'd done it. She could make it back.

Beth picked up the room phone and called the front desk. "I'll be checking out today."

"Yes, ma'am. You are welcome to leave your keys in your room when you leave," the attendant said.

"Oh, I'll stop by and pay my final bill on the way out," Beth promised, preferring to settle up with cash. Which is exactly what she did less than an hour later.

As Beth walked out of the hotel, she was temporarily blinded by the warm, beautiful New Mexico sunlight. She paused for a moment to bring her hand up and shield the light from her eyes. That's why she didn't see them coming.

Two strong hands grasped each arm right under her armpit and lifted her so her feet were no longer touching the ground. A small squeak escaped her lips, then Beth felt herself quickly propelled forward by no effort of her own. They were moving fast. There was no way for Beth to escape them.

They carried her to the back of the parking lot where the visibility was low and trees surrounded this spot. She heard the beep of a car and saw a trunk pop open.

"No, no, no!" Beth started flailing her legs. She was claustrophobic and she remembered somewhere in her past that you either broke free from captors or died trying because the chances of survival after being abducted were small. Especially when someone wanted—no, needed—her dead.

Beth glanced at their faces. They were the men who had been tracking her. Brothers dressed in all black, muscles on full display. Beth turned her head and spit in the face of the man on her right.

He swore but loosened his grip for a second. Beth used the moment to rotate her elbow, bringing her arm up and connecting with the man's mouth. The man immediately retaliated by uppercutting Beth under her chin with so much force, her head snapped backward. Pain exploded in her face and neck so hard that for a minute, she thought she might pass out.

"Told you it wasn't going to be that easy," the man on her left snorted. He took a piece of fabric from his pocket and waited until they were behind the car, the open trunk obstructing a nosy onlooker's view. He pressed the cloth to her nose. Beth tried to flail her arm at him, but her heavy cast was cumbersome and didn't hit it's intended mark.

Unprepared for the sudden motion, Beth took a deep breath and tried to breathe but only managed to inhale the chemical smell into her nose and mouth. She went limp. Her mind went blank. She had no way to know that the men quickly duct taped her mouth and tied her hands before they shoved her into the trunk, shut the door, and drove away.

42

MAK

"How did you lose the senator? What are you not telling me, Mak?"

Mak squirmed a bit in her seat in response to Wilton's question. It wasn't what he asked so much as how he'd asked it that had Mak trying to back track, bypass, and soften her response in her head. This was the story she'd been avoiding telling him. Somehow, she'd known what his reaction would be.

Wilton's eyes dared her to lie.

Mak started the car, focusing on backing out of the driveway. She'd already put the address of Langsten's childhood home in GPS and drove in that general direction. She knew she'd told Wilton the story, but she'd omitted the part where she had fired her weapon at his tire, close range, and missed. She wasn't one to lie and, in truth, she wasn't sure why she did. Maybe it was Wilton's insistence that she work on her left eye dominance factor to improve her shooting.

Mak took a deep breath. "I told you. I'd just arrived at the Airbnb when I saw him approaching in my rearview. He parked in the driveway, I pulled my gun, and I got out of the car. Just as I was about to reach for his car door, he threw it in reverse and took off. I tried to shoot a tire and missed. I was in a residential neighborhood, so I didn't want to keep shooting. I ran back to my car and gave chase. I was closing the gap—enough to see him cross over a railroad track—but the arms were down, and the train was too close when I got there." Mak sat up straighter in her seat. "He made it across, and I didn't."

"You couldn't hit a tire that was right in front of you?" Wilton's face was bright red. She'd never seen it that shade.

"Are you okay, Wilton? Are you having a heart attack?" Mak asked.

"Answer the question. After all our shooting practice, you still missed a tire that was—what, ten feet in front of you?" Wilton's voice was outraged.

"Yes." Mak pulled into a Walmart parking lot and put the car in park.

"What are you doing?" Wilton asked. "Keep driving!"

"Clearly, we need to get this all out. I'm pulling over so we can do this safely." Mak was shocked to find herself the logical one for once.

"We need to go. We know exactly where he is, and we don't have any time to waste. We should have had him days ago!" Wilton's words were coming out fast and angry.

"Wilton, you're not thinking clearly. If you rush in there in this state of mind, we're going to lose him again," Mak stayed calm.

"You don't get to lecture me about how to do my job right now!" Wilton's tone held accusation.

"Like you've never made any mistakes?" Mak asked coolly.

"Not like this!" Stephen retorted.

"Really? How about when you let Beth go?"

"That was—this is—"

"Different?" Mak finished. "Because it's not. That was a big, intentional mistake, Wilton. Huge! You made a choice to let her go knowing that Beth could ID every one of those men involved at the top level and testify to how the ring worked. She had major inside information, and you let her go. You didn't even bring her in for a statement. That recording on your phone is BS and you know it. It'll get thrown out of court in two seconds!"

Wilton glared at Mak.

Mak glared back.

The phone rang, startling Mak and breaking the staring contest.

It was Sikes.

Mak answered.

Sikes immediately started talking. "Please tell me you have a lead because I've got FBI Director Trey Masterson on the phone, and he's got teams in place, all ready to take down the names on that manifest."

Masterson's voice came on the call. "It's been a major effort, and we've worked hard for the past three days, but we're all in perfect position. If we rush in too soon, there will be a mass exodus with these criminals going underground. Can you update us on your progress? How can I help?"

"We think we know where Senator Langsten is," Mak answered. "GPS shows it's about an hour's drive from us, which will put us there around three this afternoon. We were just coming up with a plan of action when you called."

"I can take a jet and be there in less than an hour. I'll bring a few men with me to provide backup. Langsten is the key here. The first domino in this operation. We take him out, then the other leaders immediately afterward on my command. We can't let him slip away—"

Mak looked away from Wilton's glare that implied, *this time.*

Wilton cleared his throat. "With all due respect, we could be pulling up to Langsten's place when you touch down. Every minute counts, let alone an entire hour."

Mak shot Wilton a look.

Wilton clenched his jaw.

"No, this is a good plan. A solid one. Meet Masterson and his men at the airfield and go apprehend the senator together. We'll ping you the address of the airfield and estimated time of touchdown."

When the call ended, Mak and Wilton sat in the car in complete silence. It was nearly two.

"You can follow Sikes' plan," Wilton said.

"Thanks for your permission, Wilton," Mak's voice oozed with sarcasm. "I think I will."

"I assumed that. But I won't be," Wilton stated.

"Wait. What?" Mak whirled in her seat to face him.

"We're going to the airfield. We'll get a rental car for me and I'm going to keep driving to his home. You and the FBI can meet me there. I'm not taking a chance on him getting spooked and running again." Wilton's voice held no room for argument.

Mak regarded Wilton's serious tone and angry eyes. She could see there was no room for argument. Neither would she be able to talk him out of it.

"Fine." She put the car in drive. Not only was Wilton going against orders, but he might be making a deadly mistake.

43

———————

BETH

Beth's eyelids felt stuck, matted together, like she'd cried herself to sleep, and leftover mascara had run and gummed them together. She could smell the faint scent of rubber. She took a deeper breath in through her nose and decided it was a car tire. She could hear the *thump, thump, thump,* sound, and the surface she lay on bumped and jostled her body.

She couldn't open her mouth. A strong, sticky substance was taped over it. She couldn't move her arms. Her right hand was awkwardly duct-taped to her cast. It looked like they had made several loops with the tape. Her right hand was numb. She desperately pumped it open and closed to wake it up. She tried kicking her feet, but they were bound tightly together as well. Panic began to freeze her heart.

It was then that she worked an eyelid open. It was so dark, and she was so alone. A vague recollection of being picked up, walked to a car, and drugged came to her. They must have stuffed into the trunk. Beth felt her eyes begin to leak for the hundredth time since she'd fled.

This was it. They had won, which meant she was going to die. Defeat and then terror washed over Beth. She tried not to be bitter. She tried to come up with a new plan. But she defaulted to the old habits—the negativity that often shut down her brain. Was this really what happened when she finally decided to stop running and do the right thing?

It had been stupid to think she could protect herself from them. That she could go on the run and keep herself safe. She'd never been safe from them. She was the last one left who could testify against Langsten. A loose end that Langsten would tie up as soon as he saw her.

Beth could feel it in her soul. This was it. There was no reason for them to keep her alive. They were finally going to kill her.

The car slowed, but the trunk began bumping up and down. Beth's head hit something in the trunk as her body jostled over the rough terrain. Then, all movement stopped.

She heard a car door open and close. Then she heard the second one. This was her chance. Frantically, she peered around the dark trunk, trying to find a weapon. Her eyes fell on her cast. *That will have to do,* she supposed.

Beth rolled her body over so she would be facing the men when they opened the trunk. Minutes later, they did just that. Light flooded into the dark space and Beth blinked hard, but she did not hesitate. She brought both bound arms up and punched the closest man under the chin. He went flying backward and let out a string of expletives. The pain she felt in her casted hand upon impact made Beth silently echo his reaction.

Beth sat up with difficulty, swinging her legs outside the car. Where would she go? That's when she saw it. A helicopter sat in the middle of a wide-open field waiting for them to get on. The rotors were spinning. The sound was deafening. And Beth felt horror flood into her veins. They were going to push her out of it. She was going to plunge to her death.

The other man was on her. He pulled her out of the car and threw her to the ground. Beth barely registered the pain from his fist as he hit her across the face over and over again. Her eyes were glued to the death machine a few feet away. With any luck, this man would knock her out before they dropped her.

"Brent, stop!" The man she had hit with her cast said as he stood from the ground, and Beth noted with some satisfaction that blood leaked out of his mouth. Maybe he'd bit his tongue off.

"Why?" Brent, her attacker, paused.

"She needs to be alive," the man answered as he pushed Brent away and yanked Beth roughly to her feet.

Oh God, they're keeping me alive so I feel the impact of hitting the Earth! Beth realized. That's when they threw a bag over her head. Panic and terror clawed at her chest. She was going to die.

Then they had both of her arms and hoisted her so her feet no longer touched the ground. She could feel the force of the wind, like the winds of a tornado, as they walked her closer. Then, her body was thrown upward, landing on a seat. She felt the bulk of each man as they sat next to her and grabbed one of her arms. She was pinned between them in a chopper with no way to escape.

This was going to be a horrific way to die!

44

MAK

Mak sat staring at the private airfield where the FBI jet would land within half an hour, toying with her phone. She should call Sikes and tell him that Wilton had deviated from the plan. That he had gone rogue. She didn't and for the life of her, she couldn't figure out what was holding her back. *This isn't any different than when he went to Aruba alone,* she justified. He could certainly handle himself. But how would she explain if something happened to him?

Instead, Mak had let Wilton make his own plan. Let him think he was calling the shots. She'd decreased her driving speed just enough for Wilton not to notice she was attempting to run down the clock. She made the twenty-minute drive to the airfield take thirty minutes. And when they stopped at the airport rental company, Mak had parked all the way in the back corner. She'd slipped his wallet out of his back pocket as he got out of the SUV they'd been driving and let it fall on the floorboard.

When they got out of the car, she'd slowed her pace and attempted to get Wilton into a conversation so he wouldn't notice her small efforts to slow him down. She waited in line with Wilton until he got to the counter, then excused herself to go to the ladies' room. There, she sat as long as she dared, knowing she had the keys to the Range Rover, and Wilton would need them to go look for his wallet.

She found a very perturbed Wilton waiting in the lobby for her. He demanded the keys and went back out to the car. When he returned with his wallet, he'd eyed her suspiciously.

"You better not be messing with me right now, Mak," Wilton hissed before stalking back to the rental company, getting back in line, and finally getting a rental car.

That was fifteen minutes ago. Now, Mak sat waiting for the plane, which was due in soon. Before she could make up her mind about calling Sikes, her phone rang. It was John. She answered quickly.

"Hi, babe!"

"Makayla," John's voice sounded relieved.

"Is everything okay?" Mak asked with concern.

"It is—"

"But?" Mak cut in.

John sighed. "I want you to know that I'm on my way to another interview."

"Wow, that's great. They must really want to work with you." Mak smiled, feeling happy for her husband. John had always been a hard worker. Whatever he did, he gave it his all.

"Do you really feel that way?" he asked.

Mak felt confused. "Of course."

"Because I've followed you our whole marriage. It's always been about your career. Your service to our country. We agreed when we got together, and I've always honored that."

"But?" Mak asked, knowing this was leading up to something big.

"But I realized as I went through this interview process that I really wanted this," John admitted.

"I want you to feel fulfilled and successful, John. Whatever you need to be happy, go get it," Mak encouraged.

"Truly?" John was hesitantly hopeful.

"Yes, John. What is this about?" Doubt crept into Mak's mind. Was there something he wasn't telling her? Their marriage was solid. She had no concern about that, but she'd never known John to take so long to make a decision. "You were hoping to grow your business. It sounds like this will be a great new client."

Mak could see a jet descending toward the runway. She glanced at the clock and watched, wondering how long it would take them to deplane.

John cleared his voice. "It's not a new client, Makayla. It's a new career. Vice President of Business Development for Cyter Industries."

"Is it a remote position?" Mak asked. She watched the jet touch down, and she started the car to drive closer to where they had stopped. *Good, they're early.*

"No. It's a company in Tennessee. Cybersecurity, designing mobile apps compatible with banking software. It's a straight shot to president in a year or two as the current president is starting the process of retirement," John explained.

Mak was speechless for once. A small sound like a strangled cry came out. She stopped the SUV right before they opened the door to the jet and dropped the ladder.

"John, I have to go. I'm playing escort to the FBI and likely off to save Wilton's ass." Mak rubbed her forehead, glad for once that she had a reason to get off the phone.

"Right," John said with frustration and a trace of bitterness in his tone. "I love you, Makayla. Be safe."

"Love you, too," Mak said as she hung up the phone.

As she watched FBI Director Masterson and a few agents walk down the stairs, her mind whirled. She and John had always been so solid. Sure, they fought some. It was to be expected when she traveled as much as she did. But John had always understood her job. The danger of it, the distraction of being in the middle of a big job, the need for stability for Harper.

She'd never felt like she had to choose between her family and this job. She'd never been asked to, and she believed she could have it all—a career and a solid family life. Hadn't she done both for the past eight years successfully?

Where was this coming from? She'd always thought John was happy. Had she missed the signs? Maybe Wilton was right, and she hadn't been listening to her husband. Mak's confidence was shaken. She needed to get her head on straight. In minutes, they would be in her vehicle on their way to the take down the leader of a drug and sex trafficking ring. Why, in this moment, was that suddenly not enough?

45

WILTON

After driving for miles and seeing nothing but land and snowcapped mountains in the distance, relief filled Stephen when the GPS said, *You have arrived.* As he drove on past the beautiful home, sitting on acres of property with a big lake off in the distance, he saw the stolen silver Tesla sitting in the driveway. Stephen's heart picked up speed. Langsten was here.

Stephen drove further, found an inconspicuous place to park his rental car, and flipped it around on the road. From his vantage point, Stephen could barely see Langsten's house, and he doubted someone looking out the windows could see him from this angle. He wouldn't make the same mistake Mak had, practically announcing herself when she'd had him in her sights.

For minutes, Stephen studied what appeared to be a two-story ranch homestead. He'd have bet a lot of money this was the original build—Joseph Langsten's childhood home— updated and somewhat remodeled. Ornate white pillars held up the idyllic wrap-around porch. The home was a conservative gray-blue color with farmhouse modern doors with x's decorating the bottom to look like barn doors. The roof came to a point with a picture window peeking out on the second floor.

More impressive than the house was the size of what Stephen could only guess was, a stable sitting behind the house, easily double the size of the home. Stephen was sure there were horses in that building and could surmise that they were expensive ones.

"Not a lot of tree cover around the house," Stephen mumbled to himself. He would have to be stealthy to be sneaking around in daylight.

Stephen reached to the back of his rental. He picked up the Kevlar vest he'd grabbed from Mak and put it on. He pulled out a Glock and checked to make sure it was loaded and hot, then put it in his holster. He did the same with a second gun and holstered it as well. He checked to be sure his pocketknife with his pickpocketing toolset was stowed in his pocket, and he shoved handcuffs in his back pocket.

He knew he should wait for Mak and the FBI agents, but Stephen was done waiting. That meant Stephen was going to have to be careful, go slow, and do some recon before bursting in. He had to consider that the senator wasn't traveling alone. He likely had bodyguards all over the house. Stephen would only have the element of surprise one time. Then Stephen would need a plan to take out Langsten's team before he could escape.

The trickiest part was the wide-open expanse of land between him and the house. This home sat on what Stephen could only surmise was over a hundred acres of land. There was no other home in sight. He checked his clothes. What he wouldn't give right now for camo gear, but it was too late. Maybe if he followed the tree line as far as he could, he'd have more chance of staying concealed.

Staying close to the trees, Stephen set off, his focus on

point. He was surprised by how far he had to walk before the trees opened into a clearing where the lake began. Stephen stopped as he surveyed the land, guesstimating there were several acres separating him from the house. He would have no choice but to run and hope he was not spotted.

While the plan took extra time, it seemed to work because when Stephen got to the house, there was no execution squad waiting for him. Though he chose the side of the house with the least number of windows, Stephen still crouched as he approached. Upon reaching the house, he lowered below the window line and caught his breath.

Slowly, he stood to peer through the corner of the window. Surprised to find no window covering, Stephen spied into the open format of the front room and kitchen. There was no one in the room.

Walking in a squat, Stephen rounded the house and found the next window, which peered into a bedroom. It was a simple room with a perfectly made queen bed and dresser. No one was there either.

Stephen repeated this movement all the way around the house. The afternoon sun was hot as it beat down on Stephen's black, bulky vest. A trickle of sweat fell down the side of his forehead. Stephen was relieved that he didn't see one person in the home.

That was, until he got to the final set of windows. Here, the blinds were drawn. It was the only room where Stephen didn't have visibility. This was great news, Stephen reasoned. Even if there were five guys in the room, with the element of surprise, Stephen could take out several before they knew what hit them. With any luck, the senator would be his first shot.

Adrenaline surged as Stephen pulled out his pocketknife set, ready to pick the lock to the front door. But as he turned the knob, he was shocked to find the door opened with a soft click.

Senses on high alert, Stephen suddenly feared a set up. This had been too easy. He tried not to remember when he'd felt this way before. That was the night of the explosion. The one that broke Mak's back.

For half a second, Stephen considered waiting for FBI backup. Or he could backtrack and look through the stables first. But then he decided if the horses were loud, they might tip off the senator that Stephen was here.

Stephen's curiosity got the better of him. He was already in the house. He might as well look around. He pulled his gun and pointed it at the ceiling as he quietly took a step into the foyer. He paused in the large entryway to the home. His eyes swept the large, open living room, dining room, and kitchen. There was no movement and no sound. No indication of where Langsten might be hiding.

He slowly took a few steps into the room and noticed a balcony room at the top of a staircase. There was no life there, either. There was a hallway to the right. Slowly, quietly, Stephen crept down the corridor. He opened a door to the left and found a bathroom. He stepped in quickly, scanned and cleared the room before resuming his path down the hallway. He continued until he discovered a door on the right. He quietly opened the door and scanned the room. It was small with a queen-size bed in the middle. He cleared the room in minutes.

On high alert, Stephen stepped back into the hallway. He'd known the house was empty from his earlier search, but he couldn't take a chance that he'd missed someone. His eyes fell on a door at the end of the hallway. It was the room where the blinds were closed. There. He could feel it in his gut. He put his hand on the doorknob and opened the door quickly.

With both hands on the gun, Stephen pointed it straight ahead of him. "Freeze. Get your hands up where I can see them," Stephen commanded as he edged into the room.

"Stephen Wilton," Senator Joseph Langsten sat in a tall, leather chair behind a large, mahogany desk. Langsten's face lit up like a long-lost relative had returned from a trip around the world. His brown, wavy hair was now silver and shorter, but those eyes—those dark, piercing eyes that seemed to peer into Stephen's soul were the same as they had been in the picture. Dangerous and exuding pure evil. He was smiling at Stephen with triumph on his face. His hands appeared to be resting on his lap, and Langsten was the picture of calm.

"Get your hands up or I will shoot you. Maybe not in cold blood like you shot my brother, but please, just give me a reason," Stephen snarled.

Langsten put one hand up. "Oh, you don't want to shoot me. Not when doing so will hurt another person you care about." Langsten looked toward a wide-backed leather chair that matched the one he was sitting in. It was turned around, facing the corner. Stephen hadn't noticed it until now.

Langsten reached to it and turned the swivel chair like he was presenting a surprise birthday gift. Stephen's breath caught in his chest. He dared not breathe, blink, or move. Langsten smiled manically as he raised a gun, not at Stephen, but at the person sitting in the chair.

Beth Donovan sat with her arms duct-taped to each arm of the chair. *That's a lot of tape,* Stephen thought when he saw the way her arm with the cast was pinned. Rope tied her ankles together. A patch of duct tape covered her mouth. Tears streamed down Beth's face, running black rivers of mascara down her pale cheeks. Beth's hair was shorter, and it held lighter streaks of brown and red running through it, but it was unmistakably Beth.

"No," Stephen whispered. His stomach lurched as he

studied her. Blood ran down her temple and soaked into the tape. Her face was already bruising. One eye was almost swollen shut. "What did you do to her?"

Langsten grinned. "This?" His hand made an up and down motion in front of Beth's face. "This is the price of defiance. Beth and I go way back. She knew better than to put up a fight."

"You piece of trash!" Stephen wanted to lunge for him. He wanted to pound his fist into Langsten's eye until it swelled up in the same way. "I'll kill you."

"Uh-uh-uh," Langsten tutted his tongue in a patronizing way. "We are at a bit of an impasse I'm afraid. You want to kill me, and I want to kill Beth. Shall we pull our triggers at the same time?"

"What do you want?" Stephen asked. He'd keep Langsten talking as long as the arrogant senator wanted. Long enough to come up with a new plan.

She didn't feel safe with me. The words that rolled around in his brain came back to haunt him. He could not fail her now. Not when it mattered the most. Not the way he had failed Davey.

"I want you to call off your patrolmen. Lose the maps, the names, and look the other way. Beth lives and I get to continue my lucrative operation. It's a win-win."

Heavy silence filled the room.

There was no way Stephen was going to allow the senator to continue. Defeat washed over Wilton as he replayed his earlier conversation with Mak.

"Like you've never made any mistakes?" Mak asked coolly.

"Not like this!" Stephen retorted.

"Really? How about when you let Beth go?"

"That was—this is—"

"Different?" Mak finished. "Because it's not. That was a big mistake, Wilton. Huge! Beth could ID every one of those men involved

at the top level and testify to how the ring worked. She had major inside information, and you let her go. You didn't even bring her in for a statement. That recording on your phone is BS and you know it. It'll get thrown out of court in two seconds!"

Mak was right. He should have locked the car doors and kept driving with Beth or arrested her. He should have done whatever it took to keep her safe. It was his fault they were here, where Beth was not safe.

A drop of sweat trickled down the back of Stephen's neck. Seeing Beth here, like this, had temporarily immobilized Stephen. This was his fault. Davey had died to keep him alive for a moment just like this, and Stephen had no plan. He had nowhere else to go.

Then he heard quick footsteps in the hallway. Mak, he presumed. Minutes seemed to tick by and Stephen assumed Mak was clearing the house. Then, the door beside him burst open.

Mak's voice sounded by his ear. "Langsten spotted, I repeat, Langsten—"

The deafening sound of a gunshot rang through the study.

46

———————

MAK

One minute she was speaking into the cool earbud the FBI had set her up with, the next minute, Mak's ears were ringing, and the sudden silence was deafening. Not unlike another case from the past. Only, that one had involved fire. For half a second, Mak was back there, her body flailing through the air, not in control of herself until she was in pain and unconscious on the ground.

Subconsciously, she traced the small burn scar on the side of her face. She'd come so close to losing her life and everyone she loved. Her mind flashed to the conversation she'd had with John earlier. He hadn't lost her then and she wouldn't lose him now.

This wasn't fire, it was a gunshot. She did a quick check of her body. But she felt no pain. She saw no blood. That's when her heart skipped a beat.

"Wilton!" She swung to look at him. She scanned his body, not finding any wounds on him either. When her eyes made it to his upper body, she noted the way he held his gun with perfect form. His arms were still outstretched as if frozen in place. His finger was still on the trigger. His eyes were locked with the man in front of him.

Mak's head snapped up to look at the senator. A single red drop of blood rolled down the center of Senator Langsten's forehead where a bullet was lodged dead center. A gun had clattered out of his hand and onto his large, stately desk. Langsten's body slumped back in his chair. His wide, disbelieving eyes were open, unseeing.

Mak's eyes strayed to Beth sitting in the chair next to Langsten. She almost hadn't recognized her with the dramatic change to her hair and grossly beat-up face. Compassion and anger downloaded at the sight. Mak hoped Beth's face would heal okay. Anger thumped through Mak's veins.

"That was a risky move, Wilton!"

"Why? I didn't plan to miss." Wilton ran to Beth and began unwrapping the duct tape at her arms, working gently around her cast hand. He tore the duct tape off her mouth.

"Are you okay?" Wilton asked Beth.

"You did it! You killed him. You saved me!" Beth cried a torrent of tears. Her lips shook as she spoke.

"What if he would have—" Mak followed him, her teeth worrying her bottom lip. She untied a rope knot on Beth's feet.

"You provided the perfect distraction. We were at an impasse. But the minute you burst through the doors, Langsten's eyes flickered to you and I took my shot. I wouldn't have missed," Stephen explained.

"He's dead?" Two FBI agents, along with Director Masterson crowded into the room and surveyed the scene.

"Gawd, I can't believe you just killed him," someone murmured in quiet awe.

"Just like that. It's all over." Mak blinked, feeling surprised.

"Langsten is down, and we can take care of this," Wilton said to the agent closest to him as he finished freeing Beth.

Masterson nodded to his men. "Initiate the next step."

Beth stood and rolled her right wrist, wincing in pain as she looked at her cast. She looked Stephen dead in the eye. "Poetic justice. This started and ended with Langsten. He killed your brother. You killed him. It was karma."

"I was just doing my job," Wilton said with humility.

Mak snorted. "Something tells me you're gonna bring up that single shot every time we go to the gun range."

"Well, look at it. It was a beautiful shot," Wilton gloated.

"I'd rather not," Mak rolled her eyes. More blood was now pouring out of Langsten and that wasn't a part of her job she enjoyed. But she felt the shift away from Wilton's anger back to the camaraderie they typically shared. She hoped all was forgiven. But she had a feeling Wilton would be sure to double down on her target practice from here on out.

Beth wrapped her arms around Stephen. "I'm sorry I didn't trust you. You saved me and you saved Lacy, too." But there was sorrow in her eyes.

Wilton's eyes held the same emotion. Mak wondered if it was a reflection over the ones they hadn't been able to save, but she hoped they would focus on the countless number of women this moment would save moving forward.

47

BETH

It had taken a good half hour for EMT to arrive at the Langsten ranch. Beth knew she would not soon forget the horror of events from the past six hours. She'd been bound and thrown in the trunk of the car, a bag placed over her head as she boarded a helicopter—all of which were on the top of her list of phobias. And if they weren't before, they were now. Then, she'd been beaten to the point of black out.

Stephen approached, walking at a slow, contemplative pace.

"Can I talk to you, Stephen?" Beth asked as tears filled her eyes. She had been so sure she was going to die. EMT were tending to Beth's face. She tried not to think about how much the antiseptic stung her face.

"No need to thank me again, I was just doing my job," Stephen said humbly. Mak called his name, but Beth put a hand on his arm.

Stephen turned back and glanced at her hand, then at her.

"I owe you an apology, Stephen," Beth choked out. She wasn't the best at asking for forgiveness.

"You don't owe me anything." Stephen shook his head.

"I do," Beth insisted. "I've had a lot of time to think about it. I was in such a world of pain… I couldn't see past it. All of the lies I told you and the way I projected my guilt onto you… The way I pushed you away because you were too close. It was unforgivable."

"Not unforgivable. But thank you for your apology. We're good." Stephen's tone was sincere. "Listen, Beth, the FBI is taking down the whole ring. Probably as we speak. I can't let you go again. You're a loose end, and your in-person testimony would go farther to making sure nothing slips through. Will you testify willingly?"

"Yes," Beth agreed. She shuddered at the thought of life on the run. "But I have a request for when this is all over."

"What's that?" Stephen asked.

Beth smiled back, almost shyly. "I want to see my daughter."

"Lacy would love that," Stephen smiled kindly.

"You know?" Vulnerability and surprise showed in Beth's eyes.

"Yes. And she knows too," Stephen's voice was soft.

"Maybe she'll be as quick to forgive me…" Beth could only hope.

"I have no doubt." Stephen's gaze found something in the distance, but he swiftly turned back to Beth. "You know… She started a facility to help women who have been victims of trafficking. I hear she's really helping them heal."

Beth nodded, feeling pride in her heart. "I could use a little healing myself. It'll take time, Stephen. But I'm looking forward to this next phase of my life. Freedom. I don't even know what I'll do with that."

"I'm happy for you, Beth."

"Me, too!" Beth replied, and she was surprised to find she meant it. For the first time that Beth could remember, she felt hope. Hope for her future.

48

ALYAH

A party was well under way when Alyah walked into the US Marshal building. The death of Senator Langsten had lightened the intensity of having someone there to protect her twenty-four hours a day. But Sikes had expressed a concern that others who were in the process of being incarcerated might try to find the source—the person who had brought them all down. Either for retaliation or to keep Alyah from testifying to the validity of the evidence. There had been a note naming her as the leak in the senator's office after all.

It was why Alyah had taken their nightly self-protection lessons to the next level. She'd enrolled in a women's self-defense class. No more looking over her shoulder. Besides, she couldn't stomach the US Marshals in her house any longer. Especially after she'd lost her trust in them.

Alyah's eyes scanned the room for someone to talk to or stand beside. The best way for an introvert to survive a party was to find a wall to stand in front of and observe. But first, Alyah wanted to find Sikes. She had a few things to tie up with him.

As she walked by the conference room, a hand shot out

and grabbed her wrist. Caught off guard, Alyah felt her whole body yank into the dark room.

"What—" Sudden lips cut off her words as they pressed insistently to her mouth. It took two seconds to realize they were not Stephen's. That old, familiar emotion of fear made her pulse jump. She put a hand to his chest and pushed back hard only to find the dark, intense eyes of Lynn Sauder on her.

Shocked and confused, Alyah looked into his face, noting the way his hands rested on her hips, holding her in place. She searched her mind for clues or gestures that she had led him on—to the place where he thought he could touch her this way.

Anger clouded her mind. She took another step back, away from him and out of his arms. She pushed his hands off her.

"What are you thinking?" Alyah hissed.

Sauder smiled. Arrogance made his features unattractive. "Just taking what I want."

"I see," Alyah's voice was icy. "And did you consider what I want?"

"Oh yeah," Sauder grinned wider and took a step toward her.

"Stop!" Alyah put a hand up, grateful it was too loud in the main office to hear them. She gestured between them. "I don't want this."

"Maybe not now, but you will." Sauder crossed his arms, his biceps bulging.

Alyah's eyes widened. Was he trying to intimidate her? He was delusional.

"What are you doing here, anyway? Don't you have work to do?" She took another step away, this time scooting closer to the door.

"Not really," Sauder stated. "Case is closed."

"What about Pottstaff's death?" Alyah asked. It was the piece of her case she hadn't been able to cinch up. "Did you solve who murdered him?"

Sauder shrugged. "Not high on my priority list."

Shock hit Alyah. "Why not?"

"He's a criminal and he's dead. Got what he had coming to him," Sauder said off-handedly.

"You can't be serious. We need to bring the criminals to justice, not allow them to be murdered under our noses and look the other way," Alyah spat.

Sauder froze. "You accusing me of something?"

"No, I would never—"

"Don't be so naïve, Alyah. We all look the other way on stuff like this all the time. What do you think happened with Wilton? You think he wanted to bring Langsten to justice? No, he had a shot, and he took it."

"No, that's not what happened," Alyah defended.

"Then there's you. You really think anyone buys your good-girl act?" Sauder closed the gap again.

"What are you talking about?" Alyah stuffed her shaking hands in her pockets.

"Don't think I don't know how you got elected to DA. Your uncle is Scott Milternett, right? Man, you had everyone fooled. You know exactly what I mean about looking the other way," Sauder rolled his eyes.

Heat flushed into Alyah's face. She started to tell him she and Milternett weren't related, but before she could answer, Sauder's phone lit up with a text message. Alyah could see the picture on his lock screen. Her stomach lurched and her eyes widened as she looked at the picture of a young kid proudly holding up a fish and an older man standing behind him. The resemblance between the two was uncanny.

"Who's that?" Alyah pointed.

Sauder looked down. "It's me and my dad." His eyes hardened with anger. He was murdered when I was ten. It's the reason I got into law enforcement."

"That's awful." But Alyah's mind was already making connections. The man in the picture—Sauder's dad—was the fourth man in the picture that Stephen had sent her. She remembered the man standing beside Mickey Upton, Joseph Langsten, and Langsten's brother.

"...Alyah Smith. Where is Alyah Smith?" The words drifted to them, saving Alyah from reacting or saying more.

"Duty calls," Alyah said quietly as she stepped out of the conference room and made her way to the front to stand beside Sikes. She knew he was planning to announce the decision she'd made earlier today. He'd been as thrilled as her boss had been. *This is a great opportunity for you,* they both had assured her.

Alyah's eyes scanned the room until they found Stephen Wilton. They had a big, horrible problem. The least of which was Sauder's inability to accept *no* for an answer.

Quite possibly, no one had ever told him *no* in his whole life. No rules or boundaries in life often created a monster.

49

WILTON

When Stephen arrived, the parking lot at the US Marshal building was already full of cars, and he could hear loud music and raucous laughter before he even pulled the front doors open. Maybe it was his somewhat introverted nature, or his inability to just chill and have fun, but parties like this always gave him pause.

He hesitated as he thought of his brother who had been killed defending Beth. Of Trevan Collins, who had the courage to start Stephen on this path to find the truth about his brother's murder. Of David Stinnert, who had given his life to save Stephen's. Of Beth, who now had the opportunity to let go of the past and make something of her future. A celebration was due.

Stephen pushed the door open and adjusted to the noise level and the happy faces. His eyes swept over his team. Everyone was ecstatic. Word had come down that 90 percent of the men and women involved in the trafficking ring had been captured and were sitting in jail cells.

Known for their fancy gadgets, apps, and web tools, the FBI tech department had created a private webpage that the marshals were proudly displaying on a drop-down screen at the front of the room. It showed the number of women they saved during the FBI raids each hour. Stephen watched in satisfaction as the numbers continued to tick up. They had saved hundreds of women from sex trafficking this past twenty-four hours alone.

"I wondered if you would make it." Mak was suddenly by Stephen's side.

Stephen shrugged. "You know me and parties..."

Mak clucked her tongue. "I'll train you yet, Wilton."

Stephen let his eyes roam over the crowd. He told himself he wasn't looking for Alyah. But he couldn't help the disappointment that settled in his stomach when he didn't immediately spot her.

"She just got here." Mak tilted her head to the conference room, answering his unasked question.

Alyah was standing in there in the dark talking to Chief Lynn Sauder. Stephen's stomach knotted, and he wondered if someday he would refer to Alyah as *the one who got away*.

Before Stephen could respond, a shrill whistle sounded, along with Sikes' voice. "Can I have everyone's attention, please?"

The room went quiet. All eyes turned unexpectedly to Sikes. "Alyah Smith... Where's Alyah Smith?"

Stephen watched as Alyah made her way through the crowd to stand beside the boss.

"Ah, there you are," Sikes said. He turned to address the team. "Attorney General Alex Kross has put in his resignation, effective at the end of this year."

This news was met with some *boos*. Stephen looked around and noticed Kross was absent tonight. After the investigation into Gerritt's murder that Kross had subjected Stephen to this past year, Stephen definitely would not be sad to see him go.

"The good news is, our very own Alyah Smith has thrown in her name to run and will resume her previous position as District Attorney here effective immediately." To this, the crowd began to cheer and whistle. The air left Stephen's lungs. She was coming back. Alyah's eyes flitted to Stephen's, connected, then held.

Sikes went on. "As you know, Alyah was instrumental in providing evidence the FBI needed to take down this far-reaching trafficking ring." Sikes indicated to the website screen behind him with numbers ticking up. "Let's wish her well as she starts campaigning for Attorney General!"

Alyah held up a hand to quiet the crowd. "We have one more announcement," Alyah smiled, her heart-shaped mouth curving up.

She was wearing a black dress with lace edging around her bodice and sleeves with a fitted top and a skirt that flared to her knees. Stephen followed her shapely calves down to her black open-toed heels, which completed her outfit perfectly.

"Deputy Director Rob Sikes here has been promoted to Chief Deputy. Congratulations to Chief Deputy Sikes!" Alyah called out.

At the sound of more cheering, Sikes raised his palms. "It's long overdue. Just a technicality, really…"

As people rushed to congratulate Sikes, the music started up and the volume of voices rose again.

"Well, that was a lot of information!" Mak blurted, still standing next to Stephen.

"Yes, yes it was," Stephen agreed. So that meant Alyah was back for good from the sounds of it. Stephen thought about his resolve to focus on himself and give himself time to be okay with being alone. Then there was the interview he'd accepted from Senator Grant. None of that compared to the feeling in his stomach of when he'd seen Alyah alone with Sauder. Why did life have to be so complicated?

Mak's phone lit up. "Oh, I've got to go. John had a business meeting, and he told me he'd call when he was back. Don't wait up."

Stephen watched Mak go. He wasn't going to lie. The thought of having someone waiting at home for him was still appealing. His home, at the moment, was a Holiday Inn. He'd yet to find time to buy a new house, let alone look for one.

Stephen was considering pulling an Irish goodbye when he found Alyah standing at his elbow.

"Stephen, can I talk to you?" Alyah was looking everywhere but at him, her eyes roaming over the crowd. Was that fear in her eyes? Before he could answer, Alyah had grabbed his hand and was leading him away from the party. As they walked down a darkened hall, Stephen heard a voice call out in question.

"Alyah?" A deep, male voice sounded. Was that Sauder?

Stephen turned to find the source but was caught off guard when Alyah shoved him into a small space. She wedged herself and Stephen into a small closet and shut the door.

"Uh, Alyah, what are you—"

"Shh!" Alyah hissed. She held up a finger and put her ear up to the door.

Soft footsteps thudded against the wood floor. They seemed to pause and stand still for half a minute, then retreat the direction from where they had come.

"What in the world?" Stephen looked down at the petite woman, who was looking up at him as if considering what she should say. "Are you okay?"

She shook her head. She was still listening at the door.

Stephen tried not to think about how tight and cramped

this space was. His chest was inches from hers. Yet he sensed this was urgent and forced his mind away from emotions her closeness stirred in him.

She waited a few more minutes before she turned her full attention back to Stephen.

"There's something off about Lynn Sauder," she began in a low whispered voice.

"Besides his name?" Stephen quipped.

"Focus, Stephen. This isn't a joke." Alyah snapped.

Stephen remembered where they had left things. They weren't exactly friendly these days. "Okay."

"First of all, he can't take *no* for an answer," she said.

"Did he hurt you?" Stephen felt instant anger and he put his hand on the door handle. So much for staying neutral.

"No, nothing like that." Alyah shook her head. "I've told him I'm not interested in dating, but he won't give up. He shows up where he thinks I'll be. He asks me out. He walks me to my car. It's getting out of hand."

"Oh, I can put a stop to that," Stephen stated, ready to go to her rescue.

"Stephen, stop." Alyah put a hand to Stephen's chest. "I can handle all of that. But there's something else you need to know. I know who the fourth man in that picture is—the one with Upton and Langsten—where they're all standing in front of the lake," Alyah admitted.

"You do? Who?" That had Stephen's full attention.

"It was Sauder's dad."

Stephen's mouth dropped open. "What do you... how do you know?"

"I just saw a screensaver on his phone of him and his dad. I remembered him from the picture."

Stephen's jaw clenched as he processed her words.

"But it wasn't just that. Sauder made cryptic comments

here and there. And his eyes would get dark and angry…" Alyah's closed her eyes and shuddered at the memory.

"Like what, Alyah?" Stephen felt his jaw clench.

"He said there was a special place in hell for men like Pottstaff, and he got what he had coming to him." Alyah clasped her hands together. "What if—"

"What if Sauder killed Pottstaff?" Stephen finished, making the leap.

Alyah nodded. "What if he goes after the rest of them? He certainly has access to Upton while he's sitting in a jail cell."

"You're right. He does. And he might gain access to more people Langsten was working with as the FBI is capturing the criminals who participated." Stephen nodded. "What do we need to do to keep you safe?"

"Don't read into this, okay?" Alyah hedged.

"Okay," Stephen answered, his curiosity piqued.

"I don't think I'm as safe as I thought I was. Not yet. I'm afraid the election will draw more attention to me. And until we know what Sauder is up to—"

"Alyah…?" Stephen's eyes widened as he guessed where she was going with this.

"Will you come home with me?" Alyah lowered her voice, thinking of the US Marshals who left her at the office one night. "I don't trust anyone but you."

Stephen couldn't find his voice. His mind was on the text message he had gotten from Senator Grant earlier today.

Senator Grant: *Glad you're interested in the position, Stephen. Our interview is confirmed for this Thursday, Austin Government office, at 3 p.m.*

50

MAK

Mak got home to a dark house. John had told her he'd be home about the time Mak made it back from the office. He'd taken Harper to his mom's house, and they'd decided to let her sleep for the night.

Mak flipped on a light. John sat on the couch staring at nothing ahead of him. Mak let out a squeak and then recovered with a quick laugh.

"John! You scared me!" Mak put her hand to her chest.

"Have a seat, Makayla. We need to talk." John's words sounded ominous.

Mak sat.

"I really lost you during this case," John began.

"I know. I'm sorry. But you know there are seasons and cases like this—"

"I do know that," John cut in. "But I needed to talk to you more than ever. The times it was urgent, I couldn't seem to reach you. I got the job offer today."

"You did?" Dread crept into Mak's heart. "Are you thinking about taking it?"

John nodded. "Makayla, I accepted the job."

"Without talking to me?" Mak gasped, trying to understand the implications of this decision. He'd told her the position was in Tennessee, and it wasn't remote. She couldn't imagine moving at this point in her established career. How could she work this job when her husband was in a different state with her daughter? It was hard enough with all the traveling she did. Sure, Mak could transfer, but she'd built a life here, a camaraderie with this office, and Harper was in dance with friends she loved. Resentment rose like bile in the back of her throat.

"I tried and every time, you were too tied up and you weren't calling me back. At one point, you said I should do what I thought was right. So, I did. I'm excited about this opportunity. And it kills me that I don't even feel like celebrating this because we might not be on the same page about it," John looked at Mak, searching her face.

Mak tried to muster a smile. "Congratulations, John. It's been a long twenty-four hours, and I'm going to bed." As Mak made her way to her room, she tried to understand why she felt so hurt. What John said was true. He had tried to talk to her. She'd encouraged him to make his own decision.

But, where did that leave them?

51

BETH

Fresh air with a tinge of chill in it hit Beth the minute she opened the door to the US Marshal Range Rover. They had put her on a private jet and didn't say where she was going.

First, she agreed to accompany Stephen Wilton and Mak Cunningham to a local police station to give an official sworn testimony. At that point, Beth realized something important. She was no longer looking over her shoulder. The fear she had worn like a protective armor to keep her sharp was fading. She now felt safe.

It was over.

Yes, she would have to testify in court some time, but Senator Joseph Langsten was dead, and Mickey Upton was being held behind bars. She'd learned that Pottstaff was dead now too. The evil that had terrorized her life was lessening.

As she sat in that police station, Beth unloaded all her secrets. She allowed the emotions—from anger to sorrow to guilt—to flow. Sometimes it flowed down her cheeks in the form of tears, sometimes it came through a raised voice.

When she spoke about Greg and the kindness he showed,

Beth looked Stephen in the eyes. He deserved to know who his brother really was. Greg's intelligence, his protective nature, and his plan to save them all, which had led to his demise. At one point, Beth caught Stephen wiping tears from his own eyes.

The strong feelings that came out were nothing compared to Beth's first glimpse of the ranch where Lacy was staying. Set off by so many acres of land, one could not see another home. Nothing but nature in the distance as far as she could see. A privacy fence that she bet held cameras or some security around the home made her feel like she would be able to breathe. She could taste freedom like the crisp wind that whispered to her soul.

Then the front door opened, and Beth could not contain all the joy that exuded from her body. Tears spilled as her heart leapt in her chest. Lacy stood there, her own tears falling down her cheeks. Beth covered her mouth with both hands and a laugh bubbled up.

Then, Lacy was running to Beth. They collided in a warm embrace filled with loss, pain, joy, hope, and reconnection. When they finally pulled away, Beth found her voice.

"We have so much to talk about." Beth smiled.

"We have nothing but time." Lacy took Beth's hand and pulled her inside the home.

Time. That was a gift Beth had never had before. Gratefully, Beth hugged Lacy again and looked around, not seeing the simple rustic modern decorations or overstuffed, comfortable couches. Instead, she thought about what that word meant to her.

Home.

Home meant a safe place to dwell free from fear. The ability to sleep soundly at night. Space to discover who she was without someone watching her and requiring her to be a minion for them. She looked back at Lacy—her daughter. Home meant family.

Beth would find all that here. She was finally home.

THE END

PROLOGUE, BOOK 5

SAUDER

If you like *Why She Fled*, pre-order book 5 in A Mak and Wilton Thriller series—*Why He Died*.

Twenty-Five Years Ago...

The sweltering heat of the midsummer Arkansas sun was a staggering beast that had the ability to shut down the brain. The only solution to it was to strip off all his clothes and cannonball into a pond in the middle of a cow field. At least, that's what ten-year-old Lynn Sauder liked to do. But last time, he got caught, and Old Man Burt called his dad. Then his dad blistered his butt until Lynn couldn't sit down for days.

Not worth it, Lynn thought, pouting over the fact that his options were so limited.

When he wasn't skinny dipping in the cow pond, he liked to ride bikes with his best friends, Jeremiah and Nox. But Jeremiah was grounded, and Nox was at church camp, so Lynn had been hanging out on his tire swing all day.

"Church camp," Lynn snorted. Sending Nox to church

camp wasn't going to help that kid. He cussed more than the devil. Lynn snickered at that thought. Then he stopped. He could hear them again. Loud voices rose, and he wondered if Mama had the windows open because this time, they were real loud. Lynn put his hands over his ears. He hated when they fought. They fought a lot.

"Unfaithful, good-for-nothin' whore!" Daddy shouted so loud that Lynn could hear it through his hands on his ears.

Loud footsteps thumped on the stairs inside the house. It sounded like someone was running. Like a herd of elephants. Maybe they were both running down the stairs. Was Daddy chasing Mama? Lynn wished he could tell them to just cut it out. But he'd learned his lesson about telling them that. Daddy had spanked his butt and told him to mind his business. Lynn shuddered. He hated Daddy's spankins.

"No!" Mama shrieked, then there was a *thump* sound, followed by another *thump*.

Lynn sprang to his feet, fear and anger coursing through him. He ran through the front door and screamed, "Stop! Just stop!"

"You stay out of this, boy!" Daddy growled in that tone that told Lynn not to take a step further.

Lynn froze. He knew what happened when Daddy got that tone. Bad things. But Lynn also knew he usually deserved them. Like the time Lynn had climbed through the window of his neighbor's house because he wanted the cookies he saw cooling on the counter. That was the same voice Daddy had used on him.

But that's not what stopped him in his tracks. Mama lay in a pile at the foot of the stairs. There was blood dripping down her head to her cheek and onto her white t-shirt. Like she had hit her head after falling down the stairs. The blood was jarring and made Lynn's stomach feel sick.

Then he saw what Mama held in her hand. All the air

whooshed out of him, and Lynn forgot to speak. Mama held a pistol. She had it pointed at Daddy.

"No!" Lynn whimpered.

"You go right back outside, boy. This doesn't concern you." Daddy used that voice again. Lynn knew he should do something. But what?

"Mama?" Lynn took a step toward her. "Why do you have that gun?"

"Get back, baby boy. You need to listen to your daddy." Mama's voice was barely a whisper.

Lynn's eyes darted back and forth between Daddy and Mama. They were staring real hard and mean at each other. What if Mama pulled the trigger? Suddenly, Lynn knew what to do. He ran from the room and found the phone attached to the wall in the kitchen.

"Hey!" Daddy yelled. "What do you think you're doing? This is a family matter. Doesn't concern anyone else. You hear me?"

But Lynn had already dialed 911. He'd learned how to do that at school when the fire department had come to give a demonstration of what to do in a crisis.

"Nine-one-one, what's your emergency?" The voice of the lady on the phone sounded nice. Like someone who really wanted to help.

"Put the phone down, boy!" Daddy yelled.

Lynn whimpered, suddenly afraid. Daddy would really whoop him for this. Then he heard a sickening thud and a scream from his Mama.

"M-m-my Mama..."

The crack of a gunshot rang out, echoing in his ears, the sound loud and final. Then there was silence. Lynn gasped in shock and fear. He dropped the phone, leaving it dangling on its curly phone cord, and ran straight out the back door. He didn't stop until he got to his favorite tree. He climbed and shimmied up the trunk, using the footholds he had carved to get him to the first branch. He reached for it and swung his body up.

From there, Lynn could see everything. He could see straight into the living room and to the base of the stairs where Daddy lay on the floor. Mama still held the gun pointed at him. He could see a red splotch of blood blooming bigger and bigger on Daddy's chest.

"No, no, no…" Lynn murmured. Tears streamed down his face. *Was he…?* Lynn couldn't even say the words in his head. Lynn's feet dangled on either side of the tree branch as he hugged the trunk while he watched, afraid to blink. His grip tightened on the trunk, but it wasn't because he was afraid to fall. It was like Lynn needed support.

He thought he should get down and help Daddy. He was bleeding! But what if Mama shot Lynn, too? She didn't mean to do it, did she? Daddy was just coming after her and Mama got scared, right?

He could hear the police sirens now. Lynn looked up to see a black and white car speeding down the road toward his house. He stared at the red and blue lights, mesmerized by the way they circled in time with the wailing. Lynn couldn't look away. The sight and sound played on repeat in his head long after the squad car stopped in his driveway.

He watched as a young cop got out of his car. Lynn thought he looked young, anyway. The policeman pulled his gun and walked slow and easy. Lynn couldn't see him at the front door, but he heard his knock.

"Police! Open up," the man in uniform yelled.

Lynn watched Mama open the door. The officer walked in and looked at Daddy.

Lynn couldn't hear what the lawman said, but Mama was nodding and clutching the pistol in her hand. Lynn's heart pounded. Was she going to shoot him, too?

Lynn watched the man reach into his back pocket and put a white glove on his hand. Then Mama handed the gun to the cop. The police took the gun and pointed it at Daddy.

The gun went off again. Daddy's body jerked and then didn't move. The policeman didn't move for a second either —he looked frozen, standing there with the gun still pointed at Daddy. Lynn covered his mouth with one hand, and tears streamed down his face. His whole body started shaking, so he clutched the tree trunk harder. Daddy was dead. Only, it was a cop who had done it. A man he should have trusted killed Daddy. Why would he—

Through his torrent of tears, Lynn saw the officer get closer to Mama. Was he going to kill Mama too? Lynn started to scramble down from his branch. He needed to protect her. But he didn't know how. He just knew that cop in there was bad.

But then, Lynn stopped moving. He could see the policeman lean down and place the gun on the ground. Then he took two steps closer to Mama. He reached her and looked at the cut on Mama's head. Like he was checking it. Then he smoothed back her hair and pulled her into a hug.

"Don't hug him!" Lynn whispered shouted, horrified at what he was seeing. "He just killed Daddy!"

Then, Mama tilted her head up. She stood on her tippy-toes, and she kissed the man. On the mouth!

"Stop it!" Lynn whimpered. Why was Mama doing that? Daddy was dead. Lynn could see the puddle of blood underneath Daddy's body, and no one was helping him. And Mama was kissing the man who had killed Daddy.

Understanding bloomed in Lynn like the blood on Daddy's chest. That cop was bad. They were together. Was Mama bad, too? Lynn thought about all the times Mama would come in and hug Lynn tightly and rub his back after Daddy walloped him. She'd tell him everything would be alright. It had been a lie. Mama wasn't as nice as he'd thought. Would they kill Lynn if they knew he saw them?

Lynn decided right then and there that he would never tell Mama or anyone else what he'd seen. He was going to have to be the man of the house now. Daddy had told him real men keep secrets. He balled his fists up, feeling angry they took Daddy away from him. It would be his job to protect Mama from that cop. He was too little to do anything about it now. But he'd get bigger. He'd get tall and lift weights. Maybe he would become an officer too and would take down bad policemen like this one—the one who had killed Daddy.

That was the day Lynn decided to learn everything he could about this bad guy, the one who had kissed Mama.

He rode his bike all over town that summer. He listened to people talking at grocery stores and diners. He asked questions at the gas station when he used his allowance money to buy candy. He learned that cop's name was Officer Pottstaff.

Lynn decided that someday, he was going to kill Officer Pottstaff. The same way he had killed Daddy.

Buy book 5 in A Mak and Wilton Thriller series—
Why He Died **today.**

ALSO BY ADDISON MICHAEL

A Mynart Mystery Thriller series is ghostly suspense with psychological elements. If you like complex heroines, paranormal twists and turns, and gripping suspense, then you'll love this dark glimpse into the psyche.

> **Book 1** - *What Comes Before Dawn*
>
> **Book 2** - *Dawn That Brings Death*
>
> **Book 3** - *Truth That Dawns*
>
> **Book 4** - *Dawn That Breaks*
>
> **Book 5** - *What Comes After Dawn*

The Other AJ Hartford - A phantom on a train. A mysterious kidnapping long ago. Can she connect the dots before all her futures disappear forever? If you like good-hearted heroines, ghostly phenomena, and nail-biting high stakes, then you'll love this mind-blowing adventure.

A Mak and Wilton Thriller series is a pulse-pounding crime thriller series with a strong female lead, stimulating twists, and relentless suspense.

> **Book 1** - *When They Disappeared*
>
> **Book 2** - *When She Vanished*
>
> **Book 3** - *Why He Lied*
>
> **Book 4** - *Why She Fled*
>
> **Book 5** - *Why He Died*

REVIEW REQUEST

If you enjoyed this book, I would be extremely grateful if you would leave a brief review on the store site where you purchased your book or on Goodreads. Your review helps fellow readers know what to expect when they read this book. Thank you in advance!

~ Addison Michael

ABOUT THE AUTHOR

Addison Michael is the oldest of six siblings. She grew up with a golden reputation and a well-hidden dark side. Writing became her outlet. Addison's dark side emerges in the crime and mystery thrillers she writes today. She lives in the Midwest and believes in writing what she knows, so her stories are often set in the Midwest region. From cabins surrounded by acres of desolate woods to rural police departments and eclectic personalities, Addison Michael captures the essence of small-town living.

You'll find the following tropes in Addison Michael thriller books:

- Cabin in the woods
- You can't go home again…
- Unreliable narrator
- Kidnapping/missing person
- Addiction/recovery
- Femme fatale
- Serial killer